Mockingbird & Vulture

MARY J NICHOLS

EMVARR PUBLISHING LLC

Published in the United States of America by

Emvarr Publishing LLC, Michigan

Mockingbird & Vulture/Mary J Nichols

ISBN 978-1-7374523-4-8 (Print)

ISBN 978-1-7374523-5-5 (eBook)

Cover Art by Luisa Galstyan

Map Art by Erica Hogendyk

Map Fonts by Roger White

To my family who has tolerated my incessant chatter about writing, ideas, books, stress, and worries, and yet supported me through it all. I cannot thank you enough for your love, patience, and for cheering me on.

Dear Reader

This story takes place in a fictional medieval world that contains adult content that some might find difficult to read. Such as:

Language, sexual situations, alcohol use, fictional narcotics, acts of violence (weapon battles, harm/brutality toward men and women, attempts/mentions of sexual assault), and deaths.

Primary Glossary

Characters:

Javesse Tavarelle (*Ya-ves Ta-vuh-rel*) – A Bellinstarian native living in Brydasia.

Renmier Forais (***Ren**-meer For-**ā**-is*) – Known as Vulture. A former captain of the Emperor's Elite Knights of Descension.

Amalee (*Am-**uh**-lē*) – Renmier's love who has been lost to him.

Darik Nornt (***Dair**-ik **Nornt***) – Duke of Columure.

Larselis Maliage (*Lar-**sel**-es **May**-lē-ij*) – Emperor of Descension.

Samris Givins (***Sam**-ris **Giv**-ins*) – Captain of all Duke Nornt's forces.

Tredwyn (***Tred**-win*) – Former servant of an Elite Knight during the war.

Lighana (*Le-**gah**-na*) – Pleasure slaves, male or female, owned by nobles of Descension.

The Divine:

Caleb (***Kā**-leb*) – Oldest son of Fynthiar and Shaelera.

Chaos (***Kā**-ahs*) – Lord of Darkness.

Dahzia (*Dah-**zē**-a*) – Queen of the Blue Abyss.

Fynthiar (*Fin-**thē**-ar*) – Creator of Emvarr; the Father of All.

Grestin (***Gres**-tin*) – Middle son of Fynthiar and Shaelera.

Lessindra (*Less-**in**-dra*) – Goddess of Love, Mercy, and Forgiveness.

Shaelera (***Shā**-leer-a*) – Queen of the Wild.

Valorius – God of Humans. Favored by knights and warriors.

Vynia (***Vin**-ya*) – Earthen Goddess. The Healer.

Places:

Bashgrahon (***Bash**-gre-on*) – Capital of the Columure Duchy. The Blackening – A darker, colder location within the Darkness, where Sebysula dwells.

Brydasia (*Bri-**dā**-sha*) – The Eastern Continent.

Columure (*Kah-**lem**-yer*) – Southwestern Duchy of Descension.

The Darkness – Cold dark realm created by Chaos.

Delvarian (*Del-vair-ē-en*) – Home of the Serine Elves.

Descension (*Dē-sen-shun*) – Vast empire expanding most of Brydasia, made up of four duchies.

Emvarr (*Em-var*) – The world created by Fynthiar.

Fyr (*Fē-er*) Port – Largest port city of Descension, located in southern Columure.

Myndrose (*Min-drōz*) – The Northern Continent.

Ravieris (*Rā-vē-air-is*) – Capital of Descension.

Rela Sulae (*Rel-a Soo-lā*) – Also called the Darklands. Home of the Sulaens.

Ubrasia (*Ū-brā-sha*) – The Western Continent.

Yeuroth (*Yer-oth*) - The Southern Continent.

An Extended Glossary continues at the back of the book.

Emvarr

N

Onyx
Ocean

Reklusa
Sea

Myndrose

Brydasia

Silver Sea

Province Sea

Ubrasia

Yeuroth

Cobalt
Ocean

Onyx
Ocean

Dred Sea

Brydasia

N

Reklusa
Sea

Imperial Isles

Veng Island

Onyx
Ocean

Ravieris

Saurris

Venmont
Mts.

Wragorn
Duchy

Wheathfaire

Pliniur

Venzore
Islands

Bay
Woods

Charville
Duchy

Welaeda
Forest

Faytirn
Woodland

Emerasia

Bilsnir

Newburrows
Duchy

Delvarian

Lake
Diriahz

Province
Sea

Camnit

Niwfog
Woods

Dawiryn
Woodlands

Lymus

Columure
Duchy

Talgrian
Forest

Arborville

Serpent Claw
Isles

Volthany

Rela
Sulae

Bashgrahon

Cobalt
Ocean

Fyr Port

A Captured Bird

Lord Beresly's pupils devoured his platinum irises. Moments ago they'd shone almost gold-like in the campfire's glow, when Javesse accepted his proposal to live the rest of her days amongst the Serine elves as his wife. He would've outlived her by hundreds of years, yet no doubt loved her until her last breath. The song shared with their friends around the fire was joyous and their harmony perfect. So immersed in the moment, the elves hadn't heard the bandits' approach, nor seen the scattered torches beyond the tree line, closing in on their intimate celebration. This wonderful finish to their journey from the Festival of Land and Water on the eastern bank of the Dibukue River, ended in screams and shouts. Death's darkness consumed Beresly's beautiful eyes; two bolts had impaled his back, and a blade was imbedded in his nape. A large boot pressed on his shoulder as a bandit yanked the sword free, a brief fountain of blood erupting.

Javesse's veil caught between her lips with each short, hard breath as she dropped to her knees and brushed Beresly's black hair aside, her fingertips sweeping his pale-gray flesh. "Love? Love, please."

He just... stared.

"Put her with the others!" someone ordered.

Rough hands hauled Javesse from the ground; she stumbled upon numb legs.

The other four women resisted the bandits from binding their hands, their efforts answered with a slap or a knife to their throat.

The brute handling Javesse pulled her through a crowd of armored men entertained by the treatment of the elven women. Threescore of the brigands remained standing after losing over two dozen of their company. Javesse's captor shoved her forward, almost making her trip over a limp arm. "She's wearing a scarf, Captain."

"What?" A man neared, annoyance contorting his scarred face.

"This one, sir. She's wearing—"

"What do we have here?" Their captain grazed the apex of Javesse's rounded ear. "You're not an elf."

She had no strength to fight. Disgraceful for a Bellinstarian. It wouldn't be the only time she might've disappointed her family.

"What's this for?" He brushed the veil with his fingertips. "Are you so hideous the elves must hide your face?"

Laughter sounded from the gathered bandits. Humans. Horrible human men.

Javesse blinked tears free and scanned the ground. Where was her sword? She didn't remember losing it, yet it was gone.

The captain tugged on the scarf.

Jerking her head back, she slapped his hand. "Stop!"

Her captor grasped her arms and forced both behind her, hurting her more.

The captain squinted. "Bring that torch closer!"

The light's harsh dance revealed the man's unkind visage.

Javesse looked away, but another thug pulled her hair, forcing her to keep still. She cried out.

"My... that was almost a lovely sound." The captain scrutinized the cloth hiding most of her face. Once he found the loop fastened to the jewel behind her ear, he removed the veil from over the bridge of her nose.

A hush fell over the nearby bandits.

Swallowing a noticeable lump, the captain turned his head partially to the men on his left. "Kill the other women."

Chills spread from Javesse's shoulders to her hands. "Have mercy. I-I beg you."

Three thugs glanced at each other. "Sir?" one said.

"His Lordship will want none other than this one."

2

"Yes, sir."

Javesse's knees buckled as her friends screamed in anguish, but the brute forced her to remain standing. Warmth swept over her ear and neck.

"If it wasn't for the singing, we never would've found you," the captain said.

She folded forward and sobbed. Earlier, her only worry when she gave Beresly an answer wasn't that they might be ambushed, but whether Lord Euralys would accept her decision with grace. The king's nephew and Beresly, although good friends, had competed for Javesse's affection for the past three years, and Euralys had shown he did not take losing well. But this... Bringing death upon the man she loved and their dearest friends was her fault. She should've waited until they reached the safety of Delvarian.

"Foolish elves," the captain continued. "Singing so close to the Darklands."

Javesse didn't want to go into Rela Sulae, commonly called the Darklands by most humans. Those inhabitants gave great honor to Chaos and were rumored to sacrifice souls to save their own. Dread paralyzed her, and the brigands had to drag her to their horses, the captain walking alongside.

While they loaded the mounts with the valuables stolen from the murdered elves, Javesse covered her face with her hands. The bandits laughed as they walked past, slapping her wrists or yanking on her arms, the pain lingering for too long.

The captain scowled and swept his hand in her direction. "Can someone tell me why she keeps doing that? Why's she hiding herself?"

One of the two men remaining beside her shrugged. "Who knows, sir? The elves and their ways are queer."

"This isn't queer. It's bloody annoying!" He charged at her. "Why do you keep covering your face?" he shouted, spittle spraying.

Javesse quaked beneath his ire. Licking her lips, she gathered enough strength to whisper. "M-my people's c-custom."

He stared at her like she was a dolt.

"P-please?" She motioned to where her veil lay crumpled in the dirt, trampled from several muddied boots. "To prevent them from seeing m-me."

The captain released a heavy breath and scanned the party; most of the men were indeed ogling her instead of following orders. "Get her scarf," he mumbled to one of the bandits guarding her.

Javesse's hands trembled as she shook the dirt from the veil, its color already forgotten. As she fastened it to the jewel, and tried to ignore the stench, her gaze fell on Beresly. Tears burned and blurred, falling when someone grabbed her arm and jerked her to the captain's mount.

May Bryric lift your soul, my love.

Thank Fynthiar the brigands weren't from Rela Sulae, but hailed from the Columure Duchy in the southeast region. The group had traveled a fortnight before coming upon her party, or so the captain claimed. He promised the return to her new home would be prompt.

Six days after the attack, Javesse couldn't cry anymore. Terrors filled every night she managed sleep, just as seven years ago, when she'd lost her family. This time, she was to blame.

At least her captor spared her of poor treatment. Captain Samris Givins permitted Javesse to continue wearing the veil during the long trek and kept her in his company for protection. Upon learning their destination was Bashgrahon in Columure, she asked him the reasons for his being near Delvarian, the Serine elves' homeland. He left her inquiries unanswered. The captain did, however, inform her of whom His Lordship was: Duke Darik Nornt. But the reason for her capture was left unexplained.

These past many years, Javesse had never traveled farther than a few miles from Delvarian, and only a small number of the ports with her father when she was younger. Under better circumstances, she might've enjoyed exploring the region. Several lovely hamlets preceded Bashgrahon. The party didn't stay in any of them, but made camp. A shame. The towns seemed quaint and welcoming. Strange how she tried to see something good in the horrid situation.

What a fool.

The long stone wall of Bashgrahon was a dark line in the distance. The closer they drew to the estate, the partition grew taller. The muddy road passed under a wide arch, the portcullis raised, welcoming travelers. Captain Givins led the squad through the open gate. Within, the wall shrunk in the distance, encompassing Bashgrahon. Laborers worked amid acres of farmland divided by rolling fields of brown grass and bare trees; red and gold leaves scattered amid the grounds. In the center of the estate, a manor atop a hill was encircled by a wall from where guards walked, watching like hawks. As the small group approached the gate, Captain Givins raised his left fist. The sentries nodded once to him. Beyond the parapet, several smaller buildings surrounded the stronghold; smokestacks expelled dark clouds into the gray sky.

Once inside the castle, the captain ushered Javesse down many corridors, then into a bathing chamber. He must've sent a messenger ahead, for a steaming bath and servants waited. Five women in sheer garments stood by the inlaid pool. Each of them also wore a fine black leather band around their neck. Curiosity arched a few brows as their attention lowered to Javesse's veil and wool garments.

Captain Givins shoved her toward them. "Scrub the stench of those stinking elves off her."

Sorrow dominated their frowns as they began undressing her, but Javesse slapped their hands. They looked at the captain.

"Do it," he commanded.

Javesse had believed she lost every teardrop during the journey to Columure, but more surfaced. The scarf now removed, she covered below her eyes with her hands.

Captain Givins pointed at the pool. "Get her in the water!"

The women accompanied her into the hot bath, speaking with soft voices. Nothing eased her worries.

Looking over her shoulder at Captain Givins, Javesse asked, "Will you not give me the courtesy of some privacy?"

"You'll find no courtesies here, slave."

Slave. He'd never mentioned that word earlier—all those days of riding. To hear it sent a shudder throughout her. By the other women's garments and the awful neck-bands, Javesse now understood her future. She was to join the unfortunate life of the lighanas: pleasure slaves to the wealthiest noblemen and women. Sobs shook her.

The women used jasmine and rose scented soaps, fragrances that had once pleased Javesse.

"You're beautiful," the slave washing Javesse's hair said.

"The loveliest woman I've ever seen," added another.

The oldest of them, appearing in her late twenties, squeezed Javesse's hand. "Perhaps His Lordship will be gentle."

Javesse was a lighana to a man she didn't know—a duke. Why did Fynthiar permit this to happen to her?

After drying her, the women took Javesse to a chamber and dressed her in a silver garment as revealing as their own. They adorned her wrists, fingers, and ankles with silver jewelry, then brushed her golden hair with gentleness, pinning the sides atop with a sapphire-encrusted comb. Like the rest of the lighanas, she remained barefoot.

Captain Givins viewed her, then nodded.

Despite her body's exposure, Javesse continued covering her face.

"Tell His Grace we're on our way," he instructed a male servant, who then ran ahead. Grabbing Javesse's elbow, Captain Givins escorted her from the room. "Drop your damn hands."

She hesitantly lowered them to her sides.

They passed several doors, ascended a flight of stairs, then walked along another lengthy hallway before halting at a guarded door. Javesse's knees weakened as she trembled, her head lightened. After the guard opened the door, Captain Givins guided her through.

It was a small study with a burning hearth, a table of fruits and wine, and a pair of grand chairs with thick cushioned seats. A black bear rug lay between the chairs and the fireplace. There were two windows with dark-blue velvet drapes at the far end of the room, and to the left was a door. No other people were present.

Grip still firm on her arm, the captain stopped beside the table, his gaze on the other door.

Javesse made to cover herself again, but his hold grew painfully tight.

"I swear, woman," he said. "I don't care what your customs are, but if you hide your face again, I'll bind them behind you."

Arms pressed to her hips, she focused on the lined patterns of the smooth wooden floor beneath her bare feet, and wept.

The door opened and two pairs of footsteps sounded.

"I hope she's worth it, Captain. I *had* wanted an elf." The stranger's voice was mild. Kind, even.

"My aim is to please you, Your Grace."

Fine leather shoes came into Javesse's view, stopping inches from her toes.

"Now, let's have a look, shall we?" A man's hand raised to her; rings of various gemstones decorated his slim fingers.

Quaking, she flinched.

"Relax," he whispered, tilting her chin up. "I'll not harm you."

The duke appeared twice her age, possibly early fifties. Gray peppered throughout short dark hair, and his green eyes fixed on her as air rushed between his thin lips. He stepped back, whispering, "Gods."

Her muscles tense, Javesse started to cover her face, but froze when Captain Givins cleared his throat.

"I've never..." Duke Nornt inhaled deeply. "Gods."

"Are you satisfied, Your Grace?" the captain asked.

"More than you can imagine." The duke received a black leather band with a metal buckle from the servant behind him. "No." He scowled at the band. "This isn't beautiful enough for her."

"Your Grace, something'll have to be made," the servant said. "This is all you have."

Frowning, Duke Nornt nodded. "Very well. For now." He placed the strap around Javesse's neck.

It choked her. Rubbed her flesh. It itched. She wanted to claw it off, but consequences would follow should she try.

"Sell the others," the duke said. "I believe she's the one. She's all I'll need."

Javesse sputtered a sob.

"Enough," Captain Givins said.

"Oh, have compassion," Duke Nornt said. "Now leave us."

The captain and the servant bowed, then left.

The duke motioned to the table. "Are you hungry?"

Crossing her arms over her chest to clutch her shoulders, Javesse looked down. A pocket cloth appeared. She remained still.

"A proper introduction is in order," he said, dabbing her cheeks. "I am Duke Darik Nornt. And I'm your master."

Heart thudding upon that word, master, she shook her head. "No," she whispered.

"I'm afraid this is now your fate, my... my gorgeous lighana." He shoved the cloth into his pocket and gestured to the trays again. "Please?"

Javesse was starving, but the thought of eating made her ill. "No."

"Then let's begin." He hauled her to the other door, but her resistance brought him to a halt. "Don't make me send for Samris."

No. Not Captain Givins. He frightened her.

She reluctantly followed the duke into an extravagant bedroom.

A small table with a pair of cushioned chairs sat before a great fireplace. More dark-blue drapes hung from the tall windows at the opposite wall of the entrance, and a chest of drawers stood beside a door that must've been the wardrobe. A large mattress set low within a wooden frame, the four posts reaching an elaborately carved canopy ready to enclose the mattress like a tomb. Three great paintings hung on the windowless walls, one above the burning fireplace. The artworks' colors were blurs through Javesse's tears.

The duke led her to the bedside, then chuckled a nervous sound. "I almost don't know where to begin. Strange, really. Your name, perhaps?"

Trembling, she stared at the blue bedding.

"Later, then." He glided his warm hands up her arms. "To be honest, I expected elves to choose from. However, I'm not disappointed with Samris' decision to bring only you home."

More tears fell. Beresly was dead, her friends were gone, and her future was now the life as a pleasure slave.

The thin shoulder straps floated to her elbows, then wrists. Air danced on her bare breasts.

"Gods..." he hushed. "In all the travels of my lifetime, I've seen nothing, nor anyone, as beautiful as you." He removed his doublet, unbuttoned his shirt, then pulled Javesse close and kissed her.

She pushed on his chest as his fingers pressed into her arms. "No!"

"You're my lighana!" He shoved her onto the mattress.

While he untied his breeches, she scrambled to the other side. Just as she reached the corner, he grasped her ankle and dragged her to him. She slapped and shrieked until her throat burned.

The duke wept.

Javesse lay motionless, unharmed. Tears fell as she quaked, fearing he'd strike her for his body's failure.

He stumbled off the bed. Holding his pants up, he stomped from the room. The door slammed shut, sweeping the curtains with a draft and rattling items on the furniture.

She crawled to the pillows and screamed into one until her voice was gone.

Vulture

The mug cracked as it struck the tabletop. That wasn't what drew attention to the drunken fool, but several minutes of him shouting his displeasures about Darik Nornt. People could dislike the Duke of Columure, most commoners did, yet it was unwise to ruin Renmier's supper with such complaints. The drunk might've walked out unharmed, but as his rants continued, the odds grew slimmer. Renmier didn't want to deal Darik's justice tonight. He still needed time to recover from the last hunt.

"Who does that bastard think he is?" the whinger hollered, swinging his arm out. "I pay taxes to the emperor—not Nornt!"

"Ah, fill your mouth with drink and talk less," someone said.

"Yes!" The owner of the Amber Hearth glanced nervously at Renmier from behind the bar. "You've spewed enough already."

"Please, darling." A woman tugged on the drunk's sleeve. "Let's go home."

He jerked free. "People agree. Nornt deserves a slit throat!"

Patrons looked in Renmier's direction while others shook their heads at their drinks.

He watched the flames dance on the glowing amber wood. The idiot's blathering had ruined the perfectly blended herbs and spices of Renmier's meal, and this meat pie was one of his favorites. He pushed the half-finished supper aside. The chair dragged on the floor as he stood, adjusting the black stone ring on the middle finger of his right hand. It would taste blood this night.

The tavern fell silent; the young barmaid ran behind the bar to stand next to her father. The whinger paled. His wife gripped his shirt.

Renmier trudged toward them, his arms bumping into shoulders, heads, and anything else in his path.

"Vulture," someone whispered.

Clutching the collar of the petrified drunkard's shirt, Renmier pushed the woman to the floor. His fist contacting the man's gut broke the tavern's stillness, then Renmier cracked the complainer's jaw. The drunkard crumpled. Renmier slugged his mouth thrice more, blood smearing on his knuckles and the ring.

"No! Stop it!" The wife jumped on his back, trying to grab his wrist, but he shrugged her off with ease.

Her weeping and his striking the man were the only sounds in the building.

Renmier ceased the assault, blood dripping off his fingers. He was tired of beating people, but the idiots never learned not to talk poorly about Duke Nornt in Renmier's presence.

Blubbering, the woman knelt at her unconscious husband's side. "Gods," she whispered, "you could've killed him."

Renmier grabbed the drunkard's arm. "I'm not finished." He dragged the body to the exit, leaving a wet, red path.

A few chairs scuffed on the floor.

He looked at three rising men. "Follow me and you'll share his fate."

They lowered to their seats as he continued through the door.

Outside, the wife trailed. He counted on her following. And he did with this pair of fools as he'd done with others in the past: he made them disappear.

An hour later, Renmier returned with a lighter money pouch, and ready to perform. The tavern quieted as he walked to his table, which cleared of the current occupants. He nodded once at the barkeep. "Food. Drink." Renmier sat and awaited a fresh meal.

Murmurs passed between patrons; always the same word: "Vulture."

Gaping at his face, the young barmaid set a tankard of ale before him, then hurried to the scullery. She'd seen him worse than this before, so why did she act frightened now?

"Should we go look for them?" someone asked.

"No one ever finds the bodies," another responded.

Renmier grabbed a cloth from his pants pocket, then wiped the blood from his hands, chin, cheek, and mouth. The salty, copper taste hinted on his tongue as he cleaned the ring.

Brydasia lost two more of its people tonight.

Renmier had avoided Bashgrahon for almost six months, having taken leave of Columure for the autumn and winter moons. It was the same every year for the ritual. But Darik had sent a summons a fortnight ago, after the event at the Amber Hearth in Fyr Port. Renmier had wished for another month before returning. It'd taken five years to build his reputation and retain the duke's trust, and he couldn't risk losing it now. So, when Darik called for him, he answered.

As usual, Columure's gray sky greeted him. The travelers veered off the muddy road as Renmier neared. If they didn't move because they recognized him, they cleared the way because of Titan. The stallion's large hooves splattered mud, and he grunted at passersby who got close.

Renmier had trained the horse since they'd paired seventeen years ago, when he was an eleven-year-old squire. Titan knew him, his body language, and tone. The stallion was a part of him throughout his career in the Emperor's Elite. Now Titan carried him on this venture, continuing until they both breathed their last breaths.

Renmier was in no mood for Bashgrahon come evening. A tavern in a village outside the estate served better meals and provided a warmer hearth. Everything in Darik's home was cold—unfeeling—like His Grace. Like Renmier.

After six more miles, the land opened to several farmsteads: servants and slaves to His Lordship. The wealthy may pay hefty taxes, but the common folk weren't as blessed. No nobleman or woman suffered slaughter, rape, or a beating for a few missing roans, whether copper, silver, or gold. The peasants owed every coin expected of them. If the nobles built too large a debt, they made payments in other ways, women often the sufferers in Bashgrahon. Renmier had been sent to collect on one such occasion, the husband and wife now gone from Brydasia.

Most travelers dressed in thick wool and cloaks to withstand the frigid early spring. During the ride, Renmier spotted weapon bulges beneath mantles of passersby. When his appearance nor exposed sword hilt—the ends fashioned as three wicked claws curled toward the blade—sent a clear message he wasn't one to hinder, he flung his heavy leather cloak aside, showing the large flail's handle was within reach from the saddle scabbard. Would-be culprits hurried past, viewing the roads or fields. Anywhere but at Renmier. He'd smirk. They now knew him.

He pressed on while laborers worked the fields. It amazed Renmier that crops grew there. Whenever he returned to Columure, the sun refused to grace the land with its blessed light. Gray clouds always promised threats of chill and rain. With what did the farmers pay? Mud? Maybe it was Renmier who brought such conditions when he came to Bashgrahon. Perhaps the drab weather reflected his existence.

The crisp, wet trek brought Renmier upon an altercation outside a farmhouse. Five men bearing the dark-blue collector's sash were the obvious agitators. A laborer lay still on the ground while the men pushed a maiden between them. One tore the top of her dress, baring her breasts. Screaming, she tried to cover herself.

The cry echoed in Renmier's head, changing into shrieks and pleas answered by laughter and violence. He set his jaw and continued to the spectacle.

"Take her inside," a man ordered.

The collectors started to the farmhouse but hesitated when Renmier halted Titan in their path. They all wore studded black leather armor, their weapon belts providing a sword and a knife. The one who appeared in charge squinted at Renmier, then at the carrion bird pin fastened to Renmier's cloak.

"Vulture," he said. "I heard you were returning."

Renmier glanced at the weeping maiden. "Have you collected?"

"We have." The leader gestured at the unconscious farmer. "He was a bit resistant."

"Liar!" The young woman fought the men's hold but failed. "He was protecting—"

A slap silenced her, leaving a bloody smudge on her lip.

The memory of men in dark armor striking Amalee flashed in Renmier's mind. He pushed it into the shadowy mists for later. For the right moment.

"Move on," he said.

The leader sneered. "You don't control us, Vulture."

Renmier unclasped the cloak, which gathered behind him. As soon as he dismounted, the flail was out of the scabbard and in hand; the spiked ball spun, sounding in the air as it gained momentum.

The lead collector reached for his sword. That was all Renmier permitted before crashing the flail into the man's skull, caving it in. The leader collapsed into a convulsing heap. With a quick jerk, Renmier freed the spikes and had the heavy steel ball whirling again.

"Next?" he shouted.

The others released the maiden and hurried to their horses and wagon, leaving their dying comrade.

Renmier eased the flail's motion away until its swing slowed to a stop. He removed a cloth from a saddlebag, cleaned the spikes, then put the weapon back in the scabbard.

"Th-thank you, m'lord," the maiden whispered from the unconscious farmer's side.

"Is he dead?"

"No." She held the torn dress to her chest. "I don't know how he'll fare."

Renmier examined him, finding a large bump on the man's head and a bloody nose. "He'll live. Best to get him to a bed."

He carried the farmer into the house, the girl directing him to the man's bedroom.

She informed him the laborer was her father, and gave their names, of which Renmier forgot. There were more important names to remember. The maiden changed dresses, offered Renmier a washbowl, then cleaned her father's wounds while Renmier washed.

"The taverns will be full soon," she said, coming from the bedroom.

Drying his hands, Renmier grunted. "I'll have no trouble finding a table." He threw the towel aside and made for the exit.

"Please?" She grabbed his arm. "It's the least I can do."

"I don't need your gratitude."

"They would've raped me." She looked at her twiddling fingers. "All of them. And you didn't have to stop them... but you did."

His stomach twisted as he swallowed burning bile. "I despise rapists," Renmier mumbled.

"I make a grand stew. I-I promise."

So did the tavern outside Bashgrahon. Rewards were unnecessary. He would've killed all the collectors if they hadn't ridden off. The bloody cowards.

Sighing, he nodded; she brightened.

While she prepared supper, Renmier searched the collector's corpse, stripping it of any valuables. Twelve gold roans and an emerald of minor worth might come in handy. He threw the body over Titan's saddle, then rode into a cornfield, dumping it where the carrion crows could feast. By the time he entered the farmhouse, the stew was almost finished.

He checked on the farmer. The man would likely sleep through the night, leaving his daughter unprotected. Not that it mattered. The farmer did little for her as it was.

"It's finished," she called.

Renmier sat in the small kitchen. "Where's your mother?"

"She died from galnikath two years ago."

The horrible virus often spread amongst the poor, although the wealthy weren't immune. Renmier knew of nobles who'd lost their lives to galnikath. It left no survivors, and there was no known remedy. Not in Brydasia.

The maiden set a steaming pot in the center of the table, then placed a bowl in front of Renmier and the chair beside him. He had anticipated her to act, but not so early in the night.

She scooped servings, then offered a prayer to Vynia, the Earthen Goddess. They ate in silence, which he preferred. He'd said more to her than anyone over the past several months.

The girl did make a good stew, so Renmier accepted a second helping.

After supper, she offered her father's fruzae. It surprised Renmier the farmer could afford the expensive liquor. He arched a brow at the etched bottle; intricate swirls formed around apple blossoms. There was no better blend than honey apple with crueberry and cinnamon. The farmer knew his fruzae. Renmier enjoyed a second glass, then rose.

"I appreciate your hospitality." He headed for the house door.

"Wait!" She rushed and grabbed his hand. "You won't find a room this late."

"I'll get a—"

"I've a warm bed." She entwined her fingers between his. "Please stay."

He battled the knowing smile. "I must reach Bashgrahon."

"Please?" She pressed her breast to his arm.

Although he couldn't feel its softness through the leather armor, the gesture was familiar.

"I'm pure," she added. "I promise."

Six moons had passed since Renmier's last encounter and he declined several swyve offerings on the way to Bashgrahon. He didn't need anyone, but virgins were few as of late.

"What I would really like is a haircut and a shave," he said.

She blinked. "Of-of course, sir."

The maiden did a fine job providing a clean shave, including a heated towel, then trimmed his hair to his shoulders. After cleaning him off, she led Renmier to her bed; he gave no resistance.

He defeated the girl's shield-maiden. Renmier spoke no words, only grunted and occasionally moaned. She attempted to kiss him, but he denied any such contact. It wasn't lovemaking. Never was with anyone. Not since Amalee.

He turned onto his back and charted the cracks on the ceiling, wishing he could escape through other means—he felt small enough. Life was empty of any intense, emotional pleasure. The thronging meant nothing. Just another damn release giving more than he received. A heavy breath came forth as he rubbed his face. The maiden's sweet fragrance on his fingers didn't offer gratification, but images of Amalee invaded his mind. Her hazel-blue eyes flashing beneath the sun as she danced amid the fields, her blonde hair framing her slender face as she smiled. Renmier never deserved such a fine woman.

Amalee... forgive me for what I do.

The girl skated her fingertips up his arm, tracing the curves of his muscles. "You seem distant."

It was time to leave.

"Are you wedded?"

He squeezed his eyes shut.

Amalee beamed from beside their young crops. Gods, the lovemaking had been amazing.

"You are, aren't you?" The girl's nail glided over the platinum ring and circled the black stone.

Renmier licked his dry lips.

"You wouldn't kiss me," she pressed.

"It was only a swyve."

She frowned. Did she think he'd love her? The foolish maiden offered herself to him.

He eased from the bed and washed at the basin. "I'm no lover."

The blanket tight over her bosom, she watched, tears pooling. "I thought..." Her shoulders slumped. "I don't know what I thought."

"You didn't think." Renmier began the long process of putting the leather armor on.

She remained in bed. "What if I end up with child?"

Finished buckling his boots, he straightened. "You're likely not the only."

Ignoring her sobs, Renmier exited the room and descended the stairs. He dropped the vulture cloak pin on the table, then left.

Duke Nornt sat before the hearth in the great study, his hair more gray than the last time Renmier saw him. Although Darik kept his physique hidden beneath layers of fine clothing and extravagant robes, his face was thinner. The erosion had finally begun, ebbing his strength after fifty-six years.

Darik grinned over his steel mug. "I expected your return days ago."

Hands closed into tight fists, Renmier fought the desire to slaughter as the icy Darkness emerged from his core. He blinked rapidly to keep the black mists at the edge of his vision. "There were delays."

Darik rose and placed the cup on the stone mantel. "You slew one of my chief collectors."

Renmier lifted a shoulder. "The idiot drew his weapon."

"I see." Darik rounded the chair and stopped in front of Renmier. "I can't have my men slaying each other."

The chill spreading and the urge to kill intensifying, Renmier stretched his shoulders back. "They know better."

"My point is—"

"The subjects had paid their dues! They fear you already. There was no need for the girl to suffer rape."

The duke stood tall, his head almost meeting Renmier's nose. "If the farmer hadn't met his taxes, would you have still interfered?"

Renmier regarded him, then lied. "No, my lord."

"Good." Darik retrieved the mug. "Was she a fine swyve?"

Some men were real swine, and the duke was no different. During the war ten years ago, such behavior distinguished him from Renmier, but their different upbringing might've played a part. Darik respected no one, especially if they threatened his goals. That's why most of his squad had died. As for women, in the duke's opinion they were weak and meant for pleasure and servitude. Although an ass, he was powerful. People served him out of fear, not reverence.

Renmier squeezed his sword hilt, tapped the pommel with his thumb.

Laughing, Darik's cheeks reddened. "Ah, you never share the details. Such a shame." He sipped from the cup. "Did you leave a token behind to ward off others from assaulting her?"

"You sent for me."

Amusement faded from Darik's expression. "For an important matter. I've a mission for you, Vulture."

Renmier extended his fingers from the hilt, loosening the building tightness. "Who's the target?" he asked, walking toward the duke.

Darik lowered into the chair. "There's to be an attempt on my life."

Renmier froze. "Ordered by whom?"

"I know not." A loud sigh escaped Darik and into the cup. "You must find out who the assassin is and kill them." He looked at Renmier. "I fear the order may come from the emperor."

Renmier sounded a throaty laugh. "After these many years have passed, why would he now—?"

"I know not!" Standing, Darik tossed his drink into the flames. A small plume of fire and smoke billowed from the hearth.

Renmier frowned at the fire, caught in its furious dance. *How?* He faced Darik. "If His Eminence felt threatened, he'd send an army, not an assassin."

"You believe you know him, do you?" Darik squinted. "Tell me, how close to Emperor Larselis were you during service as His Elite?"

"I received orders from my commanding general and him alone."

Darik paced before the fireplace, his cheeks shading ruddy. "We may have been Elite, but we were still expendable knights to His Eminence. Despite my willingness to kill—to die for Emperor Larselis—that bastard, General Repascow, made certain I'd never gain the emperor's favor!"

Renmier remained stoic upon the name of his former general and friend.

"But oh, do I enjoy celebrating that fool's death." Stilling, the duke smiled. "Every year I pour my best fruzae and toast to the day I slit Repascow's throat."

Renmier nodded once. "He was weak. Soft."

"It's a wonder the Elite didn't fall under his leadership." The pacing resumed, Darik rubbed his chin. "Yet," he halted again, "you were much like him in those days. Not as you are now and... Are your eyes darker?"

"My lord?"

"Are they black?" Darik waved the question aside. "No matter. What I was saying was—On the battlefield you were a force to reckon with and dread."

19

Beaming from glorious war memories, he shook his fists at invisible foes. "Donning that grotesque helmet while leading lesser knights and soldiers into armies without a bloody fear." He sighed. "Gods! What a vision. I watched the enemy tremble as you charged with that flail spinning. Death on chains!" His shoulders lowered. "Off the field, your helmet discarded, there was a gentleness in your eyes—unlike now. You laughed amongst comrades, clasped arms with dying friends, and drank with your general. The very man you just called soft." Darik neared him.

"You have danced in the feast hall at the palace," he continued, "partook in His Eminence's galas, and gained his trust. Then you left it all for a simple nobleman's daughter."

The cold inside Renmier grew bitter as a brief dizziness overcame him. How did Darik know? Renmier disclosed nothing about Amalee to anyone. And referring to her as simple was a damn insult. She was a joy and peace he desperately desired after the war, and she changed her life to create a new one with him. He hadn't deserved Amalee.

"You went from one of the greatest Elites to this. What changed you?" Darik's brows lowered.

Renmier moved the tip of his tongue to the side of his mouth and bit until he felt pain. After a controlled breath through his nose, he said, "Death, my lord."

"Ah, yes. Your wife."

Renmier inched closer to the fireplace, wishing the heat could melt the agonizing chill within him.

"Galnikath, was it?" Darik asked. "Dreadful way to die. Or so I've been told."

Renmier wanted to shout the truth until his throat burned, but he contained that desire. "The matter at hand?"

Darik moseyed to his chair. "After her passing you disappeared, then returned a different person." He sat and motioned to the other seat at the small table. When Renmier joined him, he resumed. "Does losing a wife cause such darkness?"

Why couldn't Darik just get to the summons?

"Your command," Renmier said.

The duke released a breathy laugh. "As you wish, Vulture. You are to investigate the rumors, beginning in the Charville Duchy."

"That's awfully close to Ravieris."

"Best to learn if the order comes from there. Agreed?"

"Yes."

"Good. If you find no answers, go to the eastern region of the Newburrows Duchy and ask about Delvarian, but don't go to the elven country."

"Why inquire about the elves?"

"They are as much an enemy as is His Eminence."

"True." Renmier relaxed against the chair's tall back. It was almost too comfortable. "However, I don't speak their language."

"You'll have someone with you who does. In fact, she speaks and reads just about every language known on Emvarr."

Renmier didn't want a companion, and definitely not a maiden. She might interfere with everything. "It's bad enough rescuing them from your men, but to protect one on such a—"

"She goes with you. I command it. And she can fight if necessary."

Renmier shook his head. "I work better on my own."

"As you've admitted, you can't speak the Elven Tongue. In fact, avoid the pointy-eared bastards. They might try to take her back. Oh! And she speaks the underground cants."

Bloody guilds and their secret languages. And what did Darik mean about the elves wanting to take her back? Scowling, Renmier rubbed his temple. "Yes, my lord."

"Excellent! Now you'll meet her. And there are particulars you must know."

"Such as?"

The duke's visage hardened, his muscles tightened, and a slight tremor inflected his speech as he said, "She's mine."

Prey Meets Predator

avesse placed the quill into the inkwell then tugged at the neck band. Four months wearing the damn thing and she still wasn't used to its strangling presence. How had it come to this? Yes, she broke a few Bellinstarian customs and adopted some elven traditions, but such changes shouldn't have led to reprimands: suffering, loss, and disturbance of faith. If this was Javesse's path, then Fynthiar was a cruel god she could not forgive.

Things could've been harsher. Darik could have been a malicious master, but since her first night in Bashgrahon he'd not attempted to take her again. He did, however, find gratification by touching and kissing her body or watching her dance. Javesse kept his inability to perform in bed to herself, not that there was anyone to speak with. Not even her handmaiden. Javesse had learned the servant shared their conversations with Captain Samris Givins.

She had freedom to roam the castle grounds while under the watchfulness of the guards on the battlements, terrace, walking paths, or wherever they stood, and often with Samris at her side. Javesse despised him more than Darik. The leader of His Lordship's forces was a viper, and like other servants, loyal to the duke.

Even the local nobles swore allegiance to Darik, as long as they remained protected and at a heavy cost from their coffers. The peasants and laborers were terrified, not knowing if the next collection was their last day. And none dared speak of a rebellion.

There was no one to help Javesse.

She caught a teardrop before it landed on the parchment. After four hours of translating dwarven scrolls, she didn't want to start over. A heavy sigh released, she returned to deciphering the scripts from a dwarven clan of Yeuroth. As far as Javesse knew, the shorter folk lived only in the Southern Continent. What knowledge Darik desired from the stout race, she'd no inkling. Nor did she care. The scrolls held nothing of interest, only rantings from a mountain king about his cousin in a different range. Family squabbles. If such gossip piqued Darik's curiosities, and kept Javesse from his company, then she'd sit in her office for days translating hundreds of such writings.

But... there *was* a coded message that arrived from the palace in Ravieris that Darik had sent to her three nights past, the contents disturbing. Something must've distracted him, for he'd not inquired about the letter. The elves had told her the emperor of Descension was an awful man. After deciphering the Ravieris message, she came to know that truth. She could burn it and prevent Darik from learning about Emperor Larselis' orders. To do so might bring punishment to the duke, and possibly her.

Sighing, she read a few more of the dwarven words. If Darik hadn't learned of her talents, if she hadn't divulged everything to him, then... Javesse frowned. No point berating herself again. What did it matter? Even King Rainlisyr in Delvarian had taken advantage of her talents, as had her father. People always took from her. Except Beresly. He had wanted to give her everything.

No. To think once again of the lives she'd brought to an end promised smeared ink, more work, and the rending of her heart. Javesse couldn't take it anymore. Music. She needed something lovely to lighten her mood. A week had passed since the duke last let her sing.

As she glided the quill's tip on the parchment, she hummed, wishing to burst out a melody. It still brought a hint of joy. Music was her truest delight, and for Darik to limit it to his ears only was suffocating.

"Are you singing?" Samris asked from the doorway behind her.

Javesse gazed at the table lamp's flame. "If you can't tell the difference between singing and humming, you're an idiot."

His heels scraped the floor as he moved closer. "One day, His Grace will no longer tolerate your mouth."

"His Grace, indeed." She resumed writing. "Why are you here?"

Silence followed her question, yet the captain's anger pressed on her.

"He sends for you," Samris said, a hint of a growl present.

She dropped the quill into the inkwell. "Either I write the documents or... or what?"

He towed her from the chair. "The duke wants you, woman! Now move!" He pushed Javesse toward the exit.

She smoothed her dress. At least Darik didn't force her to don the revealing lighana garments anymore. "As *His Grace* wishes."

He escorted her to Darik's great study.

Javesse may have hated living at the castle, and Bashgrahon, but she loved this room. The magnificent fireplace permitted such a great blaze, it kept the chamber cozy, the plush furniture offered comfort, and sweet treats and drinks were often at the ready for her pleasures. The delights of the dark chocolates, fruit tarts, and pink wine already danced on her taste buds as she entered the room.

She slowed. Someone else was present.

He towered Darik next to the large desk, maybe standing six-foot-three; the fitting leather armor impressed a muscular body. Disheveled dark hair touched his shoulders, yet he was clean-shaven. And his black gaze locked on Javesse. At least his eyes seemed completely black—she could barely see the whites. He was unsettling. It might've been the horrific claw-like hilt of his sword. Or perhaps it was the lowering of his brows and the blackness recessing beneath his eyelids, revealing an iron color as the cold air surrounding him dissipated.

Javesse stiffened. Did she really see that? No. It wasn't possible for mists to flow in a person's eyes. Was it? The only thing certain was this stranger was the most devastatingly handsome human she'd ever seen, and he could've been mistaken as a southern Bellinstarian.

Not since her arrival at Bashgrahon had she such an urge to cover her face. Gripping the sides of her skirt, she looked at Darik and swallowed to relieve her dry throat as she stopped in front of them. "What do you want, you bloody bastard?"

He smirked while retreating a step.

The stranger's eyes widened. He backhanded Javesse right at the corner of her lips.

She half-spun, her neck hurting from the force of her head's sudden jerk to the side. The throbbing pain was immediate, and blood formed at a split.

"I'll not abide your contempt, woman." His voice was deep yet quiet, like a massive predator wanting to remain somehow unnoticed.

The duke swaggered forward.

She blinked tears free, then met the stranger's glare. No one had ever hit her so hard.

He grasped Javesse's chin; she clutched his arm, struggling. His painful hold stilled her as he slid his thumb over her stinging lips. Blood gathered on the flat, the stranger raised it to his mouth and released her. A faint grin formed before he sucked it clean.

"You..." Scowling, she shook her head. "You're appalling."

"As is your tongue." His lips hardly moved when he spoke.

It was wise to be intimidated by him. But Darik would make certain it'd not last for long.

"Vulture," Darik said, "this is my songbird."

Her disgust toward the duke for not protecting her shifted to the stranger. "Vulture," Javesse whispered. She'd heard stories about this man beating people and taking them somewhere private to devour them. She had never imagined someone so stunning, not with the moniker Vulture. "The name is fitting."

He responded with an arrogant smile.

Javesse glowered at Darik. "Was your goal to humiliate me?"

"My darling Songbird," he held her wrists tenderly "I'd never humiliate you. You brought that upon yourself."

She jerked free. "What do you want from me?"

Darik sighed. "Your expertise."

Javesse cast a frown from Vulture to the duke. "Would you just speak instead of playing these bloody games?"

"Sit." Darik gestured to the chairs. "Have some refreshments."

He knew her indulgences.

She walked a wide berth of Vulture, choosing the seat closest to the hearth. Darik served her dark chocolate and a glass of sweet pink wine. Vulture watched with low brows. He didn't know His Lordship well. Darik sat across from Javesse and explained the predicament he'd found himself in: he needed her help learning who wished to assassinate him. And she was to work with Vulture.

She grimaced from one man to the other. "I'll not do it."

"You've no choice," Darik said. "I'll tighten the band and do more than I already have."

Javesse spun from him and watched the fire while contemplating. No, he hadn't been dreadful. None of his men could handle nor abuse her... until now. Darik must've feared Vulture.

"What do I gain?" she asked. "Will you free me?"

"No," he whispered, his face twisting in a mix of anguish and fury. The expression softening, a breathy laugh escaped him. "Never, Songbird."

Tears surfaced. Looking away, she rolled her lips over her teeth and pressed. Javesse drew in a breath and nodded the slightest. "As I've no choice, what can I say?" She slammed the goblet on the table, breaking the stem, then rose to leave.

"Songbird—"

"No! I bloody hate you!"

She stormed out; Samris followed.

The pace quickened on the way to her chamber. Javesse needed to ponder what just happened, what Darik expected of her, and with whom she was to travel.

"Bastard," the captain muttered. "He believes he's something important."

The comment must've been directed at Vulture, for he never spoke against Darik.

"I don't care," she said.

Samris continued as if she'd not spoken. "I served under him during the war, but never saw his face until about five years ago, when he arrived here. Even then he seemed familiar." The captain massaged his neck. "I've scoured my mind to recall where I've seen the bastard, but I can't remember."

"How had you never seen him?"

"He always wore a helmet when addressing us *lowly* soldiers. I suppose he believed it'd frighten us." Samris shrugged. "The Emperor's Elite were a pompous sort."

That explained Vulture's arrogance and cruelty.

The elves had taught Javesse about the Elite Knights of His Eminence, and she'd read of their skills on the battlefield, learning what frightful opponents they were. She had never met one until now.

Renmier remained astonished. Too much happened too quickly. The most beautiful woman he'd ever seen shocked him with her behavior—to which he *had* to respond whether or not he liked it—then she was gone. How could such a sweet, melodious voice speak those harsh words? Yet what a remarkable sight in his bleak life: shining gold hair, large amber irises—darkest around the edges and at the pupils—and flesh so fair and flawless. And Songbird's nearness brought him a sense of warmth. Something he hadn't experienced since the initial ritual.

Of course, he noticed the jeweled neck-band marking her a lighana. Many nobles of the highest stature, including the emperor, owned such slaves they gratified themselves with. Most lighanas were women, and it was normal for masters to force their pleasure slaves to don scanty outfits. However, Darik's lighana wore the finest clothing of a modest presentation, with exception of the neck-band.

Songbird's perfume lingered in the chamber. The spirit of a memory, even though she'd been there only a moment ago. Too much time had passed in her brief absence.

Renmier didn't need reminders of her existence.

"She is quite a lot of which to—adjust, to say the least," Darik said. "The woman had lived with the elves."

Renmier nodded, then scowled. "You permit her to address you in such a way?"

His bottom lip protruding, Darik shrugged. "Perhaps it's my weakness to her beauty—my enrapture—that I can't punish her." He poured himself a drink, and still hadn't offered one to Renmier. "I've considered putting the task upon others, such as Captain Givins, but the idea of harming Songbird makes me queasy."

Annoyed, Renmier clasped his hands behind his back. Why *had* Samris even been there? Darik knew Renmier despised him. The duke made interactions between the two men rare events to avoid the tension often between them. The captain's presence had re-surged the need to kill, an urge Renmier sated upon others. But that impulse had never yielded to anyone as it had the duke's lighana. Songbird.

"You *are* to protect her," Darik said. "No harm falls upon my Songbird, and no one may touch her." Pointing at Renmier, he sneered. "Not even you."

Renmier scoffed. "No concern there."

"No?" Darik arched a disbelieving brow. "I noticed your reaction when you saw her."

"She's a beauty. Nothing more."

"She's so much more. Songbird is my most prized possession." Placing his cup beside the broken goblet, the duke frowned at the spilt wine. "You've not heard her sing." Darik's tone was soft, as if speaking to a lover. "She captures me. Holds me. I'm lost, and nearly brought to tears when she sings." A slight grin curved his lips. "Dare I admit I've shed a few?"

Soft. Renmier shrugged.

Darik chuckled. "Then tell no other." He lifted his cup and swirled the drink within. "No, you've not heard her sing. Nor shall you. Her voice belongs to me, Vulture. She's *my* songbird. Do you understand?"

The slave's hold on Darik was so strong, he permitted her to disrespect him because she could sing. He *had* grown weak.

"I do."

"And, Vulture."

"My lord?"

"Strike her again... and I'll have you hung."

Renmier bowed his head.

Fury hastened Javesse's steps along the corridor. She despised this—this Vulture! Who was he to dictate how she was to bathe, dress, and travel? The duke allowing the brute control over her was unbelievable. She had a few things to say about the ordeal, and Darik *would* listen. He talked so much the evening before, she'd have her say this morning.

The previous night, he embraced her in his bed, stroking her cheek while voicing his concern about this mission. He wished to send his men along, but they were useless. According to Darik, Vulture knew where to go and whom to look for in Descension, and most wouldn't dare stray into his path. Worried about the safety of Javesse's body and voice, Darik had forced her into a promise.

"If he touches you in harm or pleasure, or forces you to sing, you tell me, Songbird. Promise you'll tell me, and I'll kill him."

Javesse might lie just to watch Vulture suffer before death claimed him. There was no doubt Darik would ensure he'd hurt. First, she had a special request.

Samris was close behind, carrying her weapon belt, the sword bound in a peace knot. He sounded a low chuckle. "Your ass looks fine in those breeches."

Flesh heated, she glared at him. "What did you say?"

He took in the full view of her: the cream blouse, fitted brown leather vest and pants too snug for her liking. The handmaiden had braided Javesse's hair, coiling it at the crown of her head. And that was it. No perfumes, no jewelry—except the damn neck-band. Darik never let her take that off. What she hated most was she couldn't wear a veil. Vulture would have the pleasure of seeing her every day, and he didn't deserve it.

"I asked you a question, Captain," she said.

His admiration rose from her breasts to her face. "You've such a fine ass, Songbird." Samris raised the belt. "I'm curious how well this rests upon it."

Bellinstarian men never spoke in such despicable ways, and Javesse doubted any decent man did. Yet no good would come of slapping Samris. Darik's men may not have their way with her, but they got their words in when possible.

Javesse's muscles burning with the need to strike someone, she continued to the study. She slowed as they rounded the last corner. Maybe this was Fynthiar's Plan for her to find freedom. Javesse would have to put faith in the Father of All such a thought was true.

Of course, the duke wasn't alone in the smaller study. Vulture was with him. The horrid beast did a double take of her, but unlike others, he tried to hide that what he saw pleased him. He leaned toward Darik and whispered.

Javesse crossed her arms and shifted most of her weight to the left. "Can I please practice my people's custom while I'm forced in his," she pointed at Vulture, "presence?"

Darik glanced at him. "No. It'll draw attention."

"You think *that* draws attention?" she snapped.

Vulture's dark eyes darted to Samris. "We're wasting time."

If Javesse had seen correctly, loathing resided within Vulture's expression.

"Agreed." Darik nodded to the captain. "Give her weapon to him."

Samris offered the belt to Vulture.

The large man remained still, his deep breaths growing louder. He gripped his sword hilt, the air around him chilled, and a sudden stench filled the area. And there was no doubt this time Javesse witnessed black mists flowing from beneath his eyelids and toward his pupils.

She drew in a scant breath, held it. *Fynthiar's Might... what is—?*

"Vulture?" Darik said.

Vulture blinked several times at Javesse, revealing iron once more as the rank odor disappeared and the whites of his eyes cleared. "Forgive me," he said. "I ate something unsettling last night."

Guffawing, Samris thrust the sword belt at him. "Must've eaten at Star Hall. It's a lousy tavern, but you travelers enjoy that garbage."

Vulture snatched the belt, knocking the captain's arm aside. "We leave now."

"No need to be bloody rude," Samris said. "You've something to say, Bird?"

Vulture's enormous chest expanded as the darkness returned. He looked insane. "I don't like you. In fact, I'm going to kill you."

"What?" Samris half-drew his sword.

"Enough." Darik patted the captain's shoulder while giving Vulture a quizzical expression. "That was harsh, my friend." Sounding an uneasy laugh, he gestured at Vulture's stomach. "You probably haven't recovered yet. Poor Songbird."

Samris' hold on his weapon didn't loosen; Vulture's facial muscles remained tense.

Javesse retreated a few steps, yet remained transfixed by the large man and the whole bizarre event. "Di-did you say something?" she asked Darik.

"It's time to go." He held her hands and kissed her forehead. "Do be careful. Fly home to me."

She jerked away, then stretched her hand to Vulture. "My sword."

He looked from Samris to her. "Not yet."

Huffing, she headed for the door.

Vulture was right behind her, and Darik's words followed.

"Return her to me or you're dead, Vulture!"

"Hegrus, ebris Sebysula." Renmier cut his arm with the shaman's knife.

"Hegrus, ebris Renmier Forais," the shaman chanted, shadows swirling around them.

"Hegrus, ebris Sebysula. Geshuvorda, mordra, Rastnin Kirlyr," several voices replied from the dark haze.

"Rastnin Kirlyr," Renmier said. "Rastnin Kirlyr."

He repeated the name while black mists amid twisted trees filled his mind, and the coldest air he'd ever experienced danced on his flesh. Then he fell unconscious.

Rastnin Kirlyr. Renmier had stared at Samris, want for blood prodding him to kill, and reminded himself of that name: Rastnin Kirlyr. The name he'd heard four months ago, that repeated in his head before sleep, and he spoke while passing coins. A name that must cease to exist very soon. Rastnin, not Samris.

The Darkness had almost consumed him in the study, increasing the appetite to slaughter everyone in the chamber—even Songbird. It confused Renmier that Darik's voice snapped him from the thick mists. However, it was *she*, like the glowing warmth of the sun's often absent rays, who had freed his mind and strengthened his will. Songbird was his Light in the Darkness.

He didn't deserve to be near such an exquisite creature. What little soul he had left was for completing his mission. Renmier prayed to whatever god might listen that Songbird could be spared if she fell into his path.

They entered the castle stables, where Titan stood in a corner alone; the other horses crowded together at the opposite end. The large chestnut stallion snorted upon Renmier's approach.

"I hope they fed you well." Renmier patted the horse.

Titan lowered his head, tilted it, then raised it.

"Good."

Songbird gaped. She was nearly half a foot shorter than Renmier, and Titan made her seem smaller.

"He won't bite," Renmier said.

Folding her arms beneath her bosom, she straightened her back. "Must we ride together?"

"I don't trust you."

"Nor I you," Songbird whispered.

He guided Titan from the barn, noting two extra sacks tied to the saddle and the packs stocked. Renmier grasped the woman's hips, giving her no chance to fight as he placed her atop the stallion.

She slapped his shoulder. "I'm capable of getting on a horse by myself!"

"I wasn't waiting."

He climbed on behind her and directed Titan to the road. Wasting no more time, he commanded the mount into a trot. There was too much ground to cover, and his destination in the Charville Duchy was a six-day ride without interference.

Songbird's rigid posture forced her shoulders to thump his chest, and her hair brushed his nose.

Gods! She smelled like a sun-soaked field.

He had insisted she bathed with plain soap to remove the perfumes, but her wonderful, natural scent warmed him. No woman had ever affected him like that. Not even Amalee.

They rode most of the day in complete silence. Songbird would probably keep to herself if he attempted conversation anyway. It wasn't as if Renmier introduced himself kindly the night before. No. It was best this way.

"Can we rest?" she asked, breaking into his thoughts.

"Not yet."

"I need to relieve myself."

"The village is a mile away. You'll relieve yourself there."

She shook her head and clicked her tongue.

Songbird might have power over the duke, but she didn't control Renmier. No one did. Not even Darik.

They reached Volthany, a sizable village outside Talgrian Forest. With the heavy merchant traffic between communities and woodlands, many travelers and tax collectors called it a minor city. The proprietors did well in Volthany, and rumors gathered in the businesses. There were a few taverns, but Renmier had his preference, as he did wherever he frequented.

He directed Titan to the stables closest to The Long Road Tavern and paid for a few nights of the stallion's care, needed or not.

While he removed necessary packs from the saddle, Songbird practically danced where she stood. She must've been on the verge of wetting herself.

"How long must I wait?" she asked.

Renmier placed the flail into the wide, deep scabbard at his left side—the ball followed by the chains—then removed her weapon belt, his hand axe, and sword; the shield remained on the horse. He glared at the stable master, who nodded several times.

"All'll be safe, m'lord."

Renmier took an extra gold roan from his pouch and flipped it to him. "Good." He started for the tavern.

"Where's the bloody privies?" Songbird snapped.

He bobbed his head toward the outhouses located just off the road, away from the businesses.

She bolted for them, pushing people from her path.

Chuckling, Renmier followed.

The privies were amongst many of the improvements Emperor Larselis brought to the southern half of Brydasia. Before His Eminence conquered most of the continent, this region had been nothing but filth. Larselis demanded magnificence of his empire and outlawed public defecation within cities and towns. No more people dropping their pants in the streets, leaving their disgusting puddles and piles scattered. The outhouses were amid the first new structures built, and war prisoners cleaned them weekly. Rundown buildings were fixed or rebuilt, sometimes overtaken by those of wealth interested in the locations for new businesses. Elite Knights who retired, promised rewards for their service in the war, had received choice sites to build an establishment or home. Renmier knew of knights who left the larger cities for hamlets or farmsteads, seeking peace.

He frowned, recalling how quickly his reward was taken from him. Closing his eyes, he breathed deep and pushed Amalee into the thick black mists.

Songbird sighed twice throughout the duration of a long, steady stream. She came out, wiping sweat from her forehead. "Amused, are you?"

With a slight lift at the corner of his lips, he motioned to the tavern with his axe.

She stepped ahead of him. "You don't talk much, do you?"

His long strides caught him up with her. "You care naught of my thoughts."

"I believed you occupied your small mind with different methods of slaughter and devouring."

Renmier fought a laugh. "Predators think. We plan."

She gave him a sidelong look, then gulped.

Once inside, he moved ahead, clearing the way to the bar; Songbird was close behind. Good. Silence ensued as the crowd stopped what they were doing to stare.

The lanky barkeep grinned. "Welcome back, sir. I've your room at the ready, as you like." He removed a ring with a pair of keys from a wooden box and handed it to Renmier. "I'll keep your tab."

Renmier maintained lodgings in the communities he often stayed, many of them holding particular items. In the less savory cities, he hired someone to protect those rooms. The Long Road tavern didn't need protection.

Renmier looked at Songbird from over his shoulder. "Come."

Huffing, she trailed him to the steps at the far end of the room.

Only a few from the subdued crowd dared to murmur, their full attention on Renmier and Songbird.

The barkeep waved his arms. "What? Have you never seen a man and woman come in together before? Go on with your damn business!"

Renmier placed his foot on the bottom step and glared at the gawkers until they faced their drinks. He continued up the stairs, down the hall to a door, unlocking it to another set of stairs shorter than the previous. On the third floor were a few private rooms for special guests... like him. He proceeded to the last room on the right at the end of the hall, using another key. Inside, Renmier set the items down, scanning the chamber to ensure everything was as he left it seven moons ago. Satisfied, he closed the door, then checked the hooks on the shutters were in place.

Songbird hugged herself, eyeing the single bed.

"They think you're mine," he said.

She grimaced.

"Play that part," he added.

Her eyes watered. She blinked until the tears vanished. "Fine," she whispered. "Let's eat."

Downstairs, he approached his usual table next to the fireplace where three men sat. "Move," he commanded.

Smirking, a man inhaled to speak, but upon seeing Renmier, the smile and words faded. "Y-yes, sir."

The three grabbed their mugs and bowls and found a different place to finish their meal.

"That wasn't necessary," Songbird said.

Renmier pointed at an empty chair.

Frowning, she sat.

"Wait here." He strode to the barkeep and leaned over five goblets of ale. "I need a message delivered."

"I'll send for the lackey."

Many looked from Javesse to Vulture while he spoke with the barkeep. The people shared whispers, their expressions judging her. So they believed she was Vulture's lighana. It didn't matter. But Javesse hated feeling exposed in public. At Bashgrahon, she remained hidden from those outside the castle. Darik did his best to keep her to himself, then why couldn't he honor a simple wish and allow Javesse to conceal her face? Perhaps she might not draw attention. She was no fool; she was aware of her beauty. Most Bellinstarians were exceptionally attractive.

During the days of old, feuds started between many Bellinstarian clans. The king declared a new order in which the women veiled their faces, leaving only their eyes showing. It didn't immediately end all the disputes, for men swore they saw Fynthiar's White Fields in a woman's gaze. However, the bloodshed lessened within a decade. By Javesse's birth, centuries after the custom began, such quarrels amongst her people were unheard of. The only man permitted to see a Bellinstarian woman's face was her husband.

Javesse was prepared to give that honor to Beresly, an elf lord who had treated her with respect and kindness. Beresly had loved her. He died while trying to protect her, and it was her fault.

Vulture sat in the chair next to her. "What is it?"

She blinked, not making sense of the question.

"You're crying."

Javesse wiped her cheeks, finding them damp. "Memories," she whispered.

He leaned closer. Iron stared at her, showing no care, no compassion. "Present yourself better."

A barmaid arrived with two bowls, setting them before Javesse and Vulture. She hurried off, then returned with a goblet and a tankard. Before she resumed serving others, Vulture grabbed her wrist and placed a gold roan into her palm.

Her cheeks tinged bright pink. "Thank you, m'lord." The barmaid bent toward him, the slopes of her breasts pressing to the low-cut top. "If you want anything else, my name's Admona." She slid her fingers to his shoulder as she sauntered away.

Javesse wrinkled her nose.

Without a reaction to the flirtatious behavior, Vulture dug into the stew.

Javesse moved the chunks of meat aside and gathered the vegetables. Even if the first fifteen years of her life included consuming animals her family hunted, she had grown accustomed to the elves' eating habits. Meat wasn't as appetizing anymore; however, Darik had forced her to consume it. She didn't enjoy it, but did not hate it. Javesse just needed time to re-familiarize with the flavor and texture. At least the broth here was tasty. Samris Givins often insulted meals provided outside the estate, as if he could convince Javesse's life was better under Darik's care.

Vulture slammed his tankard on the tabletop.

The barmaid returned a moment later, her cleavage showing more. "Yes, m'lord."

"More stew, more ale."

Admona's confidence faltered. The bowl collected, she tramped to the kitchen.

Javesse fought the urge to titter.

"You're amused," Vulture said.

She shoved a spoonful of stew into her mouth. Chunks of meat caught between her teeth, Javesse chewed slowly. It was decent. She washed the food down with the weak wine. Darik never served her such horrible drinks.

Admona returned with another bowl and tankard, then spun to leave.

"Send more ale." Vulture's lips moved the slightest.

The barmaid paused. "Yes, m'lord." She hurried to other patrons before returning to the bar.

"Planning to have a fine time together tonight?" Javesse asked.

Vulture had just scooped stew in his mouth. Gaze still on her, he slid the spoon out.

Why did she attempt humor? He was a killer. Who ate his victims! There couldn't be joy in his life.

Looking away, she grabbed the goblet, but recalled the wine lacked flavor, so moved the cup aside.

"I *enjoyed* a farm maiden night before last," Vulture said.

Javesse wanted to say something witty. Nothing came to mind. If he believed his bragging might upset her, he thought highly of himself. She wrinkled her nose and squinted. "Now you can enjoy *Admona*."

He grunted, then resumed eating. Laughter likely accompanied his murderous acts.

Vulture hovered over the bowl, shoveling a spoonful after another. A drink of ale followed every fourth scoop. Several patrons stared his way, their discomfort obvious. He kept eating and drinking. The flail's handle, jutting from its bulky scabbard, should've been a hinderance, yet every one of his motions around it were flawless, like it was an extension of him.

Javesse finished half the stew and a quarter of the wine.

"Eat," he rumbled.

"I'm not fond of meat."

"Around elves too long." His lips hardly moved... still.

"I'd rather be with them than you."

Vulture nodded. At least they both agreed on that.

She pushed the bowl aside. "Are we meeting someone here tonight?"

He shook his head.

"Do you speak more than four sentences every hour?"

Vulture's attention remained on his meal. "Not much to say."

"You don't move your lips when you speak."

He looked at her. "And you move yours too often. Gods, woman, do you ever cease talking?"

Sitting back, she sighed. "You're dreadful."

"You're no delight either."

"Pah!"

A few people watched their interaction.

Vulture glanced at them, then at Javesse. "I suggest you remember the conversation before we came down, Songbird."

"You mean your telling me what I am, Vulture?"

"Exactly." He poked at the tiny remnants of meat in the bowl. "It's for your good you do as I say."

She crossed her arms. "For me or your reputation?"

"Do you ever learn?"

"Learn what? To be an obedient lighana?"

His narrowed glare fixed on her. "To shut your bloody mouth."

"Or what? You'll strike me?" She dipped her head toward her shoulder. "His Grace will punish you."

Vulture's brows lowered for the briefest moment. "Must you make things difficult?" He stood, his fingertips brushing the table's surface. "We're done here."

"I'm not finished—"

"You are."

They'd gained an audience from those nearby. Javesse hadn't meant to, but she pushed Vulture too far.

She followed him to the room. Arms wrapped around herself, she held her shoulders. Fear shuddered along her spine as he shut the door, locked it, then put the key in his pocket. The flail thudded on the table, making her heart patter.

Vulture sat on the side of the bed and spun a ring on his right hand. "I'm meeting someone tomorrow night. You must behave, Songbird."

Fynthiar strike him! She hated him calling her by that name, but what could she say? There was no making demands on Vulture when Darik had given him control over her.

"Whom are we meeting?" Javesse asked.

He stood, nodded to the bed. "Rest."

She scowled. "Are you telling me or not?"

"Until you prove I can trust you, I'll not tell you a bloody thing."

"Why am I even here?"

"My thoughts as well." Vulture moved the chair in front of the exit, grabbed the flail, and lowered in the seat. "Now sleep."

She placed her fists on her hips. "At least tell me how I can help."

"You might play a part in the assassination."

Was he an idiot?

A brief laugh escaped her. Then it grew. "Please explain how I can plan the duke's assassination while imprisoned in *his* home."

The spiked ball dropped, the points embedding into the floorboards; Javesse jumped.

Eyes darker, Vulture leaned forward. "Darik's got enemies, woman, even people close to him. And I don't trust you." He tugged on the weapon, freeing it from the wood. "Sleep."

If he intended to frighten her, he succeeded. Was rest possible with him present?

She turned, unbuttoned the leather vest, then dropped it to the floor. Javesse sat on the bed and removed her boots. It felt good to release her hair from the bound braid, the pressure off her scalp.

Vulture took in her every motion.

She'd never encountered someone immune to her beauty until now.

He was unmoved. Icy. As if he had no soul.

Appalling Acts

Renmier remained awake. He couldn't chance Songbird attempting an escape, not that she'd succeed. If she woke up during the night, he wanted her to see him guarding. The quiet hours gave him time to think, but nothing came from the ponderings. His mind couldn't wander in a direction leading off his path, so Renmier focused on Songbird. It wasn't hard, although boring. She must've been exhausted. Songbird had moved little by dawn.

She rolled over and stretched. Her back arched, thrusting her chest upward the slightest, her fingertips brushing the wall.

Renmier fixed on Songbird's face, but the battle against her lithe movements failed. She had the figure of a well-toned warrior.

Her eyelids fluttered open. Songbird stared at him for a moment. "Did you move at all?"

He blinked.

She looked at the flail still in his grip. "Kill anyone last night?"

The woman was witty, yet Renmier didn't respond.

Songbird sat up; her hair tangled in various places. The languorous stretch she performed enthralled Renmier, yet he controlled his body's reaction. By her adorable grimace, it was obvious Darik spoiled her with a luxurious bed.

Renmier continued observing her graceful movements. Taking a brush from a backpack was a simple task, yet Songbird made it elegant. To watch her brush her hair, the bristles transforming knots into a perfect gold curtain, relaxed him. The night before, he had loved watching as she unbraided it, the locks falling over her shoulders and back. While she had slept, temptation prodded Renmier to touch the strands, but he didn't deserve the pleasure.

She pulled the sides back and bound them, then she lifted her pack. "I must change."

"Later. I'm hungry."

Her brows furrowed. "You expect me to go down there in last night's clothing?"

"Does it matter?"

Those perfect lips parted as she huffed. "I smell awful."

"I don't care."

"Well, I bloody do!"

Renmier dropped the flail on the table and rose. "Put your boots on."

Grabbing her boots, she muttered, "Four words already? You're off to an early start."

He smiled inwardly.

They broke fast with a simple meal consisting of porridge with honey, and a thick cut pork strip; Renmier ate Songbird's share of the pork. He had coffee, a strong drink brewed from dark beans imported from Myndrose and served hot, while she enjoyed tea. Songbird wrinkled her nose at his cup, seeming familiar with the bitter drink. It wouldn't be a surprise, for Darik was fond of coffee, along with any imports from the other continents, giving him something to brag about.

The morning presented calm patrons in the tavern speaking about their upcoming day. Songbird kept her mouth shut this time; however, she still drew attention. It wasn't the poor woman's fault men ogled her. Then their comments reached Renmier's ears.

"Lucky bastard to have such a gorgeous lighana."

"I'd love to get my hands on her neck-band."

"Gods. I'd love to get my hands on *her*."

"You guys are bloody idiots. Who gives a goat's ass about the band? I want to bury my cock in her hard and slow."

Frowning, Songbird ceased stirring her porridge.

"Stay here." Renmier walked to the men.

"Vulture," she called.

"Gods," one man said as Renmier stopped at their table. "Forgive me. I didn't know it was you, an-and that she's yours."

Renmier hated the assumption, but he had to pretend... as usual. Fists on the tabletop, he leaned inward and scanned the four nervous faces. "Who's looking to bury their cock in my lighana?"

That word tasted foul.

Two men darted their eyes to the one seated at Renmier's left.

The guilty party shook his head. "You bloody bastards."

Yes, it was his voice.

There was no hesitation, Renmier backhanded the foul-mouthed dolt on the nose, nearly knocking him from the chair. He snatched the fool's shirt collar and slugged his jaw hard, a slight pain jolting through his hand.

"Stop!" Songbird shrieked as nearby patrons scurried away.

The dolt's grunts of pain sounded as Renmier continued, leaving the man's face a mess of torn flesh, broken bones, and blood.

Songbird grasped Renmier's arm, gaping at the gruesome sight. "Gods," she whispered. "What've you done?"

Renmier shrugged her off and pointed to their table. "Sit your ass down!"

Stiffening, she shuffled a few steps, then hurried back to her seat.

He looked at the other men. "Who's next?"

Their faces went paler.

"Forgive us." One blinked rapidly. "We meant... We're sorry."

Another fell to his knees. "Don't kill me."

Renmier punched the beggar's face, forcing him to prop on one arm for support. The poor bastard raised his other hand; Renmier kicked his side, the ribs caving. The beggar collapsed.

Renmier sneered at the other two men, then viewed the remaining patrons. "If I catch anyone staring at my woman, I'll tear their eyes out," he said. "If I hear any remarks about her again, I'll kill those who speak them."

Everyone looked down. Submissive.

Back at his table, Renmier glared at the trembling Songbird. "Get up," he said. Tears brimming, she stood.

He trudged to the stairs, glancing at the barkeep, who bowed his head.

Songbird waited at the steps. Good, she'd learned. Or maybe Darik trained her well enough.

They returned to the room. While she lowered to the bed, hugging herself, Renmier sat on the chair. He inspected his aching hand, where blood streaked his knuckles and fingers. He didn't always enjoy doing this, but for Songbird's sake, he licked his knuckles. It wasn't displeasing. Renmier had grown accustomed to the flavor while serving in His Eminence's Elite, when blood had splattered onto his lips during battle the times he removed his helmet. Those days, it was thrilling to taste the vitality of his enemies before they died... or after.

Songbird clicked her tongue and wrinkled her nose. "You missed a spot."

Her attempt to be condescending failed; he found the tiny lines bunched along her nose too adorable.

"Did I?" Renmier slid his finger from his ear to his chin, gathering droplets of blood, then sucked it clean. "Like a fine wine."

"You're disgusting!" She rose. "You didn't have to hurt them."

"I did."

She shook her head. "Why?"

"No one talks like that about what's mine."

Breaths heavy, her chest rose and fell. "I'm not yours," she whispered.

"They don't know that."

"They were men who—"

"Who've now learned their lesson." He stood. "No more is to be said."

Songbird looked terrified. Perfect. Her fear meant she'd do as he needed.

She stared at her fidgeting fingers. "Now what?"

He thrust his hands into the basin water, watching a cloud of pink float beneath the surface. "Now you change your clothes."

What was Javesse to do? Vulture was insane. Now he might come to believe she belonged to him, especially after the violent display in the tavern. Honest to Fynthiar, Javesse feared the man. Why did Darik trust him? She had to escape before Vulture hurt her. But where could she go? She was unfamiliar with this region of Brydasia.

Javesse finished buttoning her blouse. At least Vulture gave her the courtesy of keeping his back to her while she dressed. Spinning, she scowled. No. He'd sat in the chair and ogled her the whole time.

"Were you entertained?" she asked.

The bastard bit the corner of his bottom lip, then smirked. "You have a... lovely back."

Javesse leered at him. "I despise you."

"No doubt you'll think of new ways to say it again."

"I'm working on it."

He chuckled. "Finished?"

She grabbed the leather vest and buttoned it on. "Where are we going?"

"You'll see."

Vulture said *she* made things difficult when *he* couldn't answer a simple question?

After Javesse laced her boots, he threw on his cape and escorted her from the tavern. Rainfall had preceded dawn, leaving the grass saturated and the muddy roads spotted with puddles. The morning's chill seeped through Javesse's blouse, and she shivered. She should've worn her leather jacket, but she couldn't think in Vulture's presence.

"How long does it take for this side of Brydasia to warm?" Javesse asked.

Vulture drew in a long breath, as if enjoying the frosty spring morning. "A few more weeks."

"I pray to Fynthiar we're finished before then."

"You dislike fair weather?"

"I despise this cold. It's already pleasant in Delvarian."

"You wish to return to Duke Nornt's soon?"

Javesse readied to answer the ridiculous question, but had no response. Honestly, what could she say when Darik trapped her inside the castle for most hours of the day?

Vulture snickered at her silence.

She hated him more now than an hour ago. Javesse shuddered just to recall the savage assault he'd committed upon the two men. If he believed she'd not heard worse comments, he was mistaken. And what Vulture said about her belonging to him... She hoped he didn't think a smidgen of it was true.

With the beastly man one night, and Javesse longed for Bashgrahon. She'd rather endure Darik than this creature. Truth be told, she'd welcome Samris' company right now.

From beside Vulture, she stared at the road and rubbed her arms, watching for him to change direction. It was unnecessary, for whenever he made a sudden shift, he guided her gently by the arm. Strange how the brute showed tenderness. Javesse blew into her hands to warm them.

Vulture walked a block farther before taking another turn and stopping. "Here."

She looked up to see where they were, but she'd misunderstood.

He draped the heavy cape over her shoulders. A thin line formed between his low brows as he fastened a vulture-shaped pin to keep the cloak in place.

Javesse remained still.

He showed no emotions. Vulture must be exceptional at hiding his feelings, for why would he display concern if he felt nothing?

He tilted his head back. "His Grace would be most displeased if you fell ill, Songbird."

She wrinkled her nose. "He certainly would."

Vulture might've believed he fooled her, but he wasn't afraid of Darik. This man wasn't afraid of anyone.

As they continued through the village, Javesse's boots grew heavier with mud.

"Just where are we going?" she asked. "Another town?"

"Is it ever possible for you *not* to speak? Because that's what you must do." Vulture halted in front of a two-story building. "Don't even sigh in here. Don't look at the others."

"What are—?"

"Damn it, woman." He grasped the hair at his nape. "Can you follow one bloody command?" His iron irises glowed to a refined steel.

The transformation captured Javesse. She'd never seen an individual's eyes change so much, or at all. There was something intriguing about Vulture—the battle within his mind curious.

The bright color faded to the dull shade.

"What?" he asked.

Blinking, she lowered her gaze. "My people say the eyes reveal much." Javesse raised her head again. "I've never seen someone's divulge as much as yours."

"You think you've seen something?"

She kept a flat tone as she answered, "I have."

Vulture bent his knees enough to bring his face closer, eye-to-eye with her. "You've seen nothing, Songbird. You don't know a bloody thing about me."

There it was, lingering at the edge of his eyelids: a faint black mist waiting to engulf as it had in Darik's study. A chill raced the length of Javesse's spine. As a child, she'd heard stories about demons from the Blackening with such afflictions.

The cocky expression fading, Vulture straightened.

"I saw something," Javesse whispered.

"And what was it?"

She swallowed to wet her throat. "Th-the Darkness."

He grunted a laugh. "Then I suppose your people are correct." Vulture grabbed her arm, the tenderness absent. "As I said, mind yourself. Don't react to what they do or say. *I'll* take care of them. Do you understand?"

Sneering, she replied, "Yes, sir."

Vulture's large hand rested on the back of her neck; she stiffened. He released the band's excess from beneath the metal loop and tugged on it, pulling her ear close to his mouth. "Play your part, Songbird." The words were harsh. Gruff.

Javesse nodded, withholding the urge to cry. She now understood where they were.

He let go and knocked on the door.

After a few seconds passed, it opened a slit, and a man hushed, "What?"

"I sent word of my coming." Vulture didn't lower his tone, nor check if anyone watched.

"Yes, yes. She's expecting you."

Vulture and Javesse entered, then the door slammed shut behind them. It was dark in the small space they occupied, a dim red light coming from further down a corridor.

A man taller than Vulture, yet rotund and reeking of body odor, peered at Javesse. His round face was in a pinched expression, and small dark orbs were hard to see from beneath thick brows. His fat fingers squished upon her chin, tilting it back. "What've we here?"

She opened her mouth to tell him to remove his filthy hands, but Vulture squeezed her wrist in a silent warning. Javesse pursed her lips and held her breath to avoid the doorman's stench.

Vulture moved his arm between them. "She's mine."

The doorman dropped his hand, his beady eyes darting from Javesse to Vulture. "So she is, m'lord. So she is." Giggling, he wiped his mouth. "For now." He clapped as he spun and waddled ahead, appearing he might bounce off the walls in his haste.

Javesse looked at Vulture as they followed. "What does—?"

He tugged the collar. "Close... your... mouth. That's the final warning."

Tired of his dreadful treatment, acting like he really was her master, she grabbed his wrist and dug her nails into the flesh. "Or what, you bastard?"

Vulture slammed Javesse against the wall and pinned her, forcing the air from her lungs. Candlelight flickered from within a glazed red wall sconce, the dancing shadows making him ominous.

Their escort paused. "Is there trouble with your lighana? Shall I retrieve a whip for you, m'lord?"

Vulture's hard muscles flexed beneath the leather top, and his breath filled her ear. "I will bloody hurt you right here, right now. Then again in my room."

Uncontrollable quaking infected her.

"Wish to challenge my threat?" Vulture asked.

Eyelids squeezed shut and lips pressed between her teeth, she shook her head.

"No, what?" he continued.

Teardrops skimmed her cheeks as she looked into his eyes. "No, Master."

There it was again... a strange alteration in his visage that divulged something. The word, Master, Vulture disliked it. But he was so damn insistent she called him by that title.

He grabbed the strap and continued after the doorman.

Why was Songbird so bloody stubborn? Gods! Renmier didn't want to hurt her, but she was determined to resist. Even after he had shown her compassion on their way to the market. He was trying to keep Songbird safe, yet she still defied him. If he had told her where they were going, she might've refused to enter the building. Not that it mattered, he would've made her.

If he could have his way, he'd free all the slaves and burn the market, but another would replace it in less than six moons.

The doorman led them for a lengthy amount of time. They went upstairs, turned corners, downstairs, rounded more bends, then descended other steps, the building larger than it appeared from outside. Renmier had walked it before when seeking one of his past victims. No, not victims. Those men were criminals who had finally met justice.

The foul-smelling guide halted at a banded door and chuckled. He opened it. "Mistress, your guest has arrived. And he has a beauty with him." The doorman clapped again.

Renmier shoved him inside and entered, pulling Songbird. He gripped the doorman's throat. "You putrid—"

"Enough," said the gorgeous elf sitting behind a large white willow desk. Her tight blouse remained untied halfway, revealing more fine curves of pale-gray flesh. Powders shimmered silver on her skin from the flickering candlelight, and long white hair parted over her pointed ears. Renmier had heard a rumor she'd once been a pleasure slave to His Eminence before gaining her freedom.

Volthany might seem small for a profitable lighana market, but it was the perfect location for the proprietor to conduct her other business: a network of spies throughout southern Descension. If someone sought a particular person or persons, she found them for a sum equal to a fine lighana. Her market helped Volthany thrive with the wealthy traffic it brought, including nobles from Ravieris looking for their next pleasure slave.

Renmier released the doorman, then offered the woman a partial bow. "Mistress." He didn't know her name. Only Emperor Larselis did. The Serine elf went by the title of which Renmier just addressed her.

Songbird gasped. "No."

Renmier tugged on her strap, silencing her.

Mistress fixed her platinum gaze on Songbird as she shooed the fat bastard away. "Leave us," she said. "I am not to be disturbed."

"Yes, Mistress." The doorman's shuffling feet signaled his departure.

The elf rose. "Name your price, Vulture."

He pulled Songbird closer, making a claim that wasn't his. "No."

Songbird trembled beside him.

"I will give what you seek in exchange for her." Mistress stepped around the desk, her hips swaying. "His Eminence will pay a fortune for this one."

"She has naught to do with *our* business."

"Please?" The elf grazed her fingertips from his stomach to his ear. "I have never seen such a beautiful human... other than you."

Renmier lowered her hand. "She's mine."

Pouting, Mistress retreated. "Tell me from whom you obtained her."

He sighed. "We've business."

"You purchased a lighana from another." She narrowed her eyes. "Why should I deal further with you?"

"I have the black roans."

With noticeable longing, Mistress touched Songbird's golden hair. "Exquisite."

"Where is he?" Renmier asked.

She caressed Songbird's cheek, chin, then lips. Those perfect lips. "Let me... touch her." The elf pushed the leather cape aside and glided her fingers over the curves of Songbird's bosom.

A quaking breath flowed from Songbird. She appeared broken. Frightened.

"I would love to see her in a lighana's dress," Mistress said. "Why does she not wear one now?"

Gods! What Renmier would sacrifice to see Songbird in something that teased, but not a revealing slave's garment.

"She is for *my* viewing pleasures." He guided Songbird behind him, then removed three black roans from his pouch. "Our agreement."

"I do not blame you," Mistress said, a slight pout present. "Your lighana is... perfect." Snatching the coins, she returned behind the desk. "He is in Saurris for business matters."

Renmier grimaced. "You jest."

Saurris was on the northeastern side of Brydasia, just west of the Venmont Mountains. It would take over a week to reach the city. And Renmier didn't want to travel near the mountain range with the rise of bandit reports in the area.

"That is what my informant gathered." The elf smirked. "However, he will return to Lymus short of a fortnight. There is a tavern there he frequents."

"The name?"

Mistress nodded toward Songbird. "Tell me hers."

Renmier released an irritated huff. "Songbird."

The elf's face brightened as she whispered, "Perfect." She rolled a coin on the desktop. "Splintered Shield."

"Thank you, Mistress." He gave the neck-band a firm pull, then opened the door.

"Hold on to your Songbird, Vulture. Hold tightly."

Did a threat linger in her tone?

Renmier scowled. "Mistress?"

She half shrugged. "Lighanas have been disappearing from their masters." The elf nodded at Songbird. "Someone will snatch her the moment your attention wanders."

He stomped to the desk, shouting, "Is that a threat?"

Laughing, Mistress relaxed in her chair. "My dear friend, I am simply informing you."

Renmier grabbed Songbird's hand and stormed from the office. He didn't need the doorman; he remembered every step. The deviousness in Mistress' eyes left him uncomfortable; a rare feeling. The elf was planning.

That was the first time Javesse witnessed someone not flinch beneath Vulture's shouts and glares. The Serine elf, a seller of pleasure slaves, and a woman Javesse couldn't imagine being anything but cruel, laughed in Vulture's face. It even sounded like she threatened him. However, that threat had everything to do with Javesse.

Outside the building and a few doors away, she frowned at Vulture's back. "What have you gotten me into taking me to a lighana market?"

The beast grinned at her. What in Fynthiar's Name was wrong with him?

She tried to pull her hand away, but his grip tightened. What he'd said in the market corridor lingered, so Javesse ceased resisting to avoid his wrath. She might speak her thoughts when they returned to the inn room.

The tavern quieted upon Vulture's entry. No one spoke while he led Javesse to the stairs.

Once in the room, she asked, "Why did you take me there?"

He removed the weapons from his belt and set them on the table. "Personal matters."

"It had naught to do with—?"

He sat. "I took you to keep you safe."

"In a lighana market?" she snapped. "You're a bloody idiot!"

Vulture squinted, yet didn't raise a hand to her. "Gather your gear. We're leaving." He returned the few items he'd removed back into his pack.

Confused, Javesse blinked. "I thought we were meeting someone tonight."

"We have."

"But you said—"

"I didn't tell you the truth," he said over his shoulder. "I still don't trust you."

She laughed. "What've I done to—?"

He spun, pointing at her. "You don't listen to me!" Vulture shook his head. "I know it's only been a day, but we've had a poor start."

"Perhaps because you struck me!" She shoved him back... or at least made an effort.

He looked at her hands still on his broad chest, his lips curving. "Sometimes you're amusing. Other times, you're bloody annoying."

Javesse had never been so frustrated.

Birds of Different Feathers

Four long days on the road passed. Vulture and Javesse stayed at an inn for one night, and camped in Faytirn Forest the others, riding as late as possible the last evening. He had set up a tent large enough for one person. Apparently, he wasn't used to having company, yet he insisted Javesse slept in it while he guarded.

She wondered if he ever rested.

Javesse felt filthy, wearing the same clothes since leaving Volthany. She wanted a hot bath. She wanted chocolates and fruit tarts. And she wanted to escape Vulture. But even when he didn't look at her, he still watched. Javesse felt it.

The chilly spring nights were awful, and she damned them as she scooted closer to the fire.

Vulture had roasted a rabbit. Like a starving animal, he tore meat from the bone, flinging it into his mouth with his tongue.

Javesse shuddered. It shouldn't have bothered her; she grew up a hunter and had enjoyed the spoils of her accomplishments. Life with the elves had changed her.

He slowed his chewing and thrust a small bone with meat dangling from it at her. "Want some?"

Grimacing, she pushed a tiny leaf pile with her heel toward his foot. "Where do we go?"

He smirked. How could the condescending bastard be so damn stunning?

She leaned back and arched a brow, offering a wry smile of her own. "Is it a brothel this time?"

Vulture resumed eating.

Sighing, Javesse viewed the surrounding trees' dark silhouettes. The fresh, earthy scent of damp soil and bark helped relax her.

He drank from his flask. "We're in the Charville Duchy now."

"How do you know?"

"We passed Niwlog Woods."

Since leaving Volthany, she didn't remember seeing a forest other than the very one they now camped within. It seemed he was purposely avoiding Niwlog Woods by remaining as close to Faytirn as possible.

Vulture scowled at her. "I know the area. This path serves us better." He tossed the bones into a nearby bush. "We're continuing to Ravieris."

The annoyance she felt a moment ago faded. "W-why are we going there?"

"To ask His Eminence if he ordered the assassination."

Javesse dropped her mouth open. "You're going to ask him outright?"

"Yes."

He truly *was* a dolt.

"Do you believe the emperor will just tell you?"

Vulture shrugged. "Maybe. Maybe indirectly."

"Don't you think that's dangerous? What if he imprisons us?"

A slow grin forming, Vulture winked. "He won't."

"You're confident."

"I know him." He drank from the flask again. "Get to bed. We've a long ride tomorrow."

"Can't we stop somewhere for proper rest?" She leaned toward him. "I'd love a bath and a fine bed."

"I'm providing what I can."

A flat response. The man must feel something. In fact, he'd shown a hint of compassion before.

"Vulture, we both smell dreadful, and I—"

"Get used to it."

Clicking her tongue, she frowned. Well, Javesse could be just as stubborn. "I won't sleep in there anymore."

He glanced at the tent. "Why not?"

"You're supposed to keep me safe and from falling ill." She blinked. "Then perhaps you could show me better courtesy."

Vulture scowled. "Show you some bet—? I'm not suggesting it, woman. Get in the tent now."

"You can't make me."

He laughed. "You wish to try me further?"

His fierceness nearly had her blurting out a quick no, but Javesse straightened her back and titled her chin up. "I'm... not... sle—"

He was up and yanking her from the ground.

She punched wherever she could land a blow, be it face, neck, chest—anywhere. "Put me down! Damn you to Darkness!"

"I'll not suffer his wrath because you're a stubborn idiot!" Renmier carried Songbird into the small tent, disregarding her cupping his ear. Lowering to one knee, he dropped her onto the thin pile of blankets, enjoying the sound of her bottom hitting the ground.

"Ow! You bastard!"

"You forgot 'bloody' in there."

"Who do you think you are?" Tears filled her eyes and her lips quivered.

He pointed at the blankets. "Sleep."

"I don't want to be in here." Songbird rose to her knees.

He pushed her down, pinning her to the coverlets.

She bucked and twisted. "You'll not have your way with me!"

The vile accusation had Renmier's face burning and his ears buzzing.

"I don't want you!"

Frozen, Songbird stared wide-eyed at him.

"What?" he snapped, releasing her and kneeling upright. "You believe every man in Brydasia wants a swyve with you? They might at first, then think better of it once you open your mouth."

Her gaze narrowed and her cheeks rounded. She giggled. Why was she laughing?

"What's so amusing?" Renmier shouted.

"That's the most you've said." Laughing harder, Songbird rolled to her side, then back. "And your lips move more when you're angry."

Renmier scowled. "What?"

She blinked tears free, her merriment filling the small tent.

So she was having a laugh at him and his anger? Let her. Renmier didn't care.

He rose, staying hunched to avoid hitting the canvas ceiling. "Go to sleep."

Songbird stilled for a dozen seconds, then released a soft sigh. She slid beneath the blanket, her back to him.

This little songbird was going to make Renmier insane before the mission's completion.

While he packed the tent, she ate something light. Once everything was ready, Songbird climbed on Titan and waited. Perhaps she'd learned and things might progress easier. They hadn't spoken since the night before. She rode with her back rigid and chin up. Several times she shifted, adding a soft moan now and then. This went on for seven miles.

Fine.

"What is it?" Renmier asked.

"Nothing."

He rolled his eyes. "All right."

After a quiet minute passed, Songbird turned. "It's just…" She faced forward and sighed. "Never mind," she mumbled. "You don't care."

Her bottom wiggled against him.

Renmier wanted to stop her motion, yet he didn't. He enjoyed her nearness, smelling her hair—even if filthy—and her buttocks pressing closer; a temptation to hold her tighter. But after what he'd said the previous night? Truth was Renmier *didn't* want her. Songbird was breathtaking, but then she'd speak.

"You truly don't care, do you?" she snapped.

"About what?"

A brief, breathy laugh sounded, as if she couldn't believe his question. Silence ensued again.

His mind and body distracted by her bottom, Renmier forgot she had spoken a moment ago. He chuckled. "Interesting how you chatter when I don't wish you to, and now you keep your mouth closed."

"You want me to speak?"

"I want you to tell me why you're fidgeting so damn much."

"Are you saying you care?"

Perhaps it was good she couldn't see him grinning.

"If you don't," Songbird continued, "which I'm quite certain you do not, then I won't bother."

"Very well."

"I knew it!"

She'd never give a chance to know him. There was no point to it, and that saddened him, which was shocking. Over the past seven years, Renmier hadn't cared about such things. Yet Songbird didn't know his intention. He was going to save her. Not now, but before the end of his mission, he'd ensure she was free of Darik Nornt.

At dusk, Javesse and Vulture arrived at Bilsnir, a town currently expanding into a city. Uprooted tree stumps littered the edge of the forest where others waited their turn to be torn from the ground. Construction was underway for several structures on the village outskirts, many of them two-story tall. Tents and campfires scattered amid supply and work wagons, looking to have settled for months. A few laborers prepared meals, while some sat around sharing their day, and others likely dined in the village. Alongside the town, a narrow river flowed where dozens of boats floated beside the docks. Men came from the riverbank, laughing and chatting about their catch, happy with their ordinary lives.

Javesse envied them. She longed to experience the mundane daily life of household tasks and having a family. If it hadn't been for Samris and Darik, she'd be married by now. Perhaps even carrying a babe.

She clamped onto her lip to prevent it from trembling and fought the urge to weep. For moons Javesse had convinced herself she wasn't to blame for Beresly's death, yet she still felt at fault. She should've waited until they reached home to tell Beresly she'd marry him—they'd been less than a day from Delvarian. They never would've sung at the campfire and drew the bandits' attention. All the gods damn her for his death and the death of their friends.

Vulture directed the stallion to a stable on the other side of town. He must've intended to leave first thing in the morning. While helping her dismount, he frowned. Head lowered slightly, he arched a brow in a silent question.

Javesse ignored him. He didn't care anyway.

Grunting, Vulture handed Javesse her backpack, then collected his gear and weapons. They hadn't spoken for the past several hours, and seemed it might continue. He motioned to the right, walking in the same direction. Apparently, this was how he told Javesse what to do without speaking.

Some men on the road observed them, so she kept close to Vulture.

Thankfully the noise in the tavern didn't waver upon hers and Vulture's entrance, for the most part. Women made suggestive comments toward him, then sneered at Javesse, yet his pace didn't slow as he continued to the barkeep.

One woman gasped. "A neck-band." She snickered. "Slave."

Javesse quickened to keep up with Vulture.

"Lighana whore." A different woman elbowed Javesse in the back, knocking her into Vulture.

He glared at the woman, then moved toward her.

Javesse clutched his arm. "Please. No."

His nostrils wrinkled as he bared his teeth like an animal. "No one harms you."

"She didn't."

"No one mocks you."

Javesse couldn't have predicted his intention, he was so swift.

Vulture seized the woman's throat. "Apologize."

People scattered, and the woman's friends screamed, begging him to release her.

"Apologize," he repeated.

The woman sputtered; her eyes red as tears fell. "Fo-forgive me," she managed.

"Don't look at her." Vulture shoved the woman into her friends, one of them falling onto a chair. Swinging his arm to indicate all inside the establishment, he said, "None of you look her way."

The rest of the patrons now viewed the floor or the stained tabletops beneath them.

Javesse released her breath when Vulture's arm brushed her shoulder, and he ordered her to follow him. He stopped at the bar.

"Yes, m'lord?" The barkeep's voice trembled.

Chairs moved, the door opened, several footsteps faded, then the door closed.

The barkeep's forehead formed waves as he frowned; he'd lost business for the night. The man cleared his throat. "M'lord?"

Vulture set a black roan down. "A room, food, drink... and the guild."

Worry disappeared from the barkeep's face as he nodded. "Of course, sir. I'll provide everything you need." He signaled to a lackey. "In the meantime, I'll have your items taken to your room."

"Very good." Vulture dropped his and Javesse's backpacks on the counter, yet kept his weapons.

Javesse watched the roan disappear into the barkeeps pocket. How many black coins did Vulture carry? Black roans were the most valuable, each one equal to a hundred gold. If she asked, he might yell at her for being nosy. Javesse wouldn't blame him, for his wealth wasn't her business.

As usual, Vulture led her to a table near the hearth.

She eased into the chair next to him. "Was hurting her necessary?"

"Didn't I make myself clear enough?"

"I can endure an elbow."

"You forget you're under my care."

Drinks arrived moments later with a promise food would soon follow.

Vulture lifted his tankard. "Can I ask you something, Songbird?"

Maybe one day soon, she'd convince him to stop calling her by that name. "What?"

"What is your fascination with my lips?"

Brows knitted, she cocked her head.

"Our first night on the road, you mentioned I don't move them," he said. "Last night, you said I—"

"Oh." Giggling, Javesse twisted the cup over the table's surface.

"Are you going to tell me?"

"Perhaps." Her grin widened upon his heavy sigh.

Fish stew arrived.

She ate with a hearty appetite, pleased with the myriad of herbs. More ale for Vulture came afterward.

He continuously glanced at her.

Enjoying every bit of his frustration, she sat back. The bristles of hair on his jaw looked good on him. The man could likely adorn a beard well.

Arms now on the table, he entwined his fingers.

She laughed. "Fine!"

Some men watched, then whispered amongst themselves. Vulture's darkened irises darted their way.

Javesse lay her hands atop his, gaining his full attention.

His gaze flitted from her slender fingers curved over his knuckles, to her face.

She patted his hand. "One of the first things I noticed when we met was your lips barely move when you talk." She sat back, freeing him of her touch.

"Is that so?" His lips hardly moved.

The titter couldn't be stopped while she nodded.

"I did it just now?"

Javesse laughed again. "Yes."

"And I move them more when I'm angry?"

His lips, in fact, moved a little more than normal.

Her laughter faltered. "I-I have noticed that."

"Do you prefer me angry?" Vulture's tone had grown hostile, and he formed each word. "Keep drawing their notice."

Wonderful. Javesse had caused trouble and irritated him. A far too easy task. "I-I hadn't meant to."

"You don't know where we are," he said. "It seems like a quaint village, but it's not. It's dangerous."

"Why do you bring me to such places?"

"Because we're meeting someone who will speak the underground cant, of which I cannot. I need your help."

She nodded. "I see."

He rested his arm over her chair's back and leaned close. "I promise... tonight, you'll have a bath."

Delighted, Javesse smiled. "Thank you, Vulture."

He stared at her, then his eyes shifted to the left. "It's time to go."

Vulture led her outside, trailing a man in dark clothing. They walked several blocks, taking a few turns before coming to an alley. Holding Javesse's arm, he proceeded into the darkness.

"We have questions," Vulture said. "You received coin to give answers."

"*We* decide whether there are answers to give... Bird," someone called from thicker shadows between broken crates. "Can you even speak with stray cats?"

Vulture guided Javesse forward.

"The lovely one." A man came just within their view, scarcely discernable from the shadows. "A pearl from the sea. Exported or stolen?"

His choice of words disclosed he was from the thieves' guild. Javesse's father had rare dealings with such groups, yet she'd learned their dialect while accompanying his travels.

"Lost at sea," she said. "A shipwreck took precious treasures from me."

With a partial bow, the thief pressed his fist to his heart, and she appreciated his acknowledgment of her loss and grief.

His head bobbed, then rose toward Vulture. "What does the owner want?" he asked, disgust thick in his voice.

Javesse grazed the neck-band. "I am the one with the inquiries."

"It lets you have thoughts?" He sounded surprised. "Go on then."

Vulture growled.

Ignoring him, Javesse resumed. "Rumors spread about a blood hunt."

Vulture's forehead furrowed. "What?"

The thief snorted a laugh. "Vultures circle blood."

Snarling, Vulture advanced. "I'll circle yours."

Javesse squeezed his arm, halting him. To the thief, she said, "We inquire about such a hunt."

He shrugged. "I'm certain many would be interested."

"I see." She raised her hand to Vulture.

"I already paid."

"The fee is higher," she countered.

Sighing, he dug into his pouch and gave her two gold roans.

The thief bolted forward, skimmed his fingers over her palm, then retreated to the shadows, the act done in less than three seconds.

"We've heard there's a dog on the loose," the man said.

Javesse crossed her arms and leaned to one side, brushing against Vulture. "What's the acquired taste?"

"Uncertain at this time. Word is the trail leads south."

"Do you know anything about the dog?"

"Who's inquiring?" the thief asked. "You or the bird?"

"Paid curiosity," Javesse said.

"By you or the bird's handler?"

The thieves knew Vulture worked for Darik, so Javesse had to steer their contact to the questions.

She opened her hand again. "Something more."

Rumbling a curse, Vulture removed another coin from his pouch, then dropped it on her palm. A black roan.

Javesse widened her eyes. She'd been a child at the port in Ubrasia the last time she held one.

The thief took it and fingered the smooth stone coin while he shuffled backward.

"Paid curiosity," Javesse repeated.

"We know little about the dog. It could be a mutt, a beautiful purebred, a seadog, or a Lycan-curse."

"Then you know nothing," Vulture snapped.

"Wait." Javesse pressed on his chest, then frowned at the thief. "A Lycan-curse?"

He shrugged again. "It could be someone close to the blood, waiting for the full moon's arrival to spring the attack." He bowed. "And that's all we know... lighana." The thief disappeared into the shadows.

"Wait!" she called. "Who sent the dog?"

"Bastard." Vulture guided her from the alley.

Neither spoke on the way to the inn, where they shed their cloaks in the bedroom.

"At least we learned something," Javesse said.

"We learned nothing. It's all hearsay."

"What do you mean?" She dropped her hands to her sides. "There'll be an attempt on the duke's life."

"That wasn't what the bastard said." Vulture paced between the bed and the wall, the floor creaking beneath his heavy steps. "Blood in the south could be anyone. There are plenty of nobles in southern Brydasia."

"No target such as Duke Nornt. Though he has several supporters, many despise him."

Like a predatory bird, Vulture continued his circling.

"You understood the cant," Javesse said. "Yet you claimed to need my help."

Vulture stopped and flashed a smile, his eyes glistening. "I'm quick to learn. And I only gathered a little."

Gods, he was handsome.

She looked away. "What now?"

"We seek something more reliable."

Vulture placed the flail on the table, then sat, spreading his legs. "Come here."

What was this? No man invited a woman between his legs without expecting a favor.

Javesse shook her head.

He leaned forward and pointed at the floor between his thighs. "Right now."

Vulture had done nothing to hurt her since leaving Columure. There were opportunities he could've taken advantage of her, to force himself, but he hadn't. If anything, he was honorable in that sense, and had yet to strike her again.

Javesse stopped at his knees. He pointed to the empty space again, and she inched farther in. Grasping her hips, he pulled her closer, making Javesse's breath came faster. Vulture's fingertips glided up her arms, bringing the rise of bumps from her flesh. She parted her lips, but it only caused them to dry, especially as his fingers smoothed along her shoulders, to her clavicles, then throat. Those iron irises lowered to the neck-band as he touched it.

She stiffened.

A line formed between his brows as he unfastened the buckle, slipped the strap free, and removed the leather from her neck. Vulture lay the band over his thigh, then massaged Javesse's nape, his thumbs caressing her chin and throat, like a lover's touch.

Closing her eyelids, she breathed deeper. Easier. Javesse relaxed. For the first time in over four months, she knew a sense of freedom. And Vulture gave it to her. She opened her eyes, finding his irises the color of shining steel. Beautiful. Enthralling.

He lowered his hands and sat back, tossed the neck-band into the pack.

Disbelief stilled Javesse. "Why?"

Vulture licked his lips. "Our next contact won't speak with us thinking you're my lighana." Standing, he forced her to retreat a few steps, then he walked to the window. "Nor could I stand seeing that bloody thing on you any longer. Damn nobles and their pleasure slaves." He spat on the floor.

Vulture despised Darik had enslaved her, yet the truth...

Heart thudding upon the revelation of Vulture's feelings toward her predicament, Javesse neared him. "He never—That is, Lord Nornt didn't treat me as a lighana."

Vulture rested his fists on his hips and turned. "What?"

"Darik never forced himself on me. I mean, he did once, but—"

"You give yourself willingly?" Vulture grimaced.

The response caught Javesse by surprise. Did he care about her?

"That's not what I was saying."

His frowned deepened. "Then what are you saying? Gods!"

Javesse huffed. "He hasn't lain with me!"

Straightening, Vulture said, "No?"

"No one at Bashgrahon has." She moved closer, his warmth reaching to her. "Lord Nornt has touched and kissed me, but he's not forced pleasures beyond that."

Vulture's face smoothed, and his tense muscles eased. "Why?"

Staggered by his expression, she hesitated. "Darik is no longer capable."

"Why do you believe that?"

"He tried once—the night I arrived at his home—but he couldn't... get hard." She shuddered at the memory. "He stayed away from me for weeks. I never spoke a word of it to him nor any other. I believe that's why he's so guarded about me."

Vulture remained silent, as if in thought. Suddenly, he burst into booming laughter and fell to a knee, forcing her back.

Wishing she'd said nothing, Javesse looked away. "You're horrible."

He was quick to his feet, spinning her. "That man enslaved you as his lighana, and you call *me* horrible?"

"I don't laugh at other people's misfortunes!"

"Misfortunes?" Vulture snorted. "So you'd rather he was capable of taking you? Is that it?"

"I didn't say that." Javesse backed a step. "I'm not the one who serves him like a hunting dog!"

Vulture's eyes darkened and his face turned crimson as he pushed her against the wall. "Woman, you know nothing! I've—"

Arms folded over her torso, Javesse curled.

He retreated, appearing shocked by her reaction, even after the way he'd treated her at the slave market. Vulture grabbed his coin pouch from the table and left, slamming the door behind him.

Javesse palmed her forehead, then slid her hand to her cheek.

So Renmier had a laugh at Darik's failings, as if the duke didn't deserve it. Why did Songbird feel sorry for the bastard? It made no bloody sense. Renmier had to get his mind to the task and quit worrying about Songbird anyway. He'd take care of her later.

Games of chance occupied a few tables in the tavern. Renmier hadn't played cards in years. Winning didn't matter. He just needed to escape Songbird. He approached three men already in a game, and they didn't oppose to his joining. One player even bought Renmier's first drink. For an hour, chatter passed between the others, as did silver roans, but Renmier kept to himself. He'd yet to finish the free beer while the other men began their fourth round. The conversation amid a couple of the men implied personal experiences and knowledge of one another.

"Drink up, friend." The man to Renmier's right laughed, a hint of nervousness dropping it at the end.

Renmier added three silver coins to the pile. "I'll keep my cards."

The other two men chuckled.

"Never took you as one who sipped like a young girl having her first drink," one other said.

Amusing. A jester.

But there was a mixture of discomfort and rising energy emitting from them. These men were testing Renmier.

He shoved the mug off the table. It broke into several shards, the beer spreading on the floor and soaking into the aged wood. "I'm not that thirsty. Now place your wager."

The nervous man sounded a shrilly noise Renmier believed was laughter.

"He speaks," the third man said. "And not just with threats."

Of course there'd be a bold one.

Renmier set his cards down. He'd not give in to their goading. "If we're finished, I'll take my roans and leave."

A woman cleared her throat. Songbird stood to the side, staring at Renmier. Was she that idiotic and stubborn?

He scowled. "What are you doing?"

"You—" She glanced at the others. "You owe me a bath."

Renmier furrowed his brows. "Not tonight."

"Yes, tonight. You told me you'd—"

He rose, the chair wobbling as it scraped along the floor. "I sa—"

"That I would have a bath tonight."

"I'll bathe her," Jester said.

Renmier glared at him from over his shoulder. "Don't look at her."

Bold Man snickered. "And there's the threat."

Nervous Laugher slid his chair back, emanating the jarring noise. "We shouldn't—"

"Tell me, Vulture," Jester leaned over his cards, "does she give a good cock-sucking?"

Cold instantly filled Renmier's chest.

"That was the wrong thing to say." He flipped the table into Nervous Laugher, then kicked Jester's chest. The chair's back broke as the bastard landed on the floor, gasping.

"Stop!" Songbird shouted. "Vult—!"

Blackness clouded Renmier's vision as he grasped Jester's collar. He grew numb to the pain after each strike upon cheekbone, jaw, and temple. Jester's flesh tore and his bones cracked. The skin over Renmier's knuckles split, yet he kept pounding on him. Voices sounded distant, like yelling from the other end of a tunnel. Renmier's own heavy breathing and racing heart dominated his ears.

Someone shrieked and more shouting sounded.

Straightening, he let Jester fall to the floor. Renmier licked blood from his knuckles as he stared at the motionless body, then he spat on it. It'd been a long time since slugging a man to death. Strange how good it felt. He faced Nervous Laugher, who paled.

"I wanted nothing to do with this." Nervous Laugher waved his hands. "I swear!"

Renmier squinted, trod forward.

Nervous Laugher made inaudible noises before speaking. "I didn't know they'd do this!"

Renmier paused. Something was amiss. He looked to Songbird.

She was gone. Bold Man was missing. The players from a nearby table were no longer present. Ten feet from the exit, the barkeep lay sprawled on the floor with blood on the back of his head.

Knife drawn from the back scabbard, Renmier charged at Nervous Laugher. "Where is she?"

The man squatted and covered his face with his arms. "They took her."

"Where?" Renmier shouted.

"I don't know!"

He grabbed Nervous Laugher's arm and dragged him to stand. The blade at the man's throat, Renmier asked as calmly as he could, "What do you know?"

"They gave me twenty silver to pretend I was their friend."

"You made the wrong choice tonight." Renmier thrust the knife into Nervous Laugher's throat, withdrew it, then dropped him.

A maiden cared over the barkeep, so Renmier hurried to the inn room and collected his and Javesse's items. They'd not be returning.

Back in the tavern, he sat beside the barkeep, who was having his scalp washed by the maiden. Renmier leaned close. "What happened?"

The barkeep grimaced. "Five men in all. They took her."

"Who are they?"

The skinny man sighed. "I don't know for certain, but I've heard rumors they deal with lighanas. Collecting them and such."

Teeth gritting painfully hard, Renmier headed for the stables. After a quick look at his face, people scurried from his path.

Galloping jostled Javesse awake. She was draped over a man's spread legs and the front half of a saddle. The pommel and horn rubbed her side, the bouncing forced her ribs to thud on hard leather and knees, and her unbound hands slapped straps, the horse, and the thug's boot. The man must've been in a hurry not to have tied her; however, he gripped her belt, his knuckles pressing into the small of her back. She didn't know how much time had passed since she was rendered unconscious, nor how far the riders had traveled.

No. Someone else wasn't taking Javesse prisoner. She'd not allow it.

Feigning she was still out, she assessed possibilities for escape. The quarter moon shone enough to note two riders within view, and their group just veered off the road and onto a path into the woods. There were more riders behind her, but she knew not how many.

These men may be the lighana thieves Mistress had warned Vulture about. And the fool permitted them to take Javesse right from beneath his distracted, violent mind. Her ire toward him would have to wait. Right now, Javesse had to escape this frightening situation.

Something from the man's boot caught her attention. Fynthiar's Might! A knife hilt.

Javesse timed the perfect moment to unsheathe the weapon as the bouncing permitted, then thrust the blade into the man's leg.

Hollering, he released her and jerked on the reins.

She pushed off the horse, landing hard on her bottom, pain jolting up her tailbone and lower back. Javesse scrambled to her feet, spotting five horses in the group, then stumbled into a run between the trees.

Shouts and thundering hooves followed.

"Get her!"

Javesse prayed to reach an area too dense for the mounts. Thickets were everywhere, but not enough to deter the horses. Ten yards away, she spotted thin trees close together, and bolted for them. A couple yards within the small copse, someone crashed into Javesse, knocking her to the ground.

He sat atop her thighs. "Bitch!" He slapped her. "You stabbed my brother!"

"That's it," a different man said gruffly, "we're having our fun. I don't give a damn what the buyer says. She'll want this one no matter her use."

"I get her first," another said, limping toward them.

"Is your leg wrapped?" the one holding Javesse asked, looking over his shoulder to his wounded companion.

"It's wrapped enough."

Javesse's heartbeat pulsated throughout her. She focused, calmed her breathing, and let training combine with instinct.

The captor holding her gave his attention to his brother, who still neared. The man suggesting to "have their fun" stood a few feet away, leaving room for the limper. Perfect. To improve her situation, the young idiot straddling her moved his arm to point in the direction from where they'd come.

Javesse jabbed her right hand up, striking his throat with the heel, then punched his nose with her left, crushing it aside; he slanted back, covering his face. Fists brought quickly together, she targeted his bollocks. A couple of grunts was all he managed before releasing a strained groan.

His brother, the limper, shoved him aside and hauled Javesse from the ground.

She assisted by pushing from her heels, using the momentum to throw him off balance. Spinning within his slackened hold, Javesse unsheathed his sword, swinging out from his arm as if they shared a dance. She pierced the third man in the gut, then whirled to the limper, slashing the weapon at him.

He released her and leapt away. "Bitch!"

Javesse set one foot back and straightened her spine and chin. She readied the sword as he withdrew the blade from his brother's belt. Hurrying footsteps approached from behind her. She reeled gracefully and lifted the knife from the belt of the passing attacker while slicing his leg with the sword.

He hobbled to a stop. "Bloody Blackening!"

Two men now had leg injuries, another lay dying with a gut wound, and one rolled on the ground, holding his crotch. If Javesse recalled correctly, there was at least one more. Sword and knife ready, she nodded once.

The limper snarled. The injury wobbled his charge, yet his sword came hard and fast. Javesse dodged forward and danced around him, keeping close as he tried to land a successful strike. She evaded the attacks while being right next to him. He attempted to grab her, but she avoided the anticipated grapple.

"Just get her!" the hobbler shouted.

Javesse whirled behind her opponent, impaling the knife into his back. It wasn't a warrior's way, but they outnumbered her, especially as the limper's brother rose to his feet and another thug remained unaccounted for.

Blood trailed from the nose and over the lips of the crushed bollocks brute. His glower rose from his now dead brother to Javesse. "I'm going to kill you."

The other man grabbed him. "She's worth a lot of—"

"She's not worth this!"

The young brother shoved the hobbler, causing him to lose balance, and came at Javesse with nothing but his fists. Fool.

She dodged each swing. After a couple of dreadfully long minutes, an opening presented itself. Javesse pierced his chest with his own sword and twisted the blade. She withdrew the weapon and faced the hobbler, who leaned against a tree.

His gaze darting beyond her, he laughed. "Wickitch."

Weapons ready, Javesse turned, putting both men in view.

The hobbler wiped tears from his cheek. "'bout bloody time you got—"

Wickitch crumpled into a heap; Vulture now stood in his place.

Javesse wanted to strike him.

Axe drawn back, Vulture charged the hobbler, who irrationally brought up his hands to block.

"No... No!"

Vulture swung his weapon upward, flinging blood, and the hobbler fell to the ground, dead. It was silent while Vulture viewed the bodies.

Javesse's heart still pounded.

Hand axe swiped clean on the dead's cloak and in its holder, Vulture stepped toward her. "Nice wor—"

She kneed his crotch. When he bent forward, she pressed the knife's blade to his throat, the edge quaking against his flesh.

He bolted upright and knocked her hand away, a line of blood forming on the side of his neck. The reaction was immediate, and Javesse hadn't a chance to dodge before he clutched her throat.

"Bastard," she managed in a whisper.

His eyes darkened and the surrounding air chilled as he squeezed.

She punched his cheek, shoulder—anywhere she could reach. "If you... don't control your... temper," Javesse gasped for air, "you'll bring... my death."

Expression softening, he let go and moved back. "I didn't realize I was..." He looked away, the cold fading.

Still feeling his grip, Javesse touched her throat. "Damn you."

"Your anger is warranted." He knelt beside a body. "I... You're correct. My temper sometimes gets the best of me. And I'm not accustomed to having another to care over." Vulture looked at her. "Will you forgive me?"

Had she heard him correctly?

"I'll be more careful." He rose and inched closer. "I promise."

What was Javesse to think? This was a different side of him. Perhaps what she'd been waiting for.

"I understand," he whispered. "And I can't blame you."

Vulture searched the thugs, removing several pouches of coin and other valuables. "We'll sell their horses," he said. "The roans will help us in Ravieris."

Javesse still hadn't moved.

He reached out. "We'll camp a couple miles away."

This was a moment of trust. Did Vulture deserve it? He came for her. But if it wasn't for his ridiculous ego, those men wouldn't have taken Javesse. Yet he was there. Vulture would've hunted them to save her. And she didn't believe it was because of Darik. Vulture had shown aggressive protectiveness over her, even toward women. And he exhibited impatience and cruelty, yet compassion.

Javesse toiled over what she felt and believed about this man. It didn't matter what she thought about him. To survive, she needed Vulture.

She placed her hand on his palm and followed him to Titan. While Vulture gathered the reins of the other mounts, she climbed on the massive stallion. He fastened the leads from one saddle to the next until tying the first to Titan.

Vulture lifted in the stirrup, but dropped to the ground and strode to the last horse of the line. Bringing a black mare forward, he said, "Here, Songbird, you ride this one."

Javesse sucked in a faint rush of air. "You mean that?"

"I do."

She dismounted and petted the mare's soft mane. "Thank you."

"In fact..." Vulture unfastened her weapon belt from Titan. "Here."

Javesse stared at the sword, a gift from Beresly two years ago. Vulture was now showing his trust in her. She buckled the belt on. Over four months had passed since last wearing it.

Javesse noticed dried blood on Vulture's neck. "I'm sorry for cutting you."

Lowering his brows, he touched where she indicated and smirked. "I hadn't realized you did."

So engulfed in his rage he hadn't felt the blade. Was that good or bad?

"I'm sorry, just the same," she said.

"I forgive you." He grabbed Titan's lead. "Let's find a suitable place to rest."

They didn't speak throughout the ride, nor while Vulture set up the camp. Javesse tended to the horses, searched the saddlebags for valuable and useful items, and discarded everything else, except the saddles. Finding food in two packs, she brought them to the campfire. Vulture came out of the tent as she sat. He returned inside, came back with a blanket, and draped it over her shoulders.

"You found something to eat?" he asked.

Nodding, Javesse tossed a sack of salted meats to his feet. She'd also found a leather pouch of dark chocolates wrapped in parchment. Javesse removed three pieces and popped them into her mouth. Eyelids closed, she moaned as it melted on her tongue. The chocolate must've been imported from Salisby, Myndrose, for no other country made it to such creamy perfection. When she opened her eyes, she found Vulture staring.

"That good?" he whispered.

"The most wonderful."

"Must be. I've yet to see you smile like that." He returned to inspecting the meat from the sack. "These are fine quality. From Wragorn, I'd guess."

Javesse killed her joy as she folded the parchment over the chocolate, slid it into the pouch, then set it on the ground.

"Is something troubling you?" he asked.

Everything that had happened since she stood beside him at the tavern repeated in her mind—one moment, then another. "I wish I wasn't here. I want to go home."

The lengthy stillness that followed her confession was too much, yet Javesse refused to give in to the grief. She'd cried enough times over the past several months.

"Your sword skills are quite impressive," he said. "You dance like the elves."

She froze, her heart thudding. "How many have you fought?"

His long silence was answer enough. Vulture rubbed the side of his head, perhaps feeling a scar. "Did they teach you?"

"Some," she whispered.

"Only some?"

Javesse nodded. "I knew how to fight when I met them."

His brows twitched. "You...? You didn't grow up in Delvarian?"

There was no reason to giggle at the question, but she needed it.

Vulture appeared confused.

Settling, Javesse said, "No. I've been with the elves since I was fifteen."

"How long is that? I mean... You look young."

"Seven years." Her merriment dissipated.

Vulture turned to the fire. "I was curious about that."

"About what?"

He pulled a flask from beneath his cloak and drank. "Before we set off from Bashgrahon, you said something about your people's custom—something about covering your face." He glanced at her. "I admit I've not been everywhere on Brydasia, but I've traveled to most lands and know of no culture where people hide their faces." Vulture offered Javesse the flask. "From what country do you hail?"

She declined the drink. "I'm not from Brydasia."

A smirk played at his lips. "I suppose that doesn't surprise me."

"Why?"

"You're too stunning to be from this wretched continent." He drank again.

Javesse scoffed. "If that was true, then you're not from Brydasia either."

One of Vulture's brows curved upward. "Why do you say that?"

Her cheeks burned. Despite her earlier beliefs, he wasn't daft. How could she tell him her true thoughts? *Courage, woman. Just be honest.* Javesse raised her chin. "Because you're beautiful."

Attention now on the fire, he capped the flask and returned it under his cloak.

"Do you find it hard to believe?" she asked.

Vulture's forehead wrinkled. "Beauty is more than appearances, Songbird. Don't be fooled by what you see with me." He looked at her. "There's nothing beautiful about me." He lost his gaze to the flames again.

Javesse couldn't deny the truth of his remark: beauty lay in actions and words, and she'd seen Vulture do horrible things. Why was she desperate to see something wonderful within him?

Fynthiar, are You trying to show me a truth about this man? She tossed a pebble into the fire, losing sight of it. "I believe there's more to you, Vulture."

He snorted a laugh. Clearing his throat, he nodded toward the tent. "Go on in. Get some rest."

Javesse didn't want to be alone. She pulled the blanket tighter around herself. "I... I wish to stay out here with you."

"It'll get colder."

"There's a fire."

"Then I'll add more wood." He rose and disappeared into the trees' shadows.

No argument or forcing her to sleep in his tent? Javesse smiled.

"Where are you from?" Vulture called from around the trunks.

Thinking about her homeland, she beamed. "Bellinstar."

Leaves shuffled and his heavy steps crunched twigs behind her.

"Bellinstar?"

She craned her head back to look up at him. "Yes."

"That explains something." Vulture squatted to place several pieces of wood into the fire, then sat beside her. "Why are you here?"

Javesse stared at her fingers. "How much do you know about my people?"

"Little."

She grinned. "Of course."

"I've never been to Myndrose." He propped his elbow on his knee and his chin on his palm. "Teach me something new."

Javesse licked her lips. "What've you heard?"

Vulture smirked. "I've heard the women are exceptionally gorgeous. A rumor which has proven true."

She fought the impulse to blush deeply. "I see."

"Why do you hide your faces?"

"We only cover ourselves when around men we aren't married to."

"To prevent jealousy?"

Javesse shrugged. "Something of the sort. It's more of the foreigners we hide from now."

Vulture nodded.

"We women are also warriors," she said.

"Which I've witnessed."

Laughing, Javesse pushed on his shoulder. "Let me finish."

"Forgive me." His irises brightened from the dull iron as he chuckled. "Do go on."

This Vulture was pleasant. Enjoyable.

Javesse grabbed a stick and held it like a knife. "We begin sword training at ten years."

"I started squiring at that age. Although they didn't give me a sword until I was eleven."

"Maybe you're a slow learner."

"That's not funny." Vulture poked her side, causing her to pull away, laughing. "Now continue."

Settling, Javesse recalled the days of her youth, growing up in the stunning Bellinstarian fields between the capital city of Lunalla and the Onyx Ocean shoreline. "Father was a sea merchant and was often away, so Mother took on our training. My brothers, Jarus and Jovil, were excellent fighters. Jarus had already gained our generals' attention by the time he was fifteen."

"Your mother must've been a great teacher."

Pride swelled her heart. "She was," Javesse whispered. She bent a knee and clasped her hands around it. "Sometimes we sailed with Father to the other continents. We'd been to them all."

Vulture straightened. "Ubrasia?"

"Oh, yes."

"Fascinating."

"Their language is similar to the Elven Tongue, so it was easy to understand. I'd communicate with them for Father when he sailed there."

"How?"

"Do I speak so many languages?"

He nodded.

Javesse shrugged, drawing lines in the ground with the stick. "Like you, I'm a quick learner."

She fought a titter as he cocked his head. After a brief, breathy laugh, she resumed. "Every land we traveled, I grasped their languages, so to speak. My parents believed my studies were better used with the scholars than in the sparring yard." She sighed heavily. "But I loved holding the sword and challenging my brothers."

"How did you come to be here?"

Any happiness that had surfaced with the memories dissolved. Javesse chewed the corner of her lip. "When I was fifteen, our family sailed to Delvarian for business and pleasure. We had a friendship with the elves, you see."

She fell silent and played with the creases at the knee of her pants. "After a long visit, we sailed for home. Not two hours after leaving port, a…" Her mouth dried. Even now, seven years later, she still envisioned the massive horror beneath the water. Was it real?

"Songbird?"

Javesse released a deep breath. "Forgive me." She cleared her throat, her voice subdued as she resumed. "A storm struck our ship. We'd survived harsh weather at sea before, but never faced anything such as this." Grief tightened her throat, the nightmare she'd witnessed threatening to choke her. Javesse struggled to speak the next words, and they came out uttered. "I lost them all."

Vulture's finger dried teardrops across her cheek.

She blinked at him. "Th-the elves found me clinging to a piece of the ship. They gave me a home, treating me as part of their family."

He looked to the fire. "Forgive me," he whispered.

"You were unaware."

"Still… Loss is difficult." His warm palm covered her hand, his fingers curled around hers. Vulture sat back, his hand slipping off, leaving hers cold. "Well… I'm impressed with your fighting."

Unable to find her voice, she nodded once. Were things going to change between them?

Suspicious Behavior

Javesse agreed to slumber in the tent if Vulture did as well, pointing out he hadn't slept in several days. After a moment of hesitation, he ordered Titan to guard, then relaxed beside her, his sword at his side and hands under his head. It took little time before Vulture's breathing eased into a soft, even flow.

An hour dragged. Javesse's fascination and confusion with Vulture left her scrutinizing him from beneath a blanket. He'd shown compassion to her once again—and after violent behavior to the men in the tavern... and even toward her.

The softest moan escaped him, his brows lowered, and his chest stilled. The frown intensified; his lips parted. "Amalee," he whispered. "No. D-don't hurt her."

Javesse sat up and observed every twitching muscle and pained expression that passed his face.

"Amalee," he groaned.

She caressed his cheek with the backs of her fingers. "All's well."

The tension eased from Vulture's neck and shoulders. Javesse glided her fingertips across his forehead until he resumed a deep slumber.

She could leave now, but Brydasian men were a frightful sort. Besides, Vulture's actions proved he'd protect her. Thinking further on the matter, everything pointed to Darik. The Duke of Columure had warned he'd execute Vulture if he returned alone. Darik's concern about Javesse seemed greater than the assassin rumor. Did Vulture realize it as well?

Yawning, she lay back and pondered their next destination. They were drawing nearer to Ravieris, and his intentions were unknown.

The only thing Vulture mumbled while packing the tent was they'd no time to break fast. Once the horses were ready, he and Javesse mounted, and they ate while riding. She kept at his side. Vulture trusted her now, and she would maintain that for as long as necessary.

He shifted on the saddle and often raked his hand through his hair, many sidelong glances flitting in Javesse's direction. He even guided Titan away, putting distance between the two horses. Vulture didn't need to be ashamed for the night before; he'd already apologized.

"Vulture," she said.

Focused ahead, he lowered his brows. "What?" he snapped.

What had changed since the prior evening? Lost in the man's ever-shifting whirl of emotions, Javesse sighed. "Nothing."

"Good."

What a frustrating bastard.

Better the question went unasked. It wouldn't do any good anyway. There was naught to gain. His path remained the same, his future known to him. In fact, Songbird might find him more despicable. Disgusting. Evil. She might even laugh at him. But did Renmier care?

He wiped sweat from his nape.

Renmier couldn't blame Songbird for hating him. He'd been cruel since their meeting at Darik's. No. She wouldn't care about the truth. So why did it bother him like midsga flies having a meal of his blood?

The answer struck that morning when her fragrance enveloped him, like wildflowers in a heated field grazed by the breeze. It was as real as the warmth within his arms and the softness of her hair against his lips and nose. Songbird chased away the Darkness and brought a sense of peace he believed was lost to him. Renmier hadn't wanted to let go. Yet the debt he owed suffocated such fantasies. He would choke on the thickness of the Blackening for eternity. The fate awaiting him acknowledged, Renmier had eased his arm from beneath Songbird and escaped into the chilled morning. Shortly after, she hummed. He held his breath and listened to the loveliest melody ever to wrench upon what remained of his heart and soul. Tears welled, his throat tightened, and pressure built on his brow. Renmier almost dropped to his knees and wept. There was no doubt the gods were punishing him for the bargain he'd made. Damn Them All.

Despite how often he kept space between their horses, between him and Songbird, Renmier still gravitated to her. He needed her warmth. The tug wasn't there while they rode on Titan together, so why now?

It couldn't be done. He could not keep the gap maintained. Renmier couldn't ignore her efforts to speak with him. There was more to learn about Songbird. He wanted to share with her. And to whichever god Who might care what he desired, Renmier wished to please her—to make amends. His loss of control led to slave thieves taking her. He had to protect Songbird.

She fidgeted atop the mare, which she named Magyia.

Renmier spoke softer than earlier. "What is it?"

"I hate wearing leather."

Yet the garments formed magnificently to her fine curves. "You do wear it well."

She squinted at him. "It's uncomfortable."

"You moved with little hinderance yesterday."

Songbird gaped. "How much did you watch before deciding to help?"

"I arrived just as you felled the first bastard." He gripped the rein. "I killed the one man while you slaughtered the others. You didn't need me."

Yet Renmier's carelessness—his frightening others—almost cost her. He wouldn't dare put her in such a position again.

She huffed. "I still hate leather."

"What do Bellinstarians wear?"

After a silent moment passed, Songbird said, "Cotton during leisure times."

"And when you're fighting?"

"Heavy wool."

He withheld a laugh. How in Emvarr did wool protect a warrior in battle?

"I would think leather offers better protection if your people aren't keen on heavier material," Renmier said.

Songbird giggled. "I know it sounds absurd, especially to an Elite of His Eminence."

"It does."

"We find it easier to move and breathe."

"And gain wounds and die."

Spine stiff again, as Songbird often did when offended, she scrunched her face, a frequent expression when annoyed. "My people are excellent warriors."

"If you say."

Releasing another heavy breath, she stared forward.

Renmier suppressed the urge to laugh. "Let's get to the next village and relieve ourselves of the extra horses."

She said nothing more during the ride to Plinuir.

He hadn't meant to upset her. There was no insult meant by the inquiry nor comments, but none of what she shared made sense. Maybe Songbird would realize that in her silent annoyance.

They sold the four horses to a local stable master for five hundred gold roans. Then Renmier took Songbird to the Cracked Cauldron, his favorite tavern in the village and one of the best in the Newburrows Duchy. He promised her the proprietor's wife made a wonderful smoked trout. She seemed pleased but remained silent.

Several people at Cracked Cauldron recognized him, and the noise in the establishment softened. After Renmier and Songbird settled for a meal, the patrons relaxed. Laughter sounded at a few tables, and people came and went. Everything in the room faded as he watched Songbird.

Strange how one could eat and drink with such elegance, and that he hadn't noticed before now. Her golden irises brightened and darkened, depending on where she looked and if the flickering firelights caught the lovely color.

Renmier's mouth dried, his pulse throbbed in his throat. The tavern was warmer than a moment ago. He was only on the second mug, so he hadn't drunk too much. Wanting to feel Songbird's aura, he inched closer.

Her tongue darting over her lips, she strayed her attention to the fishbones. "Why do you stare at me like that?" she asked, moving her fingers along the rim of the bowl.

Sitting back, Renmier faced the hearth. The noise grew louder. He rolled his head from side to side, popping the sudden tension. "You finished?"

She dabbed her mouth with a cloth. "Yes."

"Then let's go. I'd like to reach Wheathfaire before too late in the night."

Renmier observed her often during the ride. Sometimes his breath caught in his chest, his throat constricted, and his cheeks heated. Reactions he'd not experienced since Amalee. He shouldn't feel this way now, not with where his path ended. No matter how much he reminded himself of the same truth in different manners, his feelings didn't change.

Once in Wheathfaire, they boarded the horses, then headed to Rabid Wolf Inn, one of the many places where Renmier had a standing room. He nodded at the barkeep, went up the stairs, and to the far end of the corridor. The key was in a pouch, along with a few others, but he didn't need one here. Someone waited.

Renmier leaned on the wall. "Knock for me, would you?"

Laughing, Songbird looked from the door to him. "Knock?"

"Yes."

She tucked a lock of hair behind her ear.

He wanted those strands curled around his fingers and her lips against his. Gods! Renmier needed to press her to the wall and kiss her with a passion he'd not known in over seven years. Stomach tight and heart thudding, he looked down the hall.

Songbird knocked a soft patting on the wood.

The pounding in his ears eased. Footsteps approached.

A burly man just over five feet tall stood in the doorway. His straw-like blond hair parted in the middle, leaving his deep-brown eyes in clear view. Thin lips opened the slightest as his pudgy cheeks rounded.

"Master," Tredwyn said with a voice seeming too small for such a round fellow. "I've been awaiting your return."

"Wait long?"

"So long, my wife left me."

Renmier forced a frown. "I'm sorry to hear that."

Wide-eyed, Tredwyn shrugged. "I'm not!"

Songbird gasped. "Awful," she whispered, yet tittered.

Tredwyn stepped aside and bowed. "M'lady, please come in."

Renmier nodded for her to go ahead. She entered the room, one of the largest of Rabid Wolf.

Tredwyn took some of the equipment Renmier carried, setting them in their respective places in the chamber. "You wished to speak to a guild member?"

Renmier produced a pouch of gold roans. "It must be tonight."

"I'll do my best, Master."

"Go on then."

Tredwyn left.

Once Renmier secured the door, he rested his forehead on the cool wood.

"How did he know?" Songbird asked.

"I sent messages ahead." He leaned against the small table near the exit. "When I left you alone last night..." Renmier lowered his gaze and continued lying. "Before I joined those bastards in the card game, I paid a lackey to ride ahead. He rides to other locations now."

"I see." She picked at her nails. "What are we to do until the meeting?"

A tease of her humming sounded in his mind, followed by Darik's words.

"Her voice belongs to me, Vulture..."

"Well?" Songbird pressed.

Renmier smirked. "We'll go to the bathing house."

Her face glowed. "Can we have some tea afterward? I would adore it."

He cringed. "*You* can have tea upon our return. I'll drink something that tastes better."

They gathered a change of clothing—clean wools for Renmier to wear under the armor—and went to the bathhouse. Thankfully, few were inside, so there was no wait. Renmier paid extra for privacy behind a tall screen painted with colorful birds.

A few feet from each tub were small chests. Songbird placed her items on one: a blue cotton blouse and black pants. She stared at him, waiting.

Renmier tilted his head.

"I won't undress while you watch," she said.

"As you're aware, I've seen women bare of their garments."

Songbird sneered.

She was a damn lighana and had seen naked men. Even if Darik failed to take her, she'd been exposed to him, so seeing Renmier without clothing shouldn't offend her.

He unbuckled the first strap of his top on the way to the crate for dirty clothing. It took several minutes to remove the armor, then the wools; the air felt good on his flesh. Renmier looked forward to the hot water since his last bath was before meeting Songbird. The aroma of jasmine filled their small space, already relaxing him.

Water lapped against the sides of the tub as Songbird sank into the bath. She hummed the softest moan.

Savoring the sound, Renmier did a slow turn, finding her head on a rolled towel and her eyes closed. Her face was smooth, tranquil.

Saliva gathered over his tongue, his heartbeat increased to hard thumps, and his nerves tingled. He stroked his arm, wanting to touch her. Throat surprisingly dry in the damp chamber, Renmier swallowed to wet it. He forced his attention to the floating flowers and herbs in his bathwater. A sluggish descent awakened his body in a rush, the heat intense on the charged nerve endings, then the fragrance filled his senses. Renmier let his body relax.

"Would you like—?"

He jerked forward, reaching for a weapon that was too far away. Glaring at the maiden peeking around the screen, he snarled. "What?"

"Wo...? Would you like me to wash you?"

"That would be lovely," Songbird said.

Renmier frowned at her. She'd grown too accustomed to Darik's servants.

"Don't I deserve this?" Her smile teased just as much as the rest of the vision before him.

Droplets of perspiration skimmed in front of Songbird's ear, running trails down her neck to mingle with the bathwater shielding her flesh. Other beads dotted her gorgeous face, glistening.

The annoyance fading, Renmier chuckled. "As you wish."

He washed while the maiden tended to Songbird, enjoying the latter's expressions and moans of gratification.

Finished long before them, he rose and grabbed the towel from the hook on the screen behind him. Twisting back around, he stilled. Both women gawked at him... and his partial erection. Songbird clamped her mouth shut.

"I assumed you ladies have seen a man before," Renmier said.

Tiny goosebumps formed on Songbird's arms. She looked away.

The bath maiden blushed. "Forgive me, m'lord." She resumed bathing Songbird, occasionally glancing at him while he dried and dressed.

Renmier was putting on the leather armor when Songbird began drying, keeping her back to him. She had such a fine bottom.

The pants and top donned, she turned, still buttoning the blouse. Songbird squinted. "Enjoy the view?"

"I did. And you?"

Ears reddening, she hid behind the mantle of hair while fastening the blouse sleeves.

Renmier laughed as he faced the bath maiden. "Our items."

She offered a bulky sack, brightening when he dropped a gold roan onto her palm. "Thank you, m'lord!"

He escorted Songbird to his room; Tredwyn had returned. While the short man spoke, Songbird sat on the bed and brushed her hair.

"The guild will meet you at the twenty-second hour. Not a moment later."

Enamored, Renmier watched Songbird perform the simple act, the bristles gliding through her long locks. He ran his fingers through his own dark strands, then scratched the young beard.

"Master," Tredwyn said.

"Yes?"

"Not a moment later than the twenty-second hour."

Looking at Tredwyn, he asked, "Who are they sending?"

"An elf, I believe."

"You do well by me. I owe you."

"You owe me nothing, Master."

"I wish you'd not call me that," Renmier whispered.

Tredwyn laughed. "I'd be dead if it weren't for you, and am grateful for what I have. Serving you is what I now live for."

The man had been a horse-handler during the war, nearly losing his life to an Elite Knight who accused him of causing his horse's leg to go lame. Renmier had witnessed the knight's lack of care for the mount, which was despicable considering the relationship between an Elite and his stallion. The knight beat Tredwyn until Renmier interfered. Not only had Renmier testified to Tredwyn's innocence, but once he did, so had others. General Repascow forced the knight to end the stallion's life, then the general removed Tredwyn from the army's services. It wasn't until nearly a year after the war, following Amalee's death, that Renmier met with Tredwyn again, when the horse-handler saved *his* life. Once Renmier recovered from the initial ritual, he sent Tredwyn to Wheathfaire with plenty of roans, and there, the man waited.

He owed nothing, but often reminded Renmier of the mission. Tredwyn stayed at Rabid Wolf, kept the room in order and protected, and answered the ring's calling when necessary.

Renmier grabbed a smaller pouch located further back on his belt and removed a sapphire. "For you."

The short man waved the offering away. "You needn't—"

"Take it."

Tredwyn sighed. "Yes, m'lord."

"Go have a fine evening."

Tredwyn's toothy grin lifted his chubby cheeks. "Thank you!" He shoved the gemstone in his pocket and hurried out.

"He's an interesting person." Songbird dropped the brush into her backpack. "He is."

Head tipped to the side, she said, "You compliment someone?"

The smirk was difficult to fight, but he won. "Let's eat, then meet our contact."

Rabid Wolf's smoked fish wasn't as good as the tavern's in Plinuir, but it satisfied Javesse enough. The tea, however, was delicious. Vulture surprised her by sharing a bottle of sweet wine after the late supper. Although he still spoke little, his expressions weren't as foreboding as in the past. Silver overtook his hard steel eyes, welcoming Javesse closer while they ate. Vulture's usual scent of leather and oil mixed strangely well with the jasmine. Perhaps the bath factored into his pleasant mood.

Javesse reached for the wine bottle, brushing her breast atop his wrist and hand. The warmth bolting throughout her was almost frightening, yet she welcomed the contact and desired more.

Stilling, Vulture breathed through his nose a tad louder while staring at the tabletop.

As Javesse poured the wine, her quaking caused the bottle's mouth to tap on the rim of her cup. She thumped the container down without meaning to.

Head tipped in her direction, he sat back, his heat still enveloping her.

She feared taking a drink might reveal how badly she shook. The bath-house replayed in her mind. Upon first meeting Vulture, Javesse had believed he was handsome, but having seen all of him, she now knew perfection. He was impeccable—even with the battle scars marring his flesh.

Jaw working side to side, he scanned the room and all within. Vulture scratched the tip of his eyebrow. "Let's go."

Javesse's stomach fluttered and twisted. What was she thinking? He'd told her he didn't want her, and she just tried to tempt him. She downed the wine and stood.

Vulture led her outside. Every confident stride sent a warning to onlookers and passersby: stay out of his way. After several blocks, they reached another tavern, The Sanctified. The name sounded promising, but the stench struck her before they entered. Not only was it the stale and fresh tobacco and body odor, but piss and vomit had Javesse almost retching her meal.

"Why this place?" she asked.

"We were instructed to come here."

Vulture grabbed her elbow and guided her to a table by the hearth where a figure wearing a green cloak sat, reading a book.

"You are early," she said without looking up, a musical lilt heard in her voice.

Recognizing the dialect, Javesse peered at the shadows beneath the hood. "Prefer Brydasia to home?"

The woman put the book down and smirked. Her Yeurothian elvish features were unmistakable, particularly the ivory flesh. Upon noticing Vulture, she smiled wider. "Oh. It is you."

He grunted. "Fancy seeing you again."

"Fancy seeing you clothed." The tip of her tongue glided over her lips. "We should take to a room afterward and discuss our last encounter."

Vulture's face shone brighter in the fireplace's glow. "Speak with me."

She closed the book and looked at Javesse. "Very well," she said in Elvish.

He scowled.

The elf swept her palm dismissively. "You know how this works."

"We do," Javesse snapped in their contact's language, the implication of the fling between the two making her seethe.

The elf jerked in her direction. "Interesting," she whispered. "Then let us continue."

Wrinkling her nose, Javesse gave a curt nod.

Vulture leaned closer, his heat pressing at her side as he glared at their contact.

"Word has it the dog comes from the north," the elf said "Whether such a rumor is true..." Raising her hands, she shrugged.

"Who in the north?" Javesse asked.

The elf sighed. "Obviously, someone in a powerful position."

"Does she want more?" Vulture asked, staring at Javesse.

"I want you," their contact replied in Common.

He didn't look at the elf. In fact, it seemed the silver had never shone in his irises. They were lead again. "Tell me what she said."

The elf tittered behind delicate fingers.

"Now, Songbird." Vulture's countenance hardened. "And the longer your response, the angrier I grow."

Frowning, Javesse said, "She claims the order is from the north."

He squeezed her arm. "You tell me what she says the moment she speaks. Understand?"

Stomach tight, she trembled. "Yes."

Vulture let go. "Get to what I paid for," he snapped at the elf.

She smiled. "Of course." She bowed her head and flitted her attention between him and Javesse.

"You mentioned it comes from the north," he said.

"I did."

"From whom?"

Looking at Javesse, she resumed in Elvish. "Some believe the trail is false. There is..." She paused, as if in thought. "There is a sense of betrayal to the target."

Javesse uttered the words to Vulture, who bore his weight upon her.

He nodded. "The fox is from the south for certain?" His choice of words was impressive. Vulture's interpretation of the underground cant grew fast.

The elf's loveliness was out of place in the disgusting tavern. "Without a doubt."

Vulture sat back, still staring at her. He removed something from the small pouch and placed it on the elf's palm; she closed her fingers around it. When he stood, Javesse did as well. Vulture motioned for her to remain at her seat, then rested a hand on the table's edge and one on the elf's chair. Bending nearer, he whispered in her pointed ear.

Flickering lights danced in her eyes. As he straightened, she bit her lip and nodded. "Absolutely."

"Good."

Vulture clutched Javesse's arm and directed her from the filthy place.

Fresh air available again, she took in a few draws. "What was that about?" She tried to jerk free.

He squeezed. "Never give yourself time to conjure a lie."

"What?" Javesse tugged harder from his hold. "I didn't!"

"I don't know that." He hauled her around a corner and down the road, ignoring stares and comments.

"Of all our days traveling together, today has been the worst," she said.

Vulture grimaced. "What are you on about?"

"You. Your behavior has been confusing."

He chuckled. "Good."

Upon reaching his room at Rabid Wolf, Vulture disarmed and sat in the large chair. Staring out the window, he moved his finger along the edge of his upper lip, seeming deep in thought.

Exhaustion pressed upon Javesse. Her mind and spirit could take no more for the day. "I'm going to bed."

He grunted. The removal of her weapon belt drew his attention.

Javesse placed it beside his flail. She unfastened her boots and slid them off, then eased beneath the fur coverlet. "I wish the warmer nights were here," she whispered.

The next morning, Vulture was gone, but Tredwyn stood before a tray of food and tea on the table. "Ah! You're awake, m'lady."

Sat up and stretches achieved, Javesse rubbed her eyes. A delicious aroma filled the chamber; she released a satisfactory moan. "What is it?"

"Porridge with honey, wastelbread, and peaches. And Master insisted on a cup of tea for you."

"Wastelbread?" She approached the tray and broke a piece of the flaky bread. It was buttery and sweet.

"It's popular amongst the nobles of northern Descension, m'lady. Master sent a lackey for it."

Javesse swallowed the delicious pastry, amazed Vulture did that for her. "Where is he now?"

Tredwyn shrugged. "M'lord has been gone since the clothing arrived." He nodded to a stack of garments on Vulture's chair.

Javesse scrutinized the items. "When was that? And what are those?"

He laughed. "You ask a lot of questions."

There was an inflection within his words. The 'ƒ' was hardly noticed, and 'qu' sounded like 'k'.

Javesse started, having heard such dialect along the border of Delvarian and the Darklands—Rela Sulae. Goosebumps formed on her arms. Why did Vulture have a Chaos worshipper serving him? Was he aware? She'd never seen a Sulaen before and didn't know what to expect. Although apprehensive, she turned to Tredwyn.

He viewed different points of her face before speaking. "M'lady?"

"I didn't believe your people lived outside Rela Sulae." Hearing her voice quiver, Javesse cleared her throat. "Are not the shadows your home?"

Nervousness fled from his eyes as they darkened. The room chilled. "Your meal gets cold, m'lady."

Fighting the urge to shiver, Javesse retreated. "As does the air around you."

He moved closer, but she shuffled backward. Tredwyn chuckled.

"You're not under any threat," he said. "Not by me, nor from him."

"I don't trust you." She suddenly recalled the black mists seen in Vulture's eyes, and the stories about Sulaens bargaining people's souls to Chaos. "What're you doing to him?"

Tredwyn sighed at the tray of food. "I do nothing. I only make certain he keeps his bargain."

"You have—?"

The door opened. Vulture entered and looked from Tredwyn to Javesse. "What is it?"

The Sulaen gestured at Javesse. "M'lady appears to have no appetite this morning," he said, no longer hiding his accent.

"Leave us," Vulture said.

"Yes, m'lord." Tredwyn bowed, then left.

Vulture pointed at the folded stack of clothing. "Are you not pleased?"

Arms crossed over her chest, she clutched her shoulders. "Why is a Darklander here?"

He glanced at the exit and stepped farther into the room. "Did Tredwyn say something?"

"Something about a bargain he intends to ensure you keep."

Vulture laughed. "Tredwyn's good for that."

She stomped to him, then shoved him back. "What have you—?"

"None of your bloody concern!" His face shaded crimson. "What is my business is not yours."

Spinning away, Javesse scowled. "Why do I feel caught in the midst of something devious?"

"An assassination *is* devious."

"You know that's not what I speak of."

The room was quiet for several seconds.

Javesse just wanted an answer. She was tired of skirting a whirlwind that threatened to sweep her into its dangerous funnel.

"Tredwyn is a part of my past," Vulture said. "We saved one another's lives."

Darklanders didn't save lives. They stole them.

"Is he not from Rela Sulae?" she prodded.

Vulture released a heavy breath. "The clothes... I believe they'll please you."

She pivoted on her heel. "Why not answer my question?" she snapped.

"I know the elves' prejudice against the Sulaens, and I'll not feed into yours." He nodded to the garments again. "Change. We leave in an hour."

Wrinkling her nose, Javesse asked, "Where's our destination now?"

He grinned. "To the palace."

How Vulture obtained garments that fit Javesse amazed her, and the comfort was more than she could've hoped. Not only did he provide cotton blouses and pants, but heavy wools, *and* a veil! Preparing for the ride, she wrapped the thick cloths around her torso while still avoiding hinderance to her arms' motions. She tucked the veil into her pack since wearing it might only draw further unwanted attention from others. But it felt wonderful to dress like a true Bellinstarian again, and Javesse was on the verge of kissing Vulture out of excitement.

He and Tredwyn spoke in muted tones in the room's corner, preventing Javesse from hearing any of the conversation. The little man bowed to her, his countenance revealing nothing. With a curt nod, Vulture began their journey out of Wheathfaire.

They rode north for two days to Ravieris, the capital city of the Descension Empire, stopping for rest in one of the many scattered copses of trees amid the plains. Despite attempts to talk Vulture out of seeking an audience with the emperor, the plan remained unchanged. And it didn't help that once he learned Emperor Larselis was having a ball, he insisted they attend. As they neared the fields outside Ravieris' walls, Javesse prayed to Fynthiar to keep her protected.

Manure overwhelmed the farming plots worked by peasants and slaves. Javesse wasn't certain if a difference existed between the two classes, and at the moment, she didn't care. She wanted to get away from the stench. It surprised her to notice Vulture didn't seem bothered by the awful odor.

Beyond the working fields, she and Vulture viewed the incline of the city walls. Lush green trees and bushes interrupted rings of white stone before rooftops of red dominated the pattern. The walls made it difficult to see past the lower city sectors. Tall towers stood sentry at the corners and intermittently throughout the long partitions, protecting enormous buildings at the top of the hill.

Javesse had never seen anything so imposing nor beautiful. Tears surfaced and her chest tightened from trying not to weep.

"Come," Vulture said, "we've places to go before the ball."

Licking her dry lips, she nodded.

An Eventful Evening

Vulture got a room at a small inn located in the second tier of the city, where the middle-class lived and most visitors frequented for affordable goods. Then he walked Javesse through the gates to the third tier: the home of the nobles and more prosperous shops. In spite of Ravieris' glorious architecture, amazing gardens, and other visual splendors, the upcoming event distracted Javesse. She couldn't imagine Vulture presenting himself well at a ball, let alone behave. He was too unapproachable.

While passing another shop displaying lovely garments, she built the courage to try once more to deter him from his intended path. "I'm certain we can get information elsewhere."

Vulture snorted a laugh. "Are you uncomfortable in the presence of royalty?"

"Of course not. I am friends with the king of Delvarian."

"And?"

"And I know *I* can at least present myself in court."

"Then I expect perfect behavior from you." Expression stern, he leaned close. "And do exactly as I tell you."

To evade the sudden discomfort of his nearness, she viewed the upcoming shop window: fine leather shoes and boots. "A-am I going as your slave?"

"No." He crossed his arms. "As my woman companion."

Javesse clicked her tongue and gasped. "You jest."

"Would you rather go as my lighana?"

"No, but—"

"The matter's settled." He pointed at the next shop. "Now let's get some clothing."

Vulture chose Javesse's gown, giving her no options. At least he had style. He selected a red silk dress with little embroidery—leafy gold vines lined the edges of the flowing skirt, low collar, and tight sleeves. And he demanded a corset, which Javesse had never worn; it looked like something meant to bind slaves. She shook her head at it, but Vulture's glare told her there'd be no quarrel.

His attire, including the blouse and doublet, consisted of black. Of course. The seamstress tried to persuade him to add color to the outfit, but his disinterested stare was the only response. He paid a heavy purse for the completion of the garments' alterations ahead of the event.

At the inn, talk of the upcoming ball occupied most conversations. Strange how the uninvited behaved with such excitement. They probably anticipated the gossip that might surface in the morning.

Vulture thudded his fist on the bar. "Baths. Now."

"Yes, my lord," the barkeep said. "I'll have the water heated immediately."

Javesse followed Vulture up the stairs to his room. While waiting, he sat on the bed and relaxed against the wall.

She chewed her nail and paced. "Do you know what you'll ask him?"

Amusement didn't mar his smooth visage. "No."

"Fine plan, Vulture."

"My concern is you, Songbird, and whether you can listen."

Javesse wrinkled her nose at him.

Did his notice just shift to the small action? She was certain he tried not to smirk.

"I-I should be the least of your concerns," she said. "You haven't an idea what to say to the emperor."

"I'll know when the time comes."

Maybe it was good Vulture could act quickly. But what if he failed? What if he lost his temper again? They'd end up imprisoned.

"Do us both a great favor." He scratched the scruff on his jaw. "Talk as little as possible."

Narrowing her eyes, she said, "I dislike you."

He shrugged.

A knock startled her.

"Baths are ready," the lackey called.

Vulture stood, removed a silver roan from his pouch, then opened the door. "Have supper here by our return."

The lackey received the coin and bowed. "Yes, m'lord."

Javesse frowned. "Aren't we eating at—?"

"No." Vulture motioned for her to follow and walked out.

Renmier groomed his moustache, then took great care to form the beard into a well-sculpted line along his jaw. He even brushed his hair. If it wasn't for the feast, he'd not bother with such details, but his presentation at the palace must be flawless. It'd been nine years since Renmier's last visit, and he wasn't certain how the emperor would receive him. Rumors had reached him about Larselis growing haughty and cruel. He hoped the emperor might remember his accomplishments during the war and not be a bastard toward him for refusing to attend the celebration that followed its end. Renmier had collected his salary, retirement reward, Amalee and her dowry, and he left Ravieris to start a fresh life. To know peace once again.

Now he prayed to whichever gods might receive his concerns that Songbird would bloody listen to him. The woman's resistance could jeopardize everything, and her beauty might tempt Larselis... and others.

Renmier started to rake his hands through his hair, but stopped as to not undo his hard work. He pinched the bridge of his nose and squeezed his eyes shut, willing the worries to flee. After dressing in simple clothing, he grabbed a knife and a pouch of gemstones, then led Songbird from the inn.

They rode Titan to the seamstress' shop to pick up their garments, then found Knights' Peak, a large upscale tavern with a stable next door. It was where most travelers of means stayed. Renmier paid for a double room for him and Songbird to prepare for the ball.

He was just putting his jacket on when she exited the adjoined room. Hesitating from straightening his sleeve, he took in the view.

She had twisted her hair within itself, holding it up with several glittering pins acquired from the seamstress; a few locks hung in front of her ears and by her temples. Soft-colored powders of autumn leaves adorned her face. The gown clung to her curves, yet allowed effortless movement with her graceful motions.

If only he could veil her from everyone's eyes.

"Is something wrong?" Panting, Songbird tugged the dress up. "I've never worn a corset, and don't know if I've done it correctly."

He moved behind her and unlaced the dress' back, which appeared she'd tied in a hurry.

She inched forward. "What're you doing?"

Holding the strings fast, he kept her still. "I must inspect your work to make sure you don't grow ill." Renmier pried the laces apart. "Pull it down."

Breaths short, she remained motionless.

"I'd rather you walked comfortably than have you collapse, Songbird."

It was a task for her to remove the sleeves and lower the top half to her waist. "Maybe we shouldn't have already eaten."

That came out breathy.

Withholding a chuckle, he inspected the ties at the corset's front, appreciating her bulging cleavage. "We'll not eat at the celebration."

"No?"

"No."

Songbird had tied the corset too tightly.

Behind her again, Renmier loosened the back strings. "I'm going to ease this so your head doesn't swim later."

"All right."

He gave an inch, keeping his finger beneath the top of the corset. "Take a deep breath." After exhibiting she needed more room, he adjusted further. "Gods, woman. Were you trying to suffocate yourself?"

"I said I've never worn one," she snapped.

Renmier retied it, then waited while she slipped her arms back into the sleeves. He restrung the dress laces into a perfect bow. "Better?"

"It is." Songbird raised her hands as high as the dress permitted. "How do I look?"

She made it ache for *him* to breathe.

"Very nice."

"Oh." Songbird looked down, her lips twitching at one corner. "You look handsome, Vulture. I didn't get to say it earlier, but I like your beard."

"Thank you." It wouldn't stay like that for long.

She fidgeted with her fingernails, a hint of pink flushing her cheeks. It took a moment for her to form whatever words she needed to speak. "My breath was stolen when I saw you upon entering the room."

The compliment had already surprised him, but her confession was unexpected.

"I thought the corset did that," he said.

Songbird's giggle was lovely. "No." Cheeks rosy, her irises glowed.

The sun's warmth shone upon him in that chamber. And Renmier didn't want to move, not from near her.

"Then I'll be honest," he said, clasping his hands behind him. "I... I can't find the words."

She cocked her head toward her shoulder. "For what?"

"How undeniably beautiful you are."

Songbird's entire face tinged pink as silence floated between them. "Thank you, Vulture."

Retreating, he said, "You can't call me that tonight."

"How shall I address you?"

So many days, and they'd yet to know each other's names. How foolish.

He bowed. "Sir Renmier Forais."

"Sir Renmier?" she said through a wide smile and barely moving lips.

He strained not to laugh. "Yes?"

"I *hate* being called Songbird."

That was almost a shame. Her voice was lovely, her humming amazing, and he could only imagine her singing.

He offered his hand. "And by what name shall I call you, my lady?"

She placed her warm and delicate hand on his calloused palm. "Javesse Tavarelle."

His tongue and lips moved the faintest, forming her name. Gorgeous. Musical. It fit her perfectly.

"A lovely name, Lady Javesse." He kissed her fingers, lingering. "Now we must go." Renmier slid the knife into the back sheath beneath the jacket.

On the way to the palace, he fell quiet. A concern deepened. Larselis would want her. While ascending the long, winding marble stairs to the entrance, the gala grew unimportant to Renmier. Keeping Javesse safe from everyone and any danger mattered most, yet he couldn't claim her. He didn't even belong to himself. Renmier was bound to another. However, he could still protect Javesse while it was possible.

They stood behind a line of guests moving slowly up the stairs.

"Won't we need an invitation to get inside?" She apparently noticed the others holding decorated scrolls.

"They'll let us in."

"Renmier?"

"Yes?"

"Can you dance?"

He laughed softly through his nose. "Yes, my lady, I can."

Javesse pulled her lips between her teeth to hide an obvious smile.

"You doubt me?" he asked.

"I have trouble imagining *you* dancing."

"Then you're in for quite a surprise."

Her delighted expression met him. "I look forward to it," she said.

By the time they reached the banded mahogany doors, set wide open from beneath a marble arch, Renmier had heard enough pretentious nobles' conversations to last another nine years. He wished there was more to say to Javesse, but it was best she knew little of his history.

"Your invitation, sir," the doorman said. Behind him stood four guards in plate armor and bearing several weapons. Elite Knights.

"Sir Renmier Forais," Renmier said.

Upon hearing his name, the knights bowed partially.

"You received an invite?" the doorman asked.

"No."

Glancing at the doorman, one knight said, "Wait here, Sir Renmier."

The doorman motioned to the side; Renmier pulled Javesse from the line of guests.

"What now?" she asked.

"We wait."

"This won't work."

"Yes, it will." He winked. "Trust me."

Five minutes passed before the knight returned with a serious-looking man beside him. He dressed like Renmier, but with a red doublet and white blouse.

"You filthy bird," the man said. It was one of Renmier's old companions during the war.

With a wry grin, Renmier guided Javesse behind him. "You dirty dog."

Laughing, he and the man clasped arms.

"Renmier!"

"Heslion."

"I never believed I'd see you again," Heslion said. "Gods! When I heard you were the Vulture, I said, 'No, not Renmier. It's not possible'. Yet here you are! I thought you were gone for good."

"I return now and then."

"And you're here for the gala?" Heslion raised his brows but waved aside his own inquiry. "Never mind. It's grand to see you. I'm certain it will please His Eminence as well. Come."

Renmier offered his arm to Javesse.

Heslion stilled. "You've an escort. And a stunning one at that. My lady." He bowed. "I'm Sir Heslion, and I'm your servant."

"Pay him no mind." Renmier smirked. "He's a scoundrel."

Heslion bellowed a laugh. "Aren't we both?"

Javesse tittered, bringing both men to silence.

"Come," Heslion said, his focus on her once more. "I shall find you a place to sit. I'm certain His Eminence shall see to a conversation with you."

Heslion escorted them into a grand chamber of white marble floors. Pillars and archways formed the decorative base of the rib vaulted ceiling, which provided acoustics for the musicians' wonderful melodies. Long tables lined in front of the arcades where walkways to doors and stairs lay beyond, and bodies filled the large, open floor, their motions precise in the same dance. Dozens of people enjoyed themselves in the whirls and dips, and several more feasted; more guests packed the tables. Renmier had never seen such an immense gathering at the palace.

At a table higher than the others, a man appearing near thirty years in age sat. Emperor Larselis Maliage. Beside him was the empress, a young woman seeming no more than twenty years old. Renmier had learned of the marriage a year ago, yet knew nothing about the woman. Not even her name.

Heslion led them two tables from the emperor's, forcing a couple to leave their seats.

Javesse's lips moved with an obvious objection poised upon them, but Renmier shook his head, and she said nothing.

"Enjoy yourself," Heslion said to Javesse. "The food will bring more than satisfaction. It'll bring a craving." He bowed, then walked through the arcade to reach the royal table.

Renmier pushed Javesse's chair in and leaned close. "Remember, don't eat or drink anything."

As he sat beside her, he spotted Heslion having a lengthy discussion with Larselis, both looking Renmier's way.

"What are we to do with ourselves?" Javesse asked.

He slouched in the chair and gave his full attention to her. "We could talk."

She simpered. "I imagine that would be quite a task for you."

"I might surprise you."

"Sir Renmier!" A man stood across from them. "Gods! You're still alive?"

"Sir Pravnus," Renmier said, his tone flat. "How do you fare?"

"Very well, as I'm certain you can see." He pointed at his own fine garments.

"You've finally earned His Eminence's good graces."

"It took long enough. Unlike you, you filthy bird. Pah!" Pravnus walked away.

Renmier returned his focus to Javesse to find her regarding him. "Yes?" he asked.

"Filthy bird?"

"Vulture."

"I should've assumed. Has that followed you everywhere?"

"Only over the past five years."

"You must've made a reputation for yourself." She raised the goblet.

He gave her a warning glare.

Javesse tilted it, but the drink didn't touch her lips.

"Sir Renmier?"

The irritation grew.

"Greetings, Sir Shargrid," Renmier said to the old companion standing at the table.

Shargrid's glazed eyes darted to Javesse. "Fine woman you've at your side."

Renmier leaned toward him. "Yes. That *I* have here. Now move on."

Fingers gliding over his lips, Shargrid stared at her as he moseyed away, already affected.

Giving Shargrid a sidelong scowl, Javesse shifted in her seat. "What was that about?"

"As I said, do not drink nor eat."

"What if I do?"

Renmier's heart raced at the thought of the outcome. Tempting, but no. He'd not let it happen. "Do you enjoy speaking so many languages?"

"No, no." Javesse gave the goblet a slow spin. "I'm asking the questions."

He grunted. "Go on."

"Tell me about the knighthood."

"The Elite, you mean?"

She nodded once.

"Elite Knights are the emperor's personal guard, and his elite force in the army."

"And?"

"I was one."

"Is that all?"

"What more is there to tell?"

The only reason he noticed she raised her shoulder the slightest was because he watched every one of her moves. Yet she performed that tiny motion with such elegance.

"What makes one knight an Elite and others not?" she asked.

"Sir Renmier." Three women stood where the previous interrupters had, just avoiding the dancers. "Are you joining us afterward?" one asked. "Please say yes."

Javesse looked from the women to him.

"Our skills, obviously," he said to Javesse. From his peripheral, he noted the women walked away. Renmier indicated the heavily armed men at the entrances and along the wall by bobbing his head in their directions. "They're Elite."

Fixated on the retreating maidens a moment longer, Javesse finally acknowledged the knights standing sentry. "They carry many weapons."

"We're trained to know many, but we focus on one or two."

"I imagine yours is that dreadful spiked ball."

Renmier grinned. "I was familiar with a similar tool prior to joining the knighthood. It still took some time and many injuries before I handled the great flail with expertise."

A passerby's hand landed on his chest. She slid it over his shoulder and off. Javesse leered at the woman's back, then at him.

Jealousy? Intriguing.

"Did you want to become an Elite?" she asked, her tone sharp.

"I was one of the youngest brought into the order."

Truth was, men from the palace had dragged Renmier from home, taking him from his parents. He was forced into the knighthood under the premise it was for the greater good of Descension. During the first two years of training, he came to understand His Eminence's desire to improve Brydasia for Her people, and he strove to gain his way into the Elite. Renmier hadn't believed he'd climb amongst the ranks to lead. He was just a farm boy.

"How young?" Javesse asked.

"Nineteen. Only two years after my knighting."

"Why so young?"

He shrugged. "I'm good at what I do. His Eminence needed men of quality leading the war."

"You mean invasion, as I've heard it called."

He waved away the comment. "The southern lands were a cesspool. Brydasia is better for what His Eminence has accomplished."

Huffing, Javesse flicked the goblet's base.

Bent closer to her, Renmier regained her attention. "Emperor Larselis has done well by taking the region from those who didn't care over it," he said. "Brydasia will be the richest continent within the next few years, and we shall thrive. His Eminence takes care of his people and rewards those who serve him faithfully."

Face red, she stared in controlled skepticism. "You truly believe that."

He sat back. "I do."

She released a soft, "*Hm!*"

"Don't you?"

"I learned from the elves about the lives lost and lands ruined because of his conquest. Did you never consider the many people killed?"

"It was war, Javesse. Death happens."

Disbelief met him. Renmier didn't mean to sound hardhearted, but did she not understand war?

"H-how many did you kill?" An unsettled expression overtook her. Discomfort. Javesse really didn't want to know.

Renmier couldn't recall most faces of those he'd slain, and why would he?

"I led a unit of thirty knights and six hundred soldiers," he said. "Many of them died believing in what they fought for, and many people died protecting their homes. Hundreds died by my hands."

Wrinkles marred her forehead and her eyes glistened with a threat of tears. "Have you no regrets?"

There were many, but none he wished to impart to her.

"Dance with me," he said.

Blinking, she looked at the dancers. "Oh, I don't—"

"Know how?"

The immediate shift of her countenance was his intention, his past no longer a topic.

Javesse squinted. "Of course I can."

Standing, Renmier bowed slightly. "Then please dance with me."

"Very well." She placed her hand into his. "Since your request was polite."

Renmier eased them into the flow of dancers. Gazes locked, he led the moves of The Blizzard, which was a difficult performance representing the survival of a winter storm to reach a lover's warm embrace. Javesse's familiarity and ability to keep up with the speedy steps and spins was a pleasant surprise. At the finale of the dance, Renmier pulled her tight against him; she entwined her hands behind his neck. Their cheeks touched while they moved their hips in a slow gyration.

He had only wanted to evade further questions. Holding Javesse like that—tasting her perfume and feeling her breath on his face and neck—Renmier needed no poison for a stirring... something he'd not felt in years. Their lips grazed each other. He brushed his fingers over her hair and lost himself in her eyes.

The music faded.

No good would come from giving in to desire. It'd weaken him. Yet Renmier couldn't remove himself from her warmth—a promise of the sun in the Darkness. He glided his mouth closer to her ear. "Javesse."

Pressed harder against him, she gripped his shoulders.

His heart raced as if he was a full man, completely alive. His own.

A staff thumping on the floor echoed in the chamber.

"Sir Renmier Forais!"

Renmier and Javesse parted and faced the royal table, from where the emperor's cheeks glowed.

"Come forward," Emperor Larselis said.

Renmier tucked Javesse's hand to the crook of his arm, then rested his palm over it. Ignoring the whispering crowd as it parted, he escorted her forward. He knelt; Javesse curtsied low.

"Your Eminence," they said.

Larselis was a fair-looking man. Like most northern Brydasians, his hair was dark, which he kept trimmed to the shoulders. He was fit, claiming he'd never be a lazy boar who grew fat while sitting on the throne. Chest expanding far, his full attention fell upon Javesse. "Gods, Sir Renmier, she's exquisite."

"Thank you, Your Eminence."

"I imagine such beauty might cause wars." Larselis touched his hand to his heart and released a rush of air. "Men might kill to take such a woman."

Javesse's grip tightened beneath Renmier's hand.

"Any man who might try will die, Your Eminence." Renmier bowed.

Guests covered their mouths, intakes of breath the only sound in the chamber. Suddenly, the emperor's laughter sliced through the thick silence.

"I've no doubt they would by your hands, Sir Renmier," Larselis said.

Javesse's hold lightened.

The emperor's eyes remained on her. "It surprised me to learn of your attendance, my friend." At last, he looked at Renmier. "Come." He gestured to his left and the chair next to him emptied. "Join me!"

Renmier sighed inwardly. He needed to speak with Larselis, yet had hoped to avoid such an invitation. To meet later in private would've been ideal, but it was too late. Renmier must improvise.

"We are grateful, Your Eminence." He bowed again, then escorted Javesse around the tables and up the arcade steps. "Remember what I told you," he whispered. "Eat and drink nothing."

"Must we sit with him?"

"We've no choice."

Larselis directed Renmier to the chair beside him, while Javesse was seated with the women to the empress' right. Renmier tried to mind her, but the emperor interfered with questions.

"Where have you been?" Larselis asked. "Hiding behind the name of a bird?"

"I travel often." Renmier saw Javesse decline offered fruits and goblets. "Others gave me that name."

"Do you no longer hold loyalty to me?"

Renmier frowned. "Of course I do, Your Eminence."

"Yet I hear Vulture gives his services to Duke Nornt." Larselis laughed. "Amusing as Darik is."

A maiden halted beside Renmier and slid her hand beneath his jacket. "I have missed you." She caught his earlobe between her teeth, then let it go slowly. "Please tell me you'll stay after the ball."

"Lord Nornt pays well for such services." Renmier removed her palm from his chest and gave her a gentle push onward. "I've heard talk about an assassination order."

Larselis chuckled at the retreating maiden. "So have I. Whether the gossip is true..." He shrugged. "Darik made many enemies, especially after murdering General Repascow in such a cowardice manner."

"Agreed." Renmier plucked a grape and rolled it between his thumb and finger. "I was curious whether the order was yours."

Lips twitching, the emperor dragged his jeweled cup closer. "Although I'm pleased with how well the southern region fares, especially the port cities, the rat won't hold it much longer." Larselis smirked. "And why would I use an assassin? I've the Elite to crush his mismatched force."

"I wouldn't underestimate Darik. He's got hidden strengths with his men and allies."

"Such as you? The Vulture."

Renmier tapped the tabletop.

"Did I not provide enough?" Larselis swept his arm the length of the ballroom. "You once enjoyed sitting amongst us, taking your pleasures in the food, drink, and women. Don't forget Love Orchid."

"My life changed."

"Ah, yes. Your wife." Larselis readjusted his position. "Her death was an ugly matter, to be sure."

Renmier set his jaw. "It was."

"I would've taken you back afterward."

"There were concerns that drew my focus."

"You're always welcomed here. I could use you—your command in the palace."

Renmier glanced at Heslion, the current Captain of the Guard. "What of Sir Heslion?"

"He's a good man, but soft. Overtaken by Orchid too often. But you?" The emperor pointed at Renmier. "No one would cross you. Right before my guests, you pressed my authority—my reign—testing my will and strength. I could've called every Elite within hearing upon you for such an act, and you would've fought to your death to keep what was yours."

Was? Renmier glimpsed Javesse eating chocolates. *Damn her!*

"The fact of the matter is I want you back." Larselis scowled. "One day, Darik Nornt shall find you no longer useful to him, and he will dispose of you."

Renmier snorted.

"Men in power do what they must to maintain an allegiance," the emperor continued. "Everyone is replaceable. Even you."

Was that sorrow in his voice?

"If you believe I don't have Elite as strong as you'd been, you're mistaken," Larselis said. "I do."

Renmier released the crushed grape.

"Be useful to me once again. You'll want for nothing." The emperor motioned to the untouched goblet by Renmier. "Drink. Think on my offer."

"I shall, Your Eminence." Renmier rose. "Forgive our early departure. Travel has been arduous, and we must retire."

Larselis regarded him. "If you must."

Renmier approached Javesse and reached around the seat for her. "My lady."

Laughing with the other women, she set a half-empty cup on the table.

"Let her stay," Larselis said. "Let your woman enjoy herself tonight."

Renmier relaxed before responding. "If she wasn't with child, I'd consider it. As such is her condition..." He patted his stomach.

"I see." Larselis raised a brow, but appeared to pass on arguing the claim. "I insist you remain here for the evening."

Damn it. Renmier bowed again. "We're most grateful, Your Eminence." He pulled Javesse's chair back, then grabbed her arm. "Let's go."

"But—"

With as much gentleness as he could muster, he guided her to stand. "Now."

She tittered as a knight led them through the arcade and up a few steps to a door hidden by an alcove. Stumbling, she clung to Renmier.

Fury and annoyance battled his control. He didn't want to stay, but because of Javesse's inability to do a damn thing he said, there they were. Once they staggered through the doorway, he carried her up the long flight of stairs to the next floor.

Arms around his shoulders, she beamed. "You're beautiful."

Renmier's cheeks heated more from her abrupt honesty, yet he ignored her.

Knights stood throughout the corridors, bowing their head as he passed. Renmier might've known some of them, but at the moment, he didn't care.

The escorting guard continued until near the end of the hall, unlocking a large door. "Enjoy your evening, sir," he muttered as they crossed the threshold.

Renmier kicked the door shut, then stomped to the bed and dropped Javesse on the mattress. "Bitch."

She curled, laughing.

The lock secured, he took off his jacket. The pacing began.

There was no way to extract the poison. Not yet. The kitchen focused on the feast, so requesting select foods might draw attention. It'd have to wait until morning.

Renmier grasped the hair at his nape. How hard was it for Javesse to listen? He spun, almost walking into her.

"You have any idea how desirable you are?" she asked. "The other women talked only about you."

"Sleep it off."

She touched his abdomen, walked her fingertips up the doublet buttons. "Join me."

Renmier's heart thumped.

Javesse rose on her tiptoes and brushed her lips over his. "I want you."

Muscles tight, Renmier caught her bottom lip between his. The familiar hint of anise danced on his tongue, revolting him. Love Orchid.

Years ago, he had tasted it after many palace celebrations, when Larselis had the food and drink laced with the elixir of desire to sate *his* lascivious moods. The emperor enjoyed involving his favored Elites in the carnal festivities. He'd once told Renmier he felt a sense of gratification while watching his poisoned knights throng women on the hall floor, tables, and arcade steps. After that admittance, Renmier avoided the feasts, for he was no one's entertainment. Then he'd met Amalee, and his life changed.

And now this lust-induced woman was attempting to seduce him.

Renmier threw Javesse's hands down. "Why didn't you just bloody listen?"

Her simper irritated him further.

"The chocolates were delicious, I couldn't resist them." She reached back, loosening the dress then freeing her arms. "However, I doubt anything'll satisfy me as much as you will."

"Stop."

The gown pooled at her feet. Wearing only the corset and red knickers, Javesse pressed her thighs together, swaying her hips left to right. Her hands glided up the front of her torso, over her breasts, then above her head. The teasing dance made it difficult to not want her.

"You don't wish me to."

Looking away, Renmier battled the yearning and lied. "I do."

Javesse neared again, her heat soaking through his clothes. "Let's remove these from you." She unfastened the first button of the doublet.

He pushed her toward the bed. "I said stop!"

"What's wrong with you?" She grimaced. "You claimed to have enjoyed the company of farm girls—" Javesse stared for a moment, then guffawed. "But now... Now I wonder if it were farm boys."

He lowered his brows. "What?"

"You prefer men. Is that it?"

Renmier curled his fingers into fists. "You're vile."

Laughing, Javesse clapped. "I now know the truth." She bent forward, emphasizing her glee. "You prefer boys!"

"I'm not amused."

"Nor are you hiding the facts by rejecting *me*." Shoulders squared with him, she sneered. "Every man at the gala wanted me... except you. You'd rather have a good swyve with the guard out there." She nodded at the chamber door. "Is that how close you Elites are?"

He squinted. "I'll not play into your game."

Javesse opened her mouth wide. "I see it now. You don't hate Captain Givins."

Frozen, Renmier gritted his teeth so hard it hurt. "Stop right there."

"You crave him."

He moved nearer, his nails biting into his palms. "Close your mouth before you regret it."

"You don't wish to kill him." She stifled a giggle. "You want to bed him."

Anger flushed Renmier's face and Darkness filled every inch of his being while he saw Samris do things he wanted to forget.

"There it is." Javesse's face glowed and her eyes brightened. "That blackness in your eyes. Lust-fury. You need Samris so badly, but you're angry he rejected you."

Renmier struck her with such force, she spun, landing beside the bed. "Horrid creature!"

"Bastard," she murmured, rising to her hands and knees. "You'll slap a woman, but you won't lie with her. Do you rough up the boys as well?"

The urge to harm Javesse more overwhelmed him. Renmier lifted her and threw her on the mattress, then he pinned her shoulders between plush pillows. "Bitch!"

She pushed on his arms. "Let go!"

"You never stop!"

Nails digging into his cheek, she raked his flesh. "Let go!"

Shouting, he jerked back. He struck her twice more; she lay unmoving.

Renmier backed off the bed, continuing until he was against the wall. Eyelids squeezed shut, he slid to the floor. Breaths came deep and slow. He had to regain control, lest the Darkness seize him. Not yet. Part of his soul still belonged to him.

After his body warmed and his mind cleared, he waited a few minutes, touching his cheek a few times to see if the bleeding stopped. Renmier hoped Javesse would stay asleep, for he couldn't endure another episode of her poison-induced behavior.

Javesse's head throbbed. She shivered. And Fynthiar damn it all, her cheek hurt.

Moaning, she rolled to her back and scrunched her nose. A horrific odor filled the chamber, coming from where Renmier stood across the room at a table. His back was to her, and he appeared busy.

"Ugh," she rasped. "What is that awful stench?"

"Your morning meal."

Their voices sounded muffled, as if spoken from outside the door.

She scratched goosebumps on her arm. In fact, they spread like an infection, and her whole body itched. Javesse sat up. Her vision spun, her heart raced, and the trembles advanced into quaking. It was terrible.

Javesse tried to recall what happened the night before, but after being force fed a wonderful piece of chocolate, she remembered nothing. Not a bloody thing. Smacking her tongue against the roof of her mouth, she gathered a trace of anise. How strange.

"What am I breaking fast with?" What Javesse needed was more of that delicious chocolate and wonderful wine.

"Grospies."

"I've never heard of them. They smell revolting." She scooted to the edge of the bed and swung her legs over the side, finding she wore only the corset and knickers. Javesse pulled the coverlet to her chest as Renmier approached with a delicate-looking bowl, small brown balls steaming within.

His jaw flexed as he neared, his motion rigid. The man was ready for her resistance. As he should've been. What a fool to believe she'd eat even one of those disgusting pieces of meat.

There were scratches on his cheek. Javesse was about to inquire of them, but the stink coming from the bowl drew her attention. No. She wasn't eating whatever the emperor had provided. Javesse lowered the blanket and bent forward, hoping a tease of cleavage might calm Renmier's tense demeanor. "Chocolate sounds lovely."

His gaze remained on her face. "Open your bloody mouth."

"You know I don't care for—"

"Now!"

Nose wrinkled, she leaned back on her elbows and crossed her legs. "No." She kicked the bowl from his hand, scattering grospies on the bed and floor.

There wasn't the slightest hesitation; Renmier scooped a handful from the mattress. He knelt over her, clutching her cheeks to pry her mouth open. "You'll eat these!" He shoved two meat chunks deep inside.

Javesse attempted to spit them out, but his large hand covered her nose and mouth, his iron eyes hard. There was no choice but to swallow the foul meat. Renmier repeated the feeding. After a third time, Javesse gagged; he leapt aside. She fell to the floor on her hands and knees, and vomited not only the grospies, but everything she'd consumed at the feast.

His palm traced comforting circles on her back. "Good. Get it all out."

How dare he touch her. The knights at the ball were correct: Renmier was a filthy bird, and Javesse wished to get away from him.

Once her stomach could purge nothing more, she sat on her heels and wiped her lips with the back of her hand. "I hate you."

"That's fine." He lowered to the chair and gestured at the mess. "But this was necessary."

"How was this necessary?" Javesse snapped.

"I instructed you to eat and drink nothing."

She climbed upon wobbling legs. "They forced it into my mouth, just as you did those—those... Whatever they are!"

"Goats' testicles."

Her jaw dropped. "What did you just feed me?" she whispered.

"Something I knew you'd retch right back out, along with last night's poisoned food." Renmier rose. "Get dressed. We're leaving now."

"I'll go nowhere with you."

"You don't have a bloody choice!" He huffed a laugh. "Unless you'd rather stay and become His Eminence's next lighana. That's what he has planned for you."

"How do you know?" She walked around the vomit and reached for the dress from the chair while trying to keep as far from him as she could.

"I know him."

The sleeves were still difficult to manage. "Damn dress." The gown on, she adjusted the collar.

Renmier moved behind her, lacing the back with the same care as the prior evening.

Javesse stilled. "What happened?"

"Nothing of which you need to worry."

"Your face—"

"You."

She waited for him to say something more, but Renmier must've believed one word was enough. Spinning, she slapped his hand away. "What about me?"

He searched her eyes for a quiet moment. "You weren't yourself."

How much did the wine and chocolates alter her?

Javesse crossed her arms beneath her chest. "You don't know me, Vulture."

Appearing hurt, Renmier scowled. He sounded a heavy sigh as he put his jacket on. "You're correct about that."

She pointed at his face. "Why did I do that?"

The obvious inward debate was short-lived before he spoke. "The poison they add to the food and drinks is called Love Orchid. It heightens the craving for sexual desire." There was no smug expression, nothing to hint Renmier took pleasures with her.

Javesse looked away and prayed she'd not done something regrettable.

"And it remained in your body, pushing you to need more," he continued. "That's why I forced you to eat the grospies, so you'd expel it all." Renmier sheathed his knife. "There're mint leaves in Titan's saddlebag. Are you ready to leave?"

Mint leaves? Her breath must be awful—it tasted horrible to her. Nodding toward her toes, she said, "I just... just need my shoes."

He waited by the door, silent and patient.

"Why didn't you warn me about the poison?" she asked while tying the slippers.

His shoulders slumped. "I should've." Straightening, he released a heavy breath. "But I don't know that you would've listened anyway."

Javesse slammed her foot and pushed the skirt down. "Maybe you should try being open with me," she snapped. "I thought you trusted me."

Renmier's shoulders lowered again. "I'm sorry. I wasn't sure if I could trust you here."

That admittance hurt as much as her cheek. She touched it and winced.

"Forgive me," he murmured. "I struck you."

She glared at him. "Is that why I scratched you?"

"You spoke rather foully. I regret I—lashed out in response. I'm sorry." Renmier tucked his chin and moved his wrists in circles.

"Dare I ask how foul?"

"Please don't."

His answer shocked her, but she nodded. "I... I forgive you for that, I suppose. If you'll forgive my behavior."

"As I said, you weren't yourself." Renmier opened the door and raised his elbow to her. "May we leave now?"

She straightened the dress and accepted his offer. "Please."

A knight escorted them downstairs, along the arcade, and around dozens of sleeping bodies in the ballroom—many naked and entwined. Javesse owed Renmier great gratitude. But if he had told her the truth before, maybe last night's events wouldn't have happened.

Just as they reached the palace exit, someone called out Renmier's name.

"Leaving so soon?" Sir Heslion approached, gripping his sword hilt. "We've yet to break fast." Lust resided in his glassy eyes, which settled on Javesse. "*I'm* still hungry, and there's a mighty tempting delicacy standing right before me."

Renmier punched him in the face; Javesse jumped from the sudden action.

Heslion fell flat on his bottom, holding his bleeding nose. "What the—?"

"I said I'd kill a man for trying to take my woman." Renmier's voice was so low, it sounded like a growl. "Speaking like that was bold."

Heslion narrowed his watery eyes and spat a bloody glob near Renmier's foot. The effort to rise was sluggish while they stared at each other. Heslion laughed. "You haven't changed, Sir Renmier."

"Good day, Sir Heslion."

"Safe travels." Heslion's countenance didn't show the same sentiment as the words.

Renmier moved with slow, deliberate steps down the long, winding stairs.

"Was that wise?" Javesse whispered.

"They won't do anything to me yet."

"Great Fynthiar, I pray not."

"Once we gather our things from the inn, we're leaving Ravieris."

"Let's gather them as hastily as we can."

Grinning, he patted her hand. Just what did he find amusing?

Truths & Lies

Thank Fynthiar the itching came to an end. And with the corset discarded in Ravieris, Javesse could breathe without restraint beneath her cotton and wool garments. She had considered wearing the veil, but people might stare with fascination or curiosity, which meant unwanted attention. Did it matter when Renmier didn't look at her the same?

Within his heat during The Blizzard, she'd fought the yearning to kiss him. And it was amazing how Renmier's irises entrapped her, which they often revealed his emotions. His muscles, expression, the way he whispered her name in her ear, divulged everything. Vulture wanted her. Yet when the opportunity arose, when he could've taken advantage of her, he hadn't.

Javesse gave him a sidelong glance. Was Renmier more honorable than she had first believed possible?

He looked at her from the corners of his eyes. "What is it?"

She couldn't let him know her beliefs of his desires, nor that the sensual dance continued in her memory. Words failing, she stammered noises. Javesse rubbed the back of her neck and released a breathy laugh.

"Are you well?" His brows curved low. "I know of no such effect from Love Orchid."

"I am." She repositioned atop the saddle. "I... I was wondering if you found the answers you sought. From His Eminence, that is. You said nothing about the conversation." Relief eased the discomfort from her chest.

"I have." Renmier's attention shifted forward... to the south.

She slowed Magyia. "And?"

He halted Titan and twisted enough to look at her. "And now we—"

"Return to the duke." Gaze on the mare's mane, her mood lapsed.

For a couple minutes, she nor Renmier moved from atop the shifting horses.

What did Javesse believe might happen? Darik owned her, and Renmier worked for him. Of course Vulture would return her to his master. Her master.

"Javesse." Renmier directed Titan closer. "I must do this."

Everything blurred. She blinked, freeing the pooled tears.

His warm palm pressed on her cheek, his thumb stroking the droplets away.

She closed her eyes. "Please don't take me back to him."

The warmth disappeared and the teardrops' trails chilled.

"I must complete my mission." He commanded the stallion back, then nodded once toward the path.

The heartbreak trapped air in her chest, hurting. Javesse sniffled and directed Magyia onward.

Renmier hated the deception, but he couldn't tell Javesse the truth. The road wasn't the place nor time anyway. At least six days of demanding travel lay ahead to reach Columure, then another day to Bashgrahon. But Fyr Port was Renmier's first destination, the trek there would take nine days—without counting the hunt. The port city was the busiest in Brydasia, drawing most trading ships. Renmier dealt with many sea captains but trusted only a few. He prayed to whichever god might grant him a favor that an earnest captain would've docked when he and Javesse arrived.

In the meantime, he had to restrain the growing feelings for her. The previous night made his path difficult enough. It wasn't Love Orchid; effects of the poison were something out of Javesse's control. It was her reaction upon hearing they were riding to Darik's, the way she leaned into his palm, and the sidelong looks. Despite how things had been since the mission began, she reciprocated his feelings. The timing couldn't have been worse.

As they rode onward, he berated himself. Renmier had made foolish decisions throughout his lifetime, but nothing as idiotic as this. To open to Javesse would be a mistake. He'd benefit from nothing, and she'd gain heartbreak.

That's what Renmier could do. The cruelty's return should ensure Javesse despised him again, making their parting easier. It was a perfect plan.

After a few miles of silent riding, he directed Titan over a small hill and toward scattered groupings of trees. The nearest privies were more than an hour away and Renmier wasn't waiting. Not while an unknown party followed.

A soft command to Magyia was the only sound from Javesse as she trailed him down the slope.

Renmier alighted, tossing the rein over the saddle. "Into the trees," he said, nodding to the copse across a narrow gap from the one he stopped within.

She looked from one cluster to the other. "What does it—?"

"I need to piss."

Sighing, she rode to the other copse of trees.

"Javesse!"

She slouched as she stared at him.

"Stay there until I call for you," he said. "Can you follow that instruction?"

One nostril wrinkled as she sneered. "I'm certain I can manage." She rode slowly to the trees.

Renmier moved the sword from the saddle to his belt and hooked the hand axe to its holder on his back; he left the flail on Titan. Once he concealed the stallion between a pair of budding bushes as best he could, Renmier hastened to outside the edge of the tree line, making sure he stood in plain sight. A dozen silhouettes on horseback had just reached the hill's apex, the sun glinting off steel plates and studs. The men weren't knights, but they weren't plains patrol either.

He walked thirty feet into the woods, keeping his back to the approaching group, then proceeded to relieve himself. Pissing during battle would only ruin the leather.

Hooves drumming grew nearer, as did voices.

Javesse, please stay where you are. Damn it. I should've warned her.

Then again, she was a smart woman who would recognize the forthcoming trouble. However, her stubbornness had proven her talent for getting into a predicament.

Renmier fastened his breeches. As he grasped the sword hilt, footsteps thudded outside the trees. A slow draw left the scabbard flat, and as he faced the men, he unhooked the axe.

Their black leather and silver studded armor were of high quality—better than Darik's men. It was the orchid pin on their cloaks that belied their origin. Would the emperor have sent them after Renmier? It made no sense, not when Larselis had just offered him a position at the palace.

Renmier tipped the axe forward a few times. "Is Captain Heslion sour with me?"

A man, guard One, stepped forward while drawing his sword. He released a slow breath. "You assaulted the Captain of Palace Guards, sir, and must face punishment."

"He had the opportunity to deal his punishment before I left. Yet did he?"

One glanced at the other eleven. "Sir, Captain Heslion was feeling rather... unwell at the time. Turn the woman over to us or die."

Javesse. This wasn't about Renmier striking Heslion, but the captain wanting her. Men truly were willing to kill for Javesse. But then Renmier would kill to protect her.

"He sent you to your death. You know that, don't you?" Renmier viewed each face, noting the plate bracers and greaves over the studded leather. "Heslion's a bloody coward," he continued, "and not one of you will leave these woods because of him."

A few of them laughed, unsheathed their weapons.

Wait... Was Javesse still there? She could've left for Delvarian and he'd not know until the battle was over. If she had, there was naught he could do now. He needed to survive these advancing fools before focusing on her.

Renmier threw the axe. Not exactly balanced for throwing, but he'd done it plenty of times before and knew just how to accommodate for the weight. The sharp edge planted on the right side of One's face. Damn. Renmier had aimed for the center. Either way, the effect was the same. Shock stilled the others for a couple seconds, giving him a start. He charged, drawing the knife from the back scabbard. He plunged it into Two's chest, driving it up while parrying Three's attack with his sword.

Like an arrogant idiot, Four came around the collapsing One, shouting.

Renmier ducked, pulling the knife from Two and backed into Five, using his weight to knock him off balance.

Four crashed into Three, slowing his pursuit.

Spinning around Five, Renmier slashed the knife up the man's throat and chin, the keen blade parting flesh. He blocked Six's attacks, retreating while doing so. When the man chased, Renmier impaled him with the sword. With a few trees at his back, he readied to face the remaining eight guards.

Three and Four charged, swinging at the same time.

Renmier blocked Three, allowing Four's weapon to strike his side. Turning his wrist, he locked Three's hilt within the claws of his own and thrust the knife into the man's gullet. Renmier freed both blades before Three fell, spun to block another attack from Four while Seven and Eight moved in. Warmth pulsated at his side, a gash bleeding.

Four's eyes were wide with maniacal joy as he repetitively swung hard. The man hoped to hurt Renmier again. That wasn't going to happen, because Eight bellowed a roar as he lunged, revealing the perfect time for Renmier to side-step the attack.

Eight's blade pierced Four's abdomen. Four stared at Eight in disbelief, and Eight froze.

Renmier threw his knife at Eight, the point driving into the man's ear. Unfortunately, the action gave Seven the advantage of a precise attack, and he sliced across Renmier's stomach. Thank any god willing to accept his praise that his armor was far superior to theirs; only the sword tip cut through enough to wound him. Grunting, Renmier dodged back from another swing, stumbling over one of the dying guards. He clutched a branch to maintain balance.

Seven chased, Nine followed with Ten right behind, and Eleven and Twelve aimed crossbows at Renmier. Bastards.

Renmier pushed from the tree, his sword impaling Seven's chest, but Seven managed a nasty cut in Renmier's left arm. At least it wasn't his sword arm.

Leaving his blade in Seven, he hurried to One and yanked the axe from his skull. Renmier turned and blocked a swing from Nine, but couldn't dodge Ten's piercing attack in his side—the same spot Seven had struck. Just flesh and muscle. Renmier roared as he threw his shoulder into Nine's chin, then slammed the axe's head into the man's jaw; bones shifted beneath flesh.

While Nine staggered back, Renmier whirled to avoid Ten's rapid swings. He brought the axe down, chopping just as quickly, but Ten proved worthy with his swift blocks. The snap sounded from Eleven or Twelve. Renmier jumped back, avoiding the first bolt, but he struck a tree and the second bolt planted into his right shoulder. He dropped the axe as the point and barbs tore through muscle.

Ten hollered as he charged, swinging with renewed vigor.

Renmier side-stepped and used his left arm to block the attacks while trying to avoid tripping on the fallen guards. He waited for an opening to tackle Ten, but the man was quick and fierce. While he evaded the continued assaults, Eleven and Twelve reloaded their crossbows. He might have to endure another strike just to escape the crossbowmen from killing him.

Javesse arrived, attacking Twelve first, her sword piercing the man's chest from the side. He collapsed.

Knowing Renmier was taking her back to Columure, she had stayed.

Eleven spun, releasing a bolt at her, but she was already dancing around him to evade the attack.

Ten's blade impaled Renmier's rib, into his lung.

Why did he let Javesse distract him?

He fell to the ground. Darkness pulsated at the edge of his vision and coldness crept over his flesh. *I'm not dead yet.*

"It is inevitable," Amalee said.

Ten grinned over him. "Now you lose your life *and* the woman. Don't you feel like a fool?" He chuckled. "And to think... I killed Vul—"

Blood sprayed from behind him, his eyes and mouth widened. He fell to his knees.

Javesse kicked him aside, then knelt next to Renmier. Her gaze dropped to his chest. "No," she whispered. "Please tell me you have elixirs or herbs."

His breath came in rasps as he nodded. "Titan," he uttered, pointing to the bushes.

She bolted from the ground, at her feet in astounding speed. "Titan!"

Burning pain expanded in his chest and blackness grew in his vision while he waited. Yet his thoughts were not on death, but on Javesse. Why did she stay? Renmier gave her no reason to remain with him. The woman could've been free.

Javesse returned with his healing case. She removed two vials, one containing violet liquid and the other blue. "Which one?"

"Why?" he managed in a whisper. Gods. It hurt to speak that simple word.

"So I can heal you, you bloody idiot!" Frustration reddened her face, tears brimmed her eyes. She straightened, seeming to understand his question. "I... I thought about leaving." Nodding, she wiped her nose on her sleeve. "But I couldn't leave you to die. And I still won't." Chin set, Javesse raised the vials. "Now which one?"

Renmier shook his head. "Free," he barely said through gritted teeth.

The teardrops finally broke. "I'm not letting you die, you bastard." Looking at the vials, she continued. "I'll shove them both down your throat if you don't tell me."

If only he could laugh. With what strength he could muster, Renmier tapped the violet bottle. It was the strongest healing elixir in Brydasia, and would even completely heal the scratches from Javesse.

She wasted no time. Before his hand returned to the ground, she was pouring the contents into his mouth.

In a few minutes, he'd rise. In half an hour's time, he could ride.

"You will be mine soon enough," Amalee said.

Renmier didn't need the damn reminder. Chasing her voice away, he pressed Javesse's hand to his lips. "Thank you."

She scanned the bodies, a few of them wheezing their last breaths. "Why did you send me away?"

Because he was a fool. Renmier had tried this once before and failed. Why did he believe the outcome might be different? This wasn't a battlefield with comrades at his side. He was alone. But then he wasn't. This time Javesse came to his aid. And while he lay amid the dead and dying palace guards, he marveled at the woman still holding his hand and staring at him with such fury.

Renmier didn't answer her.

"You're a bloody idiot," she whispered, then wiped her eyes.

Once he was well enough, they resumed travel, leaving the extra horses behind. No need to get into trouble for selling Imperial mounts. Let Heslion find them and the dead guards.

At a tavern in a small village, Renmier ate little and said nothing. The acreus elixir healed all ailments, including hunger, which left him with no appetite. There was no healing remedy that matched acreus nor came at such an extravagant cost, for finding an apothecary who could handle the divine root was rare. Renmier had only one more vial, but it was at Fyr Port. At least he had other herbs, although simple.

Javesse bent over her food, picking at it. The constant commotion in the establishment, not even her chair getting nudged, brought a reaction. She showed no improvement in the inn bedchamber. Javesse removed her boots and weapon belt, then climbed beneath the coverlet, keeping her back to him.

Renmier disliked this silence. Before, she chattered often, her principal topic: his lips. Now her deflated spirit left her muted.

He stared from the chair. What harm was there to reveal everything? It was puerile to withhold his true intentions. He nodded. In the morning, he'd tell her their true destination.

She stirred an awful lot beneath the thin blanket. It didn't help that the night's chill entered through the worn fur hanging at the window. Renmier should've found a better place for rest, but his mind had been busy and he stopped at the first village they came upon.

Leaving the weapons on the table, he sat on the edge of the bed. "Javesse."

"It's bloody cold."

Renmier had nothing to offer; the extra blankets were on the horses. Except...

"Want me to hold you?" he asked. "To give you some warmth, that is."

Her head turned, the blanket covering everything below the bridge of her nose. Was she that cold? After a slow blink, she sat up. "All right."

He situated behind Javesse, positioning her between his legs. Once she rested against him, he pulled the flimsy coverlet over her and pressed his arms and thighs to her sides. It took a moment for her tense muscles to relax, then everything felt almost perfect. Like she belonged there.

Renmier drew in a deep breath and released it, trying to clear his thoughts of unobtainable desires.

The breeze whistled beneath the old fur window hanging, the draft dancing over the floor and up the bed, like an invisible arm stretching to infect them.

"Remember when I told you about the shipwreck?" she asked, slicing into the silence.

He welcomed her sweet voice and the distracting topic. "Yes."

"There... There was something I hadn't told you."

Brows low, he glided his chin along the softness of her hair. "And what would that be?"

She hesitated twice. "Promise you won't laugh?"

"Why would I laugh about you losing your family?" He stroked her arm—to offer comfort, of course.

"It's not about that." Javesse sighed, her head tilting to the edge of his shoulder as she looked at him.

For the first time, he noticed just how thick her eyelashes were, and just beyond them, the curves of her cheekbone and chin came into view.

"I'll make no jests about anything you wish to say," he said.

"Promise me. You mocked my people's choice of armor."

A chuckle rolled in his throat. "An entirely different matter. Now please share with me."

She straightened her head, seemed to reconsider in silence. Her fingers curled around his wrist, gently holding. "I had been below deck in the family's quarters, translating inventory scrolls for my father. It may be why I survived, for my family was above deck."

"Why?" He encompassed her with his arms, needing to protect her from an unseen danger.

"While I was put to work, they were enjoying the lovely weather. It had been a gorgeous day, which is why it shocked me when the storm struck." Javesse shook her head the slightest. "The ocean and winds had been perfect. A sailor's dream. Then gales came, and the waves rose higher in mere seconds."

She trembled.

He combed his fingers through her glorious hair with his free hand. And as much as he had fantasized about touching those golden locks, his mind remained focused on her. "Go on. I'm listening."

"A storm didn't wreck the ship," she whispered. "It was..." Javesse sniffled. Swallowed. She cleared her throat. "Something tore it apart."

He stilled. "I'm listening, Javesse."

"You'll not believe me. I know you won't. It'll sound absolutely absurd."

A teardrop landed on his wrist, right between her thumbs as she clutched tighter.

"Speak with me," he whispered.

She nodded, yet needed a moment to gather herself. "I-I saw something in the water. Something... I don't know. There are nights I wake up from horrible dreams of it coming for me because I had escaped. But I often think it was a false vision from the fright and panic, and from swallowing the water. It couldn't have been real." She craned her neck enough to look at him. "Do sea serpents exist?"

He cocked a brow.

"You do think I'm a fool."

"No." Renmier rocked gently from side to side. "I've been to the taverns at Fyr Port on many occasions, and have heard stories about monstrous serpents that travel the waters doing Dahzia's bidding."

"Do you believe them?"

He shrugged. "I've never voyaged the seas, Javesse. But the sailors' fears ring a truth. From the tales they've shared with those willing to listen, it sounds as if the captain of your ship hadn't paid the Queen of the Waters for safe passage." He caressed her cheek, drying tears away. "Do you know if he gave a gemstone of great value to the ocean shortly after you set sail?"

Javesse's lips quivered and her eyes watered again. Unable to answer, she shook her head. "I was occupied with the departure—watching the sailors work. I hadn't paid mind to the captain," she nearly shouted.

Renmier pulled her closer without crushing her. "I've heard rumors that Dahzia is a cruel demigoddess who'll punish ships with her serpents and sea elves if homage isn't paid."

"But why *my* family?" Javesse turned sideways and curled against him. "We were innocent." She wept.

Why did the gods abandon Renmier at *his* greatest time of need? He had no explanations for what gods and demigods did. But he hated them all.

"And you," she said, straightening and glaring at him. "You're cruel as well." Javesse scooted to the foot of the bed and kept her back to him. "Get off. I don't need you."

Harsh. But she'd learn in the morning.

"Very well." He swung his legs over the side and eased off. "Sleep. We've a long ride."

Grimacing, she buried herself beneath the blanket. "Bloody bastard."

"Javesse." Renmier pushed on her shoulder.

She squinted at him.

"Time to go."

She snuggled into the pillow once more. "I don't wish to."

"Doesn't matter. Up!" Smirking, he slapped her butt.

A squeal escaped as she twisted within the coverlet. "How dare you!"

He chuckled. "Must I slap your rump again?"

Eyes wide, she sucked in a breath.

"And it's a fine bottom," he added. What was he saying?

At least Javesse's cheeks showed color and her gaze flickered as she stumbled from bed and charged at him. The blanket wrapped around her foot, and she fell forward, flailing her arms.

Renmier caught her. The warmth of the sun's rays over a summer field surrounded him. Once he assisted her to stand, he asked, "Are you always clumsy when you're angry?"

Javesse slapped him.

There was no avoiding the grin, yet it faded as he held her in a loose embrace. Renmier lowered his arms and swaggered back.

Her hands slid down his chest, fingertips grazing his abdomen before falling to her sides.

The nearness missed, he cleared his throat. "I've a surprise for you."

Javesse sucked on her bottom lip. "I don't believe I can endure another one of your surprises... Vulture."

The address stung.

Disregarding it, he said, "This just might please you. However, I'll withhold it until later."

"Fine." She collected her items and readied.

Their morning meal was light and quick. Renmier wished to leave the previous day behind and move forward.

He frowned. *Forward to what?*

The question slugged his head. Only one path lay before him: revenge. He could view Javesse's fate as part of it. Bitter and sweet. Just to have her warm his coldest moments was a gift he wasn't worthy of, and Renmier thanked any gods willing to receive his appreciation. What he couldn't forget, what Javesse might never accept, was that he was a killer. She'd witnessed his rage and felt the sting of his ire.

Then why did she look at him with those sidelong glances, golden irises thinned by enlarged pupils? Why had she touched him when it was avoidable?

Renmier drew in a deep breath, releasing it in Javesse's direction. She was a fool's dream.

Javesse glanced at Renmier, who chewed on his lip, appearing deep in thought. The clean, handsome man from the emperor's celebration was preferable. The one who had shared his life and danced with her. Not this fool who nearly got himself killed while facing those Imperial guards alone. *And* he's taking her back to Columure.

Why didn't she just leave for Delvarian when she had the chance? But the memory of Renmier dying almost had her in tears... again. So she thought about his expression while they had danced at the feast. That, however, reminded her of the women who attempted to gain his attention, then the conversation she and Renmier had had at the table. There was something he'd said that prompted her to recall the message Emperor Larselis had sent to Darik. It revealed how naïve Renmier was about the men he served.

"Emperor Larselis is breaking his word," she said.

Renmier frowned. "What are you talking about?"

"At the ball, you said the emperor takes care of those who serve him."

"And he does." He looked so certain.

Javesse shook her head. How could she convince him of the truth? She'd have to just tell him. "I've seen a letter in which he declares all widows and orphans of knights and soldiers—"

"Are secured." Renmier halted Titan. "They'll need not worry about food nor shelter. His Eminence cares for those who had served him."

"How can you say that after those men just attacked you?"

"He didn't send them. Now move." He commanded the stallion into a trot.

She'd not allow Renmier to remain ignorant of his emperor's lies. Javesse caught up to him. "Larselis has them murdered! Slaughtered by the dukes' men!"

He jerked on the rein so hard, Titan whinnied. "Lies!" His scowl deepened and his face turned crimson. "They lost their lives for his glory. He swore an oath to care for the families of the fallen. His Eminence would never murder innocent peop—"

"He already has! Think of those you've killed in his name!"

Renmier drew in a long breath, his glare a horrid mask. "Ride," he said between clenched teeth.

They rode for three hours in a peculiar silence. Over the past few days, they had traversed a path meant just for them, albeit one full of snares, thorny brambles, and sinkholes. Then the sun broke through the canopy, the colorful flowers shared their fragrances, and birds sang... for Javesse and Renmier.

This had to be Fynthiar's Plan.

Gods, what was she thinking? Renmier was returning her to Darik! Did she believe him as honorable as Beresly?

"I've something to..." he mumbled.

Why did she think he was anything more than a bigger thug with scarier weapons than Darik's men?

"I'm not taking..."

That's what he was: another cruel soldier caring not about whom he trampled beneath his boot for a greedy duke and emperor!

"We're riding to the..."

How could Javesse believe he might care or... or even love her after what just happened?

"I can't return you..."

Renmier really was a beast. A bloody vulture! He didn't care about her or anyone.

"Did you hear me, Javesse?"

She scrunched her face in his direction. "What?"

Brows low, he licked his lips. "If—" Renmier chuckled. "It wasn't the response I anticipated. If you'd prefer returning to Bashgrahon, so be it." He looked forward.

Javesse tugged on Magyia's rein. "What did you say?"

"I said if you wish to go back—"

"Before that."

He faced Titan southwest. "It'd be wrong to return you to him." Renmier scratched behind his ear. "Weren't you listening?"

Was she breathing or not? Javesse replayed what he said while she'd been contemplating.

"I've something to tell you. I'm not taking you back to Duke Nornt. We're riding to the west coast. I can't return you to Bashgrahon. It's wrong."

Her mouth dried. "You...? You're not taking me to Darik?"

Renmier smiled, appearing more handsome than ever. His complexion was smoother. Brighter. His shoulders relaxed and his back straightened, as if free of an unbearable weight. Directing Titan closer to Magyia, he said, "I'm taking you somewhere safe."

"When did you decide this?"

Patting the stallion's neck, he said, "Days ago." With easy flicks of his wrist, he flipped the rein back and forth over the saddle rise. "To be truthful, I believe I decided the moment I saw you."

"Before or after you struck me?"

Renmier frowned at her and commanded Titan onward.

Javesse bit her bottom lip to prevent a joyous squeal.

Naked beside the river, she adored the sun's warmth on her flesh. What a joy to have such pleasures again. In Delvarian, she'd lain beside waterfalls and rivers, the breeze dancing over her body. Beresly had accompanied her on two occasions; they sang, then made love.

Renmier was only yards away, on the other side of the brush. If he came to the riverbank, would *they* make love? The confusion he caused was maddening. Yet during the gala, in spite of those tramps trying to steal his attention, Renmier had shown complete interest in Javesse.

Memory of his hardness against her at the dance's end brought a soft moan. If the women hadn't poisoned Javesse that night, might she and Renmier have made love? And would it have been as wonderful as the dance suggested?

Once again, excitement expanded her chest. Javesse yearned to know this man called Vulture. The mysterious and muddled behavior was overwhelming, but she couldn't deny Renmier's physical allure. Upon seeing his body at the bathhouse, pleasurably invasive thoughts had struck her. Such fantasies overtook her now.

Javesse shouldn't have permitted the carnal whims to heat her body, yet how could she not enjoy succulent imaginations about Renmier? He protected her, freed her of that damned neck-band, and even touched her with affection. He had attempted to save Javesse from the slave thieves, shielded her from the emperor, laughed and danced with her, and held her close to offer his heat and comfort. And he frustrated her more than anyone.

But who was Amalee?

The name spoken in his sleep never left Javesse. Was Amalee a lover? Renmier had admitted to having pleasures with a farm maiden before meeting Javesse, but it didn't mean he wasn't committed. Plenty of people were unfaithful to each other.

Javesse cleared her thoughts and focused on the music of the water's flow and the sun's heat. Renmier remained. Leather and oil invaded her senses. She could taste his nearness. After a heavy sigh, she propped up on her elbows and scanned the surrounding trees and across the river. No one was there. Just birds flying past and diving in the water for a meal. Renmier was so deep in her mind, she felt him. The whole thing was ridiculous.

And it was time to dress.

She slid the clean blouse on, the warmth enveloping her. Eyes closed, she imagined Renmier holding her from behind again. Gods! She'd never be ready to leave if she continued these thoughts. To distract herself while gathering her pants and socks, she hummed one of her favorite songs. After the first chorus, the love song battled to escape. Humming was no longer an option. Javesse let the words out in a whisper, which grew in volume as she tied the pants' strings. Her body throbbed with anticipation of the next verse's inappropriate words, and she released it, the octave in a sultry note.

Thuds came in her direction.

She wrapped the blouse around herself and looked for her sword.

Leaves ruffled and panting sounded.

"You're singing," Renmier said.

Javesse relaxed her shoulders and eased out her held breath. "And you frightened me."

His tear-filled gaze darted from her untied blouse to her face. "I heard your voice." Although he remained still, he took in the perimeter. Renmier's eyes dried. "And I'm not the only one," he uttered, his lips unmoving.

What could Javesse say? She'd drawn attention by foolishly losing control.

"Come to me," he whispered, reaching for her. "Make it convincing."

She frowned.

"Do it."

Javesse inched closer.

"As if you mean it." His voice was soft, but his brows were still low, uncertainty saturating his eyes.

"You bastard," she whispered.

"You think I want this? Do it."

Renmier's chest stiffened beneath her touch, and his breaths came heavy out his nose. Shaky.

Javesse brushed her fingers through his jawline beard. Her heart palpitated. Wasn't this what she'd been fantasizing? On her tiptoes, she caught his bottom lip and sucked.

Renmier remained frigid until she clasped her hands behind his neck. He pulled her closer, the cool studs from the armor heating against her exposed skin. The kiss deepened with deprived passion, a moan rolling in his throat.

Javesse lost herself in him, in that moment; their tongues touched, then danced.

He broke for the slightest second. "Gods!" he gasped. Kissed her again... and again. His calloused hands moved beneath her shirt, his fingers pressing lines into her back.

She tugged on the strap below his neck.

Renmier pulled her leg over his hip and clutched her bottom, crushing her to him. Her blouse parted, throbs resonating throughout her the moment he squeezed her breast. His tongue thrust into her mouth, intensifying Javesse's desire. Craving him more, she clumsily unfastened the first buckle of his top, then began on the second.

The kiss slowed, the touches softened. It felt... meaningful. Intimate.

Renmier released her and pulled away, panting. "They're gone," he whispered, swiping his sweat dampened hair aside. He retreated through the bushes. "Dress!"

Heat infected various places of Javesse's pulsating body. She swallowed, wetting her dry throat, then squatted and wept quietly.

Renmier needed the rest of the beard to fill out, yet hair didn't grow well on his throat. It often itched. Shaving the unwanted scruff shouldn't have been much of a task, but envisioning what had happened at the riverbank interfered with concentration. Honestly, Renmier would rather make love with Javesse than shave, but the heartbreak that'd follow wasn't worth the risk. The dark contract prevented him from having a future, and pretending love could sever it was foolish. Still, he glimpsed her looking at him in the mirror's reflection now and then.

"Was anyone really there?" she asked.

He performed a soft laugh to show amusement, then lowered the knife. "You think I wanted you to kiss me?"

"Your reaction belied you."

"Yes, well, your lips are fine." He scraped the soap from the blade onto a stone and resumed the task. "There were elves. Two."

"What?" She straightened. "I... I could've returned to Delvarian with them."

"I hadn't wanted you to accompany me." He cleared another path of hair off the center of his throat. "Yet here you are. And now you'll help me finish my objective."

"But they—"

"And had they come to your aid," Renmier peered at her from over his shoulder, "I would've killed them. Is that what you wanted?"

Arms wrapped around her knees, Javesse looked away.

"The kiss wasn't special anyway." A mumbled lie.

Renmier resumed shaving in silence. Too long a silence. It made him uncomfortable she hadn't responded. Maybe he hurt her, but it was necessary. Let her sulk. Let her hate him.

A rock struck the back of his head, the blade scraped his throat.

He dropped the knife and spun. "What the bloody Blackening are you—?"

Tears welled, one skimmed down her cheek. "Damn you."

"I told you I didn't want it. I regret it." Renmier pointed at her. "Throw something at me again, I'll swat your ass."

Javesse hurried into the tent.

Deep, slow breaths calmed his annoyance. He hated lying, but it'd been a part of life the past seven years. He was nothing but a lie. Holding Javesse that afternoon, the passion and magnificent kiss were emotions he'd not experienced since Amalee. Feelings for Javesse were stronger. Dangerous. It was impossible to love her. How long could he ignore that truth? At the end of this mission—

He cut the thought short and slid the blade near the trail of blood on his throat.

The next day commenced with a long ride. A boring, silent one. Javesse looked at him several times, a question poised on her tongue. After a few more breaths, courage arrived. "Who is Amalee?"

Renmier yanked on the reins, then twisted to face her; Titan grunted. "Where did you hear that name?"

She looked to the sky, the horse's mane, Renmier's knee, anywhere but at his heavy glare. "I... You've said it in your sleep."

Brows meeting briefly, he turned and commanded Titan forward.

Javesse watched. He'd never open to her. Sighing, she followed.

It remained quiet into the night. Renmier ignored her during supper, then proceeded to the inn room alone. Apparently, mentioning Amalee resulted with such an effect.

He chose not to guard this night, but rest, cringing when Javesse joined him beneath the blanket. The small mattress left little room, forcing them to touch. Renmier moved his arm to his stomach.

"Lumpy pillow," he muttered.

That made no sense.

"Better than the ground," she said.

"Perhaps for you."

The muffled shouts and music from the tavern filled the room's stillness. Javesse needed to make amends now.

"I'm sorry for mentioning Amalee."

He stiffened.

"I hadn't meant to offend you by—"

"She's my wife."

Everything Javesse believed Renmier might've felt was a farce. He hadn't wanted that kiss.

She forced a laugh. "I suppose I understand why you regretted it. The kiss, that is."

The pounding in her ears drowned the noise below as she tried so hard to understand.

He clasped his hands on his chest. "She's dead."

Javesse looked at him. "Oh, I'm... sorry."

"Are you?" A grimace darkened his face.

"Have you forgotten I know such loss?"

Renmier's scoff cut. "You didn't lose a lover."

It hurt from how hard she bit her lip. "The night Captain Givins took me from my elf friends was the night they murdered the man I was going to marry."

The rage subsided from Renmier's visage. "Javesse," he whispered. "Forgive me. I'm sorry for being an... ass."

Tears broken free, she shook her head. "You *are* an ass."

He grazed her cheek with his thumb. "What was his name?"

She stared at him, disbelieving he truly wished to know. But Renmier didn't break eye contact as he waited for an answer.

"Lord Beresly Greinlyn." Javesse could imagine Beresly's platinum irises and dark hair, and hear his laughter. She swallowed the urge to cry. "He-he was a fine man who intended to love me the rest of my days." She sniffled, guilt pressing on her soul. "It's my fault he's gone. All of them."

"It's not."

"We were returning from the Festival of Land and Water at the Dibukue River, the music still living within us. I felt more connected to Beresly after dancing and singing on the riverbank with him, and I... I knew I wanted to be his wife." She sucked in a scant breath, released it along with a few teardrops. "I had just accepted his proposal, and we were celebrating with our friends." Javesse couldn't avoid the horrors of that dreadful attack: Samris and his men slaughtering her lover and friends. "I should've waited until we returned to Delvarian, but the idea of a new life excited me."

"I'm sorry."

Wishing to forget that evening, she tried to think of something positive, but dancing with Renmier, and the connection she had felt with him, was all that came to mind.

"You said it was seven years when you lost your family?" he asked.

Confused by the change of subject, she nodded.

A slight hesitation. A private debate. "It was also seven years ago when I lost Amalee. She was... murdered."

Javesse's heartbeat paused. "Renmi—"

"Then they left me for dead!" The blanket tossed aside, he bolted from the mattress. "Some of them have already paid." Chest expanding with deep breaths, darkness misted from beneath his eyelids again as the strange cold resurfaced. "And there are more to suffer."

"Renmier." Javesse moved into his path, but what could she say?

His shoulder knocked into hers as he continued to the bed and sat. "They forced me to watch."

The strain in his voice wrenched her heart. She hugged his head, bitter ice awful against her. Javesse frowned, yet heartbreak stilled her retreat, and she wept into his hair. "I'm so sorry."

Ragged breaths and huffs interrupted his sorrowful groans. Suddenly, Renmier's arms surrounded her. His body shook as his sobs muffled upon her bosom. The chill faded.

Petting his mane, Javesse rocked and did what felt natural—what felt right: she hummed. As the tune flowed, his weeping lessened. She eased into a song.

"Hold tight, never release me, there will come a time when we shall part. No matter the powers that be, I shall always remain in your heart. The waterfalls halt, the sun falls, the mountains crumble, and forests dry, but my love for you is forever and shall never die. Hold tight, never let go, there will be a day when the gods call. No matter the powers that flow, I shall always be there when you fall. The waterfalls halt, the sun falls, the mountains crumble, and forests dry, but my love for you is forever and—"

Renmier's lips were upon hers with the same passion as at the river: hungry. His damp cheek brushed hers as his mouth traveled to her chin, throat, reaching her blouse's opening.

Javesse loosened the strings and parted it, cool air flowing over her bare flesh. A moan escaped, and she arched her back the slightest as he latched onto her nipple. Oh, Fynthiar! Bunching Renmier's blouse bit by bit, she tugged it to his armpits.

He cast the garment aside, then stood and pulled her close.

That same slow, intimate kiss. Unlike any Javesse had ever experienced. Time crept while that immaculate kiss continued as they untied each other's pants and pushed them down. On the mattress, their bodies interlocked, and within minutes, Renmier became one with her.

Javesse welcomed him. Wrapped herself around him, not wanting to let go. Ever.

Euphoria gripped her twice during their lovemaking, stars spinning inside the shadowed room the second time. Renmier whispered against Javesse's neck, then relaxed.

She swiped hair from his temple. "What was that?"

"Nothing." He lay back. "You are... wonderful."

Although curious as to why the endearment remained secret, she pushed it aside. "I'm wonderful? I fear I'll not be able to walk for the next fortnight."

Renmier's laughter was an unusual sound this time. Pleasant. He pulled her close and kissed the side of her head. "You're an adorable creature."

Was *this* Renmier? An intimate and playful man? An amazing lover? Javesse hoped this was the truth of him.

Forehead snuggled to his jaw, eyes closed, she thought of the two words he'd kept silent: *My mockingbird.*

To make love with Javesse was an undeserved experience, as was she. She awoke with a ravenous demand, and Renmier accommodated her appetite. Within the afterglow, they calmed from the throes of ecstasy. She rested against him, sliding her fingers over the dark hairs below his navel, her gaze lost on the sun peeking through the missing shutter planks. A glow illuminated her face, enrapturing him.

Tracing the curve of her shoulder, Renmier wondered on the possibility the Father of All sent Javesse to save him. She offered a view of a future other than eternal torment. Javesse was hope.

Yet it couldn't be true. Despite Renmier's devotion and victories won in the name of the battle god, Valorius had ignored his prayers at his greatest time of need. Not even Lessindra could forgive Renmier for the bargain he'd bound himself to. No god would hear his prayers nor care about his desires. He'd waste no more time fantasizing about hope. Not for his damned soul.

Javesse pressed her ear to his chest. She sighed, then giggled.

Even within his dark considerations, her warmth brought him a touch of joy.

"What's so amusing?" he asked.

She tapped her fingertips in a quick, rhythmic beat, slowing them to a steady thump. "I'm listening to your heart."

He smiled. "Does it surprise you to hear it at all?"

"What if I said yes?"

He combed his fingers through her hair, watching the dark trails disappear as the soft strands fell into place. "You're the first woman I've kissed since Amalee."

Javesse leered at him. "Now I know you're lying. You've claimed to have been with many maidens."

"Meaningless swyves with women I didn't know nor cared about."

Her expression softened. "You care about me?"

"I kissed you, didn't I?"

Another snort, another giggle. "Oh, I see. A kiss means so much more than—"

"I never made love to them." Renmier scowled. "I did with you."

Javesse fell silent.

"A kiss... I don't know," he continued. "It means something more when sharing a kiss. A promise, so to speak."

She had the nerve to laugh at him.

"And thrusting into her means little?" she asked. "You have an odd view of affection, Vulture." Javesse rolled and sat up at the bed's side.

Renmier grabbed her arm. "You're not listening."

"Then you're not speaking clearly!"

She always had to be difficult. Or was Renmier afraid of speaking the truth? The answer was obvious: he didn't want suffering for either of them, but grief was eminent.

He let her go and turned, raking his hair back. "I love you."

It was silent.

Was he to look at her? No. Mockery instead of reciprocation might stare back.

"What was that?" she whispered.

"I'm certain I spoke clearly enough."

The other undeniable truth, one Renmier couldn't be free of, attached itself to the longing for a new life.

"It doesn't matter," he said.

"What do you mean?"

He stepped into his trousers and jerked them up. "My life isn't my own."

"Darik doesn't own you."

"I speak not of him!" Renmier snatched his blouse and put it on. Frustration weighing his brow, he spun. "I am who I am—What you believe I am: a killer. And my path has an end of nothing but Darkness."

"Then walk a new one with me." Javesse hurried to him and clutched his wrist. "You needn't continue like this."

"You'll never understand." He watched dust float in the streams of sunlight shining through the broken shutters. "I've no choice. There're men who'll die by my hands, and that won't change."

"But it can."

"No!" He swung his arm away. "Despite my feelings for you, my course won't alter."

Tears surfacing, Javesse shook her head. "I've heard stories about love overcoming darkness. You must want it."

A life from Darkness, to be encompassed in Javesse's radiance, was more than Renmier could ever want. But unfeasible.

He leaned down, their noses nearly touching. "I choose *my* path." Straightening, he frowned. "Now dress. We leave in twenty minutes."

Renmier resumed with putting his armor on, ignoring that a minute passed before Javesse dressed. If breaking her heart made him a bastard, then that's what he was. Best to do it now than cause greater pain later.

Truth Changes Nothing

None of it made sense. It was illogical. The passion shared with Renmier had been glorious. For him to cast it aside, claiming it was unwanted, had to be a lie. He admitted to loving Javesse. How was she supposed to accept the nonsense he spewed before leaving the inn? At first, she credited it to him being frightened of the choice now presented to them. As they rode southeastward, pain eased in, engulfing Javesse's heart. Despite his feelings, Renmier would discard everything. While passing merchants, travelers, soldiers, and others, she frowned at his back, furious at how easily he chose murder over love. Bloody ridiculous! Did she mean nothing to Renmier? How could she change his mind? He was a stubborn ass.

Javesse commanded the mare to catch up to Titan. The thumping of her heart competed with the horses' hooves on the dirt road.

"What?" Renmier asked, still looking ahead.

It felt like cotton from the fields of Bellinstar gathered on her tongue, making it difficult to speak. She swallowed enough times to clear the nervousness. "I need to understand—"

"How much clearer can I make it? You're an intelligent woman." Renmier still hadn't looked her way.

"I'm intelligent enough to recognize your amazing performance back there."

He jerked on the reins so hard, Titan snorted then whinnied. Renmier narrowed his eyes. "Performance?"

There was no retreating, no matter the intimidation he exuded. Yet harm wouldn't come to Javesse—not physically.

"The man at the inn wasn't you."

A wicked grin curved creases into Renmier's cheeks, his dark eyes gleamed. "You think you know me, do you? A fortnight on the road and one night with my cock in you, and you know me."

Disgust twisted her stomach. "Why?"

"I'll not explain it again. Move. We're meeting someone." He continued onward.

No length of time watching him would change Renmier's choice. There was no room for Javesse in his path of shadows.

She swallowed the sob trying to burst free.

The next day, two hours after breaking fast, they entered the Columure Duchy and arrived at a hamlet called Camnit, located across the Tebazryl river. Javesse wished she was more familiar with this region, which was more welcoming than Bashgrahon. The small stone buildings were mostly homes, but businesses dominated the crossroads, of which there weren't many. Moss grew on the rooftops, between stones, and on several window shutters. The largest structure was a mill beside the bridge, where a waterwheel splashed in the river in a surprisingly relaxing rhythm. Burly men stacked logs on the dry, sunny side of the tall, long building. Sturdy wagons with massive steeds waited at the back end, while shirtless men loaded planks into waiting carts.

Some Delvarian villages had waterwheels, but the elves used those for grains. This was the largest mill Javesse had ever seen, and the first that produced wood materials.

"Come," Renmier called.

Shaking away the amazement, she followed him.

Several villagers tipped their heads in a greeting. It wasn't their fault, but Javesse didn't have it in her to return the friendly gesture.

The tavern was a quaint establishment providing a bar long enough for four people, eight tables, and a modest fireplace. Open shutters permitted the afternoon's sun to illuminate the room, leaving shadows at every corner and the blackened wicks cold behind unglazed sconces and in the triangular iron chandelier. Stale tobacco filled the air, as did the aroma of roasting meats, bread baking, and a mixture of drinks.

Renmier strode to the corner farthest from the door and sat.

Before, he'd guide Javesse through the taverns, but now he wanted nil to do with her.

There was a strong compulsion to walk out. She shouldn't have to suffer this behavior from him. Tears stinging, shoulders slumped, Javesse dragged her heels as she followed.

It was hard not touching his boot to Javesse's, graze her fingers, or look at her. It was difficult playing the uncaring bastard, especially after admitting his true feelings. Idiot. What Renmier wanted most was within reach, to a point. Love and warmth was right there, yet he couldn't have them. Not Javesse, not love, and not warmth. A foolish bargain made while he was enraged now held his fate. Renmier's soul was lost. The chance Tredwyn might reveal a way to change this path was unlikely. Still, Renmier twisted the black stone ring and waited for the Sulaen.

Tredwyn arrived during Renmier's second ale; Javesse drunk only a sip of wine. The Darklander sat without invitation, his portly face beaming within the shadow. It was strange how things reversed between him and Renmier. Tredwyn was once the servant, and now Renmier was the enslaved. If Emperor Larselis had known Sulaens served in his forces during the war, he might've taken advantage of the powers available to him. He might've bargained his soul to have claimed all Brydasia. Renmier considered it was best Larselis remained ignorant to a lost opportunity.

"Good evening, sir," Tredwyn said.

Tiny wrinkles marred Javesse's nose, her irises now amber. "What is *he* doing here?"

Tredwyn fixed on her from beneath the dirty strands of blond hair and snorted.

Dark and light, ice and warmth. They trapped Renmier between them. Obligation and desire clawed at him, tearing from the middle like the seams of a worn blouse.

"Go to the bar," he instructed Javesse. "Wait until I call for you."

Disbelief and hurt stared back. She might try to protect him from the Darklander, but it'd be futile.

"Go." He focused on Tredwyn.

The little man watched Javesse retreat, then his attention shot to Renmier. "All you requested is in your room at the port city. You're almost finished."

Renmier curled his finger around the bottom corner of the tankard handle, slid the cup closer. He wished it didn't matter that just about every roan and gemstone he owned waited at Fyr Port. For Javesse, it did. "How do I change this?"

Tredwyn's spine straightened, a thick brow disappearing beneath his parted hair. No emotion showed upon his face, yet a chill emanated from him, as if in warning. He squinted. "Change what?"

Jaw working side to side, Renmier considered how to answer the question. It came as a whisper. "My fate."

"What was that?"

Renmier thumped his fist on the table. "My fate!"

If they had gained an audience, he knew not, for he didn't look from Tredwyn. Renmier never backed from any man. Gods! He'd challenged the emperor. Yet now... Now he slouched and fiddled with a splinter at the table's edge.

"I see you know the answer," Tredwyn said.

Renmier bit on his tongue, withholding a dangerous truth, but spoke the only truth he could. "I don't want it anymore."

"*She'll* see to it you keep your bargain." The Sulaen inched closer. "I do like you, Renmier. You've done well by me, and I wanted to return the favor by—"

"By helping yourself." Renmier glared at him.

The memory of Tredwyn leading Titan through the young wheatfield flashed in his mind, as did brief images of the stout man kneeling beside him and dragging him back into the farmhouse, all while whispering strange words. How had the Sulaen been there in time to stop Renmier from dying? Or had *she* guided him?

"Tell me what you gained by bringing me to her?" Renmier asked.

Arms folded over his chest, Tredwyn sat back. The transformation from servant to master never failed to amaze Renmier. He rarely doubted this path, yet when those times arose, Tredwyn was quick to act and set him back on course. A dark power came from the little man, although not his own. It was from one of strength outmatching Renmier by centuries. The Sulaen's muscles and expression relaxed. "I'll not suffer eternity in Darkness, but she will devour my soul upon my arrival into that realm."

Renmier ached from those words. "I was the path to your freedom from torment."

"You were... sir. And I'm sorry for that." Tredwyn placed a supportive hand on Renmier's shoulder. "I know you want—"

"I want away from this violence." Renmier shoved the friendly hand off. "I want the promise stolen from me."

Tredwyn leaned close. "You can't have any of that, my friend. Darkness is all you'll know once you've fulfilled the bargain, which shall be soon." The little man's face took on a distinct glow of excitement. "You are less than a day's ride from Lymus, and your next victim shall soon be there."

An icy chill throbbed from Renmier's core, as if roused from a deep sleep. Every doubt he felt a moment ago vanished, overtaken by the hunger for blood—for vengeance. "I'll be there waiting."

"Good." Tredwyn glanced at Javesse. "And the woman?"

"You needn't concern yourself about her."

"Your end meets at the completion of her journey." Tredwyn squinted. "Remember that."

No. Javesse will never reach Bashgrahon. Renmier nodded once. "I'll await word of his arrival at Lymus."

The Darklander stood and bowed. "Good day, sir." He thrust his hand forward. "It was an honor to have known you."

The impulse to knock it aside and tell Tredwyn to go to the Blackening nearly came to fruition; the Sulaen believed he'd done a great service. In truth, he'd done nothing more than convince Renmier to unknowingly switch their souls for eternal suffering.

Standing, Renmier ignored the gesture. "Perhaps in the war, but not for what you've taken from me."

Tredwyn's shoulders dropped and his expression changed to that of an upset child. "I took nothing, sir. You willingly gave your blood and oath." He started for the door.

Javesse watched until the Darklander was gone. Her gaze lowered before meeting Renmier's. Without a command, she returned. "Are we staying?"

Gone was the lilt in her voice and the glow from her cheeks. Javesse was a broken woman. For him? Renmier never deserved her.

He dropped a silver roan next to his cup. "We ride east."

The darkness of the Sulaen's land and people showed as Tredwyn leered at Javesse on his way out. What did he have to do with Renmier? Tredwyn's presence evoked a response within the large man almost as dark as the Sulaen's soul. Renmier moved with a purpose driven by anger. His steps were heavier, his brows fixed low with a deep line between them, and freezing air radiated from him. It was the Vulture walking beside her once again, yet there was something different. A battle raged within those iron eyes.

Perhaps Javesse could sway Renmier into changing the direction he trod. Even if Tredwyn had cursed him, Javesse knew Fynthiar had confidence in her to break the spell. Renmier loved her, and she refused to believe otherwise. There was still a fight within he desperately wished to win, and she would stay at his side to give him strength against whatever foe he kept hidden. Getting Renmier to drop the partition he built between them was a struggle.

They collected the horses and rode in an easterly direction. Such a shame to leave the village. Javesse had hoped to spend at least one evening there.

After two hours, she convinced Renmier to stop at a tavern near busy crossroads. There was a stable, mercantile shop, bathhouse, and guard post also nestled inside the tree line just off the roads. Javesse adored the buildings, which were amongst the finest craftsmanship she'd seen. Different animals adorned each archway, seeming to watch those who entered and exited the establishments. The wildlife's likeness were remarkable, right to the details of fur, feathers, and scales.

The Weeping Willow was across a land bridge over a creek, and small by tavern standards. Even compared to the one in Camnit. Three tables lined both sides of the room with a large one at the far end. From the only inner door came the mouthwatering aroma of savory foods cooking, and two shouting voices. Wooden beams supported the walls and ceiling, the sun shining through the gaps between planks of the walls and rooftop. Patches of grass scattered amid the dirt floor, and at the northeast corner stood a twisted trunk of an enormous willow tree; scars from sawed away or broken branches marred the inside half of the tree. Outside the window, several leafy whips swayed in the light breeze.

Eight plains patrolmen spread amongst two tables, often glancing toward the scullery door while chatting.

Javesse remained close to Renmier on the way to the table at the end of the tavern. Hopefully, the men here didn't know him well.

A woman bustled from the kitchen, carrying a platter piled with sizzling meats and steaming vegetables. She hurried to a table of patrolmen, bending over the legs of one of them. He pinched her bottom, drawing laughter from her and the other men.

The act surprised Javesse. The barmaid wasn't particularly attractive, yet these men rained attention upon her as if she was the most exquisite woman. Compliments poured from their lips as their hands grazed various parts of her body. She withstood it better than Javesse imagined tolerating.

She nodded at Javesse and Renmier, then pushed a guard's hand from her hip, whirling out of his grasp. "Go on and eat, you oafs!" The woman practically glided over the dirt.

"Wynna! What 'bout us?" a man from the other table shouted.

She half spun and waved. "Aw, your supper'll be out soon!" Her cheeks red from exertion, she continued with a slight limp and rounding spine belying her energy as she neared. "What can I do for you, loves?"

Renmier looked toward the other tables. "What they're having'll do."

"And a drink?"

"Cider and wine."

Javesse straightened. "Cider sounds delicious."

"Lovely." Wynna picked up the pace as she approached the patrolmen. "More ale?"

Faces bright, they raised their mugs with a cheer. Their good mood continued while she served the other table food and refilled mugs. Two of them proposed to Wynna, but she slapped their shoulders and laughed. "You're far too young, boys!"

Javesse giggled.

"They adore her." Renmier adjusted his wrist bracer.

"You've been here before?"

"A few times. Although Wynna's not always present."

Javesse reached for his hand, but the barmaid arrived with the ciders.

"There you are, loves. Your supper'll be out soon." She swept past the patrolmen occupied with their meals.

Javesse inched her fingers closer to Renmier's hand. Before she could grab it, he lifted the mug and drained it. She watched. Waited. The cup thudded on the table, leaving a dent in the wood. "Renmier... I—"

"Here you are." Wynna set the platter down.

Roasted quails covered in herbs and a fruity glaze, surrounded by potatoes, carrots, and cabbage, was the most enticing meal Javesse sat to since leaving Bashgrahon.

"More cider." Renmier thrust a fork into the nearest bird.

Wynna smiled at Javesse. "Anything else for you, love?"

"No," Javesse said. "It looks wonderful."

Wrinkles formed at the corners of Wynna's eyes as she beamed. "I'll be back with another cider." And she was gone, hurrying to the scullery.

Javesse lifted the fork from atop the napkin Wynna left next to the platter. "This is... I didn't expect a meal like this."

Chewing, Renmier nodded. "I've never been disappointed."

She was hungry, but convincing him to change his path was more important. "Renmier, I—"

"Your cider, love." Wynna placed a full tankard on the table and collected the empty one.

Glaring at her, Javesse snapped, "That's enough for now."

The guards fell silent and looked in her direction.

Hurt showing, the barmaid straightened. "Oh. Yes, m'lady."

Renmier frowned at Javesse. "You needn't be rude to her."

"It's all right, sir." Wynna smoothed her apron.

"No, it isn't," he said.

Trembling from embarrassment and shame, Javesse traced the fork handle with her fingernail. "Forgive me."

"All's forgiven." Wynna rested her warm palm on Javesse's arm and winked. There was peace in her touch.

"Thank you."

"You're welcome. Enjoy your dinner." Wynna gave a sorrowful glance at Renmier before returning to the guards.

The men gestured Javesse's way, but the barmaid waved their concerns aside and drew their full interest with a story.

Wynna's forgiveness still flowing throughout her, Javesse listened to the tale of Lessindra's Mercy and Love giving hope to those who believed there was nothing left to cling to. "Now promise me, my dears, that you'll share Her Mercy with those in need."

Serenity showed in the patrolmen's faces. It exuded from them. "Anything you want, Wynna," one said.

"Anything," another voiced.

More sincere promises poured forth from the guards.

Would these servants of Descension truly give their hearts to Lessindra?

Javesse scoffed. "Can those who serve under Emperor Larselis Maliage possibly forgive?" she whispered.

"The plains patrol in this area are known to be quite forgiving," Renmier said. "As surprising as that might sound to you. Even their captain shows compassion." He bit another junk of quail meat off the bone.

Did Wynna affect the emperor's guards here? Who *was* she?

If Renmier had heard the barmaid's story, he made no sign of it. But Lessindra, the very Love of Fynthiar, was the way to help him.

Javesse clutched his arm. "Please reconsider the path you're choosing. It mustn't be that way."

He stopped chewing, then swallowed. "You know nothing, woman."

"I know I love you, and you love me."

A rumble resembling a chuckle sounded in his throat, yet his face showed little amusement.

"Those weren't lies." She tightened her grip.

He blinked, his jaw flexed, yet he didn't look at her. "Eat. It's your last meal until tomorrow."

Tears blurred Javesse's vision. "Renmier," she whispered. "Please."

He jerked from her grasp.

Feeling lost, she stared at her empty hand.

Disheartened, Javesse followed Renmier late into the night, beyond the twenty-fourth hour. Shivering beneath a blanket, she wondered why they hadn't stayed in the hamlet or camped.

"Why aren't we stopping?" she asked.

"I wish to reach Lymus before morn."

"How far is that?" Clenching her teeth, she tried to keep them from clattering.

"A few hours."

Javesse pulled on Magyia's reins. "That's too far. We need to rest."

The large silhouettes of master atop stallion slowed to a stop. "Keep riding."

"No."

Renmier commanded Titan alongside the mare. In spite of the long hours on the road, he sat upright, proud. Like a knight.

Javesse's lips quivered. "P-please. A f-fire."

A heavy breath escaped him. "Fine."

He guided them into a small copse of brown maple trees, which emitted a sweet aroma. After starting a fire, he fed the horses, removed the heavier gear off their backs, then commanded Titan to guard.

Javesse observed Renmier's motions, and that he avoided looking in her direction. Several minutes passed by the time he sat across the fire from her. The distance between them felt unnatural. The silence was worse.

Crickets chirped and rodents moved in the tall grass. Wood crackled from the fire's powerful heat, sending tiny dots of red and orange toward the canopy, the glow enclosed within the grouping of trees.

Javesse pulled the blanket tighter for warmth and found Renmier staring at her.

His tongue peeked out to wet his lips. "I can't lie anymore."

Was this it? Was he letting go of the foolish path he insisted on traveling?

The iron melted from his eyes, appearing as refined steel. "My life belongs to another."

Like everything else about Renmier, the statement made little sense.

"My soul is not mine to keep."

"Of course not. Our souls join our gods," Javesse said. "Mine shall rise to Fynthiar's White Fields, and I assume yours shall go to Valorius' Great—"

"You don't understand." Brows low, Renmier continued. "They took everything from me. And I gave my soul to hunt and kill them."

"You're correct. I don't understand." Yet Javesse believed she did. The Darklander's presence, a man who gave honor to Chaos, explained everything. A pull on Javesse's chin changed into a tremble as she fought to maintain her composure. Yet she wouldn't surrender this battle—not to Chaos and not so easily.

Hands clasped, Renmier watched his fingers fold and straighten. "Amalee and I married two months after the war ended," he began. "Emperor Larselis promised the Elite who took leave a reward for their service. Many started a business, and some started families. Amalee and I wanted a farm." Renmier nodded the slightest. "I requested prime land to the southwest—not far from Camnit. His Eminence obliged and gave us fourteen acres. We used my military wages and Amalee's dowry to pay the laborers to build our home."

Javesse remained still, imagining Renmier as a happily married farmer tending to crops and livestock. It was difficult while staring at the killer across from her.

"Six months later, the house wasn't finished, nor was the barn and larder," he continued. "Yet the house was livable, so we planted seeds and dreamed of our future." The steel pooled beneath surfacing tears, exposing a hint of green. "I wanted a family." The words were barely heard above the crickets' chirping and the campfire's crackles.

He pushed grass and dirt with his heel, forming a grave-shaped mound. "One morning, men arrived just after Amalee and I broke fast." The dull steel suddenly overthrew his green irises. "I thought they might've been sent from His Eminence, yet I didn't recognize their armor." Renmier's voice rose above the night's singers. "They declared I owed taxes to the new lord. I wasn't letting them take anything from us."

Javesse moved closer to him.

Deep lines creased his forehead as he drew in several long breaths. "I had killed *hundreds* on the battlefield, but couldn't stop twelve men from overpowering me." Disgust contorted his handsome face, but it shifted into shame. "I was foolish, thinking I could—that I could defeat them all without anyone at my side. They brought me to life's last breaths, forcing me to watch while they violated—" Renmier sniffed hard, then pressed his eyes shut and swallowed.

With great tenderness, Javesse squeezed his shoulder. Silence and warmth were the best she could offer, even though he hadn't sought comfort, not even as a chill radiated from him.

Renmier swiped his palm down his face, then pant leg. "Afterward, they left me to die. Tredwyn found me. He tended to the wounds until I was able to travel to his homeland."

Javesse withdrew and sat back. "Rela Sulae."

Renmier bobbed his head once. "There I learned how to make certain those men, and the one responsible, would meet justice. To suffer as Amalee had suffered... and more."

"Why didn't you go to His Eminence?"

"I knew only their faces." Lowering his elbows to his legs, he hunched forward. "The Sulaens showed me how to find them. I remained there until I was healthy and ready to hunt. And I'm near the end."

Javesse took his hand between hers. "Renmier, the Sulaens are people of Chaos. To have even consider asking for his aid was—"

"The Soul Eater aids me, not him."

His demeanor revealed surety... and remorse. Renmier knew his fate, yet he now regretted the decision made seven years past.

"My soul is hers once I've killed them all," he finished.

It mattered not how many times nor how long Javesse shook her head, there was naught she could do. She wanted to shout and hit Renmier for being such a fool. The tears surfaced, but she restrained the anger and hurt. "Then don't kill them. Leave with me."

The smallest smile played at the corner of his mouth. Not mocking, nor amusement, but gratitude. "I've given too much already. There are only three men left, and I shall kill one tomorrow."

"No." She wrapped her arm around Renmier's and rested her cheek on his shoulder. "You don't have to. We can ride past Lymus. Or ride to shore. We... We'll sail."

For several years, the thought of boarding a ship terrified her, but now Javesse was ready to brave the oceans of Emvarr for Renmier.

His lips touched her hair, then pressed to her scalp. "I want that more than anything... but I can't."

It couldn't be that simple. How could someone say they wanted something, yet reject it so damn easily? It was preposterous.

Those thoughts sparked anger into fury. Javesse shoved him, but he braced himself. She shifted to her knees and swung her fists, hoping to land a successful blow just to hurt him back. "You bastard!"

He winced from a few strikes, then twisted and caught her wrists. Sharp pain jolted through her arm and to her fingertips, yet she fought his hold.

"Stop!" he shouted.

"You stop, you bloody fool!"

"I can't!" He jerked her close. "I can't, Javesse."

Her lips quaked as she searched his eyes for hope.

He blinked, then let her go and busied himself with retying a wrist bracer. "Don't... Don't expect to find love with me. There's nothing inside me to love." Renmier turned. "Nothing, Javesse."

She wiped her nose on her sleeve. "*I* decide that, not you."

The night remained still as the crickets resumed their song. Javesse continued silently willing Renmier to gather her into his arms. Promises of a lifetime together never came forth; they never would. He'd rather give his soul to the demoness in the Darkness than share his life with Javesse.

Rastnin

Lymus was what Brydasians called a passing village: a place for passersby to rest, get repairs, food, and supplies. The only residents were the business owners. There was one barrack for plains patrol, who were present to maintain order. A nearby lord handled disputes in Emperor Larselis' stead, as it was for many villages. Lymus' prime location gave it plenty of travelers and business, filling the coffer of the local lord and His Eminence.

Renmier only stayed there on a couple of occasions, so had no reserved boarding. The innkeeper was quick to provide a room for two gold roans. After a brief discussion about Rastnin Kirlyr, a well-known patron of the adjoining tavern, Splintered Shield, Renmier paid the innkeeper a black roan to send a lackey upon Rastnin's arrival.

"If you so much as utter about my inquiring of him to anyone," Renmier said, "and he learns before I speak with him, I'll shove this roan so far up your ass you'll taste the stone."

Wide-eyed, the innkeeper promised that Rastnin, nor anyone, would learn of the conversation having taken place.

Renmier and Javesse remained in their room, waiting.

She'd been quiet since the previous night. He had hoped revealing some of the truth might help her understand, but she only grew angrier. Women were difficult to comprehend. A man could do nothing right by them. If he lied, he was a pig. If he was honest, he was a bastard.

Renmier didn't want to break Javesse's heart, but he hadn't expected to fall in love with her. The gods must be punishing him for embracing Chaos' Darkness.

The ring on his finger vibrated, and a frigid breath worked its way up his throat, coming out in a small white plume. Renmier froze and watched it float.

Rastnin Kirlyr was in Lymus.

Fifteen minutes later, a lackey arrived with a message from the innkeeper. "The man you await is here, sir." The young boy swiped his dirty hair aside.

A silver roan flipped swiftly over Renmier's knuckles, one at a time. "Is he staying here?"

The boy watched with amazement. "Yes, sir!"

Renmier tossed the coin to the lackey.

"Thank you, sir!" The boy traipsed off, trying the neat trick himself.

Renmier locked the door. Needing to concentrate on Rastnin's exact location, he paced with his eyes closed, taking five steps to the window before taking five steps to the bed. Everything had to be precise, even the approach on his victim.

"Now what?" Javesse asked.

"Please be quiet."

She huffed in obvious irritation. "You don't have to do this."

"I do more than you realize."

"Why?"

"I needn't answer to you."

He'd only taken a few more steps when the bitter cold clutched his spine, pulsating as the chants from the Darklands commenced in his head.

"Hegrus, ebris Sebysula. Geshuvorda, mordra, Rastnin Kirlyr. Geshuvorda, mordra, Rastnin Kirlyr."

The chant repeated while the biting chill ran its course throughout Renmier's body and blackness edged his vision. The only words he knew were the names and *mordra*. That word he came to understand after the fourth hunt. *Mordra* meant murder. But this wasn't murder. This was justice.

"There's the real Vulture," Javesse said. "I miss Renmier... the man who loves me."

She was a saving glow that reached for him. Renmier wanted to pull her close and chase the shadows away, but the chants held him captive, reminding him of what he must do.

"He's not here." His voice was as if another spoke with him. Gravelly. Evil.

Renmier placed the hand-axe, knife, and flail in their respective sheaths and holders. "Do not leave. I'll return when I do."

He opened the door, but it slipped from his fingers, slamming shut; splinters scraped his flesh. He blinked at Javesse in disbelief.

She shivered beside him. "Don't go."

Containing the rage, he gently shoved her back. "If you're not here upon my return, I'll hunt you down, Songbird."

Renmier headed for the stairs. Each step sent a resonating, freezing throb of blackness and ire, growing stronger as he drew nearer to the target. The chanting almost deafened him, as it always did, the victim's name louder than the other words. Renmier didn't have to search since *she* directed him to Rastnin. The chants now silenced to murmurs as he entered the tavern.

Rastnin sat with two others, holding a tankard while he chatted and laughed. He appeared innocent, as if he'd never done a bloody thing wrong. Ever. He was nothing more than a thug—a rapist and murderer. And he'd pay for the unpunished crimes.

Gripping the knife hilt, Renmier walked right to him, unaware if others noticed. The blade slid free from the scabbard.

Rastnin glanced at him, then did a double take. His smile dropped as he let go of the mug and reached for his sword.

Renmier's knife cut right through the man's shirt sleeve, blood quickly soaking the material. The wound was only to scare Rastnin. Renmier couldn't do his business in the tavern. No. Rastnin would ensure to take it elsewhere.

He jumped to his feet and retreated, his chair falling over; the other patrons cleared the immediate area. "What's the trouble?" Rastnin shouted, holding his injured arm. "I don't know you!"

Renmier spun the knife around and swung at the man's shoulder, but Rastnin dodged back, practically tripping over a vacated chair.

Shouts and gasps surrounded the two men. Someone hollered.

Renmier only heard mumbles, for the chanting grew louder, Rastnin's name dominating once again. "I'm going to kill you."

Rastnin grasped his sword hilt... then ran, leaving the tavern.

Perfect.

Renmier trod after him, giving the coward time, for distance from Lymus and the authorities was important. On the way to the exit, he grabbed a mug of ale and downed it, throwing the empty tankard on the floor before leaving. The dark voices pressed him, but he'd not heed them just yet. *She* should know his methods by now.

Just as he reached the stables, Rastnin was riding away.

"Titan!" Renmier bellowed.

The stallion neighed from within.

"Come! Now!"

The horse's hooves thudded on the stall door twice before the sound of wood cracking and breaking followed. Titan trotted out, and the stable master trailed him, shouting, "My door!"

Renmier mounted the steed. He commanded Titan into a canter, then at a hard run. It mattered not if someone was in his path. This was vengeance. If people got in the way, that was their own fault.

Travel had no effect of tracking Rastnin, for *she* informed Renmier of the direction with the trail of black mists only he could see. He rode for two miles, just entering Niwlog Woods. During the ride, beyond the chants and blackness at the edge of his vision, his mind replayed the crimes Rastnin committed. Renmier still felt the man's sword point drive into his back and slide out, and Rastnin's laughter as Renmier collapsed to his knees, spitting blood. He remembered Rastnin's boot on his throat, forcing him to watch the others assault Amalee. Then he witnessed Rastnin have his way with her as well.

Once the memories ended, the Darkness left Renmier numb, just as it had during the other hunts.

The black mist gathered behind a bush ahead off the path. The foliage trembled. Renmier pulled the flail, and with skilled expertise, whirled it, building momentum. With a signal from his legs, Titan charged. Renmier brought the heavy spiked ball into the bush, the points impaling the concealed man, who buckled with a cry of pain. He then used the weapon to propel Rastnin from cover, the spikes tearing free, along with cloth and flesh.

Rastnin stumbled face first into the dirt and leaves, a large patch of blood expanding on the back of his right shoulder. He attempted to rise, but failed.

Renmier stopped Titan twenty feet away, dropped the flail, then alighted. Withdrawing the axe, he walked to Rastnin within a tunnel of shadows twisting with dark chants and song.

Rastnin struggled to a kneel, his right arm remaining low as he stared, his eyes like wide pits of black upon a pale field. His shaking left hand ascended. "Please. Please don't."

The chanting was so loud, *her* voice above the Sulaens', commanding the kill, that Renmier barely heard Rastnin's plea. He raised the axe.

Upon hearing the commotion downstairs, Javesse dashed for the exit, but stopped. The man who left the room wasn't Renmier, and she didn't know which might return: him or Vulture. Upsetting Renmier while Darkness still enshrouded him was the last thing she wanted.

Then shouting and furniture moving ensued.

She paced. Halted. Why did Renmier pace so often? It didn't help ease Javesse's worry.

A knock startled her. She threw the door open, but it wasn't him.

"M'lady," the scowling barkeep said. "Your man's—Well, he's attacked another." He swallowed. "And he chased him from my establishment. Forgive me, m'lady, but you'll have to..."

Javesse turned, no longer listening.

Renmier did it. He sought revenge against another for something that had happened seven years ago. Was there no end to his rage?

She spun. "Do you know where they are?"

He shrugged. "Someone said the stables for their horses."

After gathering their gear, she thrust the heavier items into the barkeep's hands. "Send these to my horse."

"I don't know which—"

"Tell the stable master the black mare that accompanied the beastly chestnut!"

"Very well then!" Stomping out, he left the door open.

Javesse collected the lighter items and hurried out, hoping to catch up to Renmier in time to stop him.

Dusk had settled, making it difficult to follow the fresher tracks, but people coming into town pointed in the direction of the two riders. Noticing broken branches in the trees off the road, she lit a lantern, then walked Magyia along the trail. No doubt Titan's. Renmier hadn't anticipated anyone to look for him.

She heard a man shout in anguish. Releasing Magyia's lead, Javesse hurried toward the pleading. She came to an abrupt halt as Renmier's axe cut right between a man's widespread fingers, continuing to his wrist. The man screamed, jerking his arm down just as Renmier freed the axe and tossed it aside. The poor victim brought his gushing hand to his chest and curled into a ball, blubbering.

Frozen, Javesse whispered, "No."

Renmier strode to the flail beside Titan, grabbed it, then walked to the wretched man weeping on the ground. The ghastly spiked ball moved in a perfectly blurred circle. In a swift motion, he swung the ball upward.

"No!" she screamed.

The stranger landed flat on his backside

"Renmier, stop!" Javesse stepped toward him, hesitating as the weapon was once again in motion, but in the opposite direction.

He stood over his victim, the flail rising. Renmier pushed up from his knees then brought the weapon down, the spiked ball contacting with a moist thud. The impact cut short a hint of a groan.

Javesse's stomach lurched.

The flail descended in repetitive strikes, Renmier grunting with each blow.

She swallowed the bile collecting in her throat. Drawing her sword, Javesse crept behind him and timed the rise and fall of the flail. Just as it came to the right of its descent, she braced herself and thrust the blade into its path, catching the chain. The sword was almost pulled from her grasp, but she held tight.

Renmier roared and yanked the weapon forward, disarming Javesse and sending the sword toward a tree. He spun, his flesh pallid and black eyes wide. A snarl curled his lips as he charged at her, a rancid odor surrounding him.

"Renmier." She raised her hands. "He's dead."

The horrid grimace lessened, and the blackness receded enough from his pupils to reveal a little white. "No," he whispered in his own voice.

"Please," Javesse said. "Please stop."

"Not her. No." He tossed the flail aside. "I won't do it."

Her heart beat so hard, so fast, she grew dizzy. Javesse's whole body quaked.

Renmier blinked a few times. He jerked his head to the side, then dropped to his knee, bellowing a deep moan.

"Renmier!" Javesse went to grab his arm, but he pushed her away.

"Go!" He fell onto his back and shuddered. "Leave... me!"

Javesse remained still while he convulsed.

His eyes rolled back as putrid, black mists billowed with his shouts. As the last of it snaked into nothing, he silenced. Renmier didn't move.

She knelt and touched his faintly rising chest. He was freezing. Tears flowed as she glanced at the corpse less than ten feet away, regretting that she did. The mutilated face hardly looked like a face had once been there at all. She returned her gaze to Renmier. Why had he sought such grotesque vengeance? He should've taken this man to the magistrate or the emperor. Surely, His Eminence would've tended to the matter.

This was her life. And what a disturbing situation she found herself in. The man she loved was a murderer.

Javesse could leave. She should. No one was keeping her there. She could go to Delvarian and start life over again. But she wanted a life with Renmier. Not Vulture. Could Renmier separate from the creature living within?

His color improved to pale, but he still shivered.

"Renmier?"

He didn't stir.

What could Javesse do? Someone might kill him if she left him behind.

Fynthiar, please help me. Javesse removed her cloak and spread it over Renmier.

They couldn't stay there; she could not stand the sight of the nearby bloody mess. Javesse was no weakling. She could drag Renmier somewhere in the woods to hide. At least until he regained consciousness.

Javesse stared at his weapons, both covered in gore. He'd be furious if she left them behind, so she retrieved her sword, then gathered his axe and flail, wearing one of his gloves to avoid his victim's blood. The items now wrapped in a blanket, she fastened them atop the tent behind Titan's saddle. Javesse then led Magyia to the stallion, tying the mare's lead to his saddle horn. Patting Titan's neck, she said, "Follow me. I'm taking Renmier somewhere safe."

Elves communicated well with animals. But she wasn't an elf, nor was she Renmier. And Titan listened to him like a shepherd's dog to his master.

After a few deep breaths, Javesse grabbed Renmier from beneath his armpits. He was so heavy, but she managed to drag him several feet before having to drop him for a break. It took Javesse an hour to find a proper place. A fallen trunk surrounded by blooming bushes and trees displaying their spring leaves offered suitable cover and a clearing for a fire. She feared drawing attention, however, Renmier needed warmth. After feeding the horses two apples each, Javesse set up the small camp.

She threw two blankets on the ground, then retrieved Renmier's fur coverlet. Unfortunately, dragging him to the makeshift bedding caused the blankets to bunch and left him with the hard ground to lie upon. She rolled them into a pillow and placed them beneath his head. Javesse started a low fire. By the time she sat beside Renmier, exhaustion coaxed her to lie down.

There'd be no sleep. Javesse must watch him closely. And during that time, she'd pray to the Father of All for some sort of answer.

Dawn's fierce orange glow illuminated the tree trunks, making them look bloody. Brydasia was truly beautiful, if only it wasn't so damn violent. Javesse shouldn't judge the Eastern Continent so harshly, for Myndrose was no better. In spite of Myndrose's magnificence of colorful people and cultures, greed for power soaked the lands in blood. Why couldn't these kings and emperors leave the people alone? Why was peace so hard to obtain? It's all Javesse wanted. It's all most people wanted... wasn't it?

After her contemplation, she examined Renmier; his condition hadn't changed. It was hard knowing if that was a blessing or not. What would've happened if she had given in to the desire to lie beside him and he'd woken up during the night still consumed by dark hatred? Thankfully, the fear of waking to him crushing her throat had prevented her from falling asleep.

Many months had passed since she last practiced the Bellinstarian customs used during prayers. Although a veil came with the garments Renmier bought for her, she hadn't worn it, not when she wanted his attention. But now she bound her hair up, tucked it beneath a wool scarf, and hooked the veil around her ears. The tugging might take some getting used to, like it did when she first wore them as a young girl. Knelt beside Renmier, she moved her arms up and down in smooth motions, the right, then the left; her wrists twisted clockwise. Javesse continued doing this, and on the third time raising her arms, she began singing, although in a whisper. No need to warn anyone of Renmier's location. The song was of praises to Fynthiar.

For too long she had only spoken quick prayers—or curses—to her god. Of course the Father of All knew she was angry with Him. He knew everything. But after all Wynna, the simple barmaid, had said about Lessindra's Forgiveness, Javesse had to make amends.

The song finished, she released a slow breath and relaxed her hands upon her thighs. "Father of All... I am furious with You." Tears blurred her vision as she stared at Renmier. "You know why. I don't know what to do anymore. I need Your Guidance. Please." Her eyes squeezed shut, she spoke clearer. "I need *You*, Fynthiar."

Birds flew from branch to branch, and the breeze rustled the leaves.

King Rainlisyr's kind face came to mind.

Javesse opened her eyes. She must return to Delvarian to seek help? *If* the elves might consider lending aid.

After accepting the answer from Fynthiar, she packed enough food to start the eight-day ride, tucked the fur coverlet around Renmier, and kissed his quivering, stiff lips. "Titan shall protect you. If you awaken while I'm gone, please stay. Wait for me." She caressed his jaw, ignoring the dried blood spotting his face. "I love you, Renmier, and I'm going to save you."

Javesse strode to the tall stallion and tugged his rein. "You keep him safe. Do you understand me?"

Titan grunted.

"I know you do," she said, petting his nose. "Please protect him."

Looking back at Renmier once more, she thought another prayer to Fynthiar. Javesse must ride hard to make the journey in less time, the breaks sparse. She couldn't risk losing Renmier.

The twisted trees revealed the familiar path Renmier trod after every hunt. Other than arriving at the realm sooner than usual, something was different. The thick mist was colder, the crooked limbs reached for him, and roots jutted from the damp, puddle infested ground to trip him. Renmier avoided their grasps. The dead forest had never behaved like such before. He found the meeting place and sat on the fallen trunk. No fire awaited him. None ever did. The Blackening didn't welcome warmth. He felt *her* approach, a freezing air reaching deeper into his soul.

"You're displeased with me," he said. "After the prior hunts, you permitted me time to reach a safe place to recover."

"I told you to kill her." Amalee came into view, crossing the large clearing. "Yet you disregarded my order."

It felt like ages had passed since Renmier last saw her. She was petite, reaching only his shoulders when he stood. Her blonde hair usually hung to her waist, but she had braided it this time; her lithe body moved to a private rhythm, for Amalee loved to dance. Renmier missed her lively hazel-blue eyes. He was never given the pleasure of seeing them here, but pure-black pools instead.

"She's not part of our bargain," he said.

Amalee knelt and rested her hands on his knees. Her colorless eyes were far too large. "You care about her."

Renmier looked away. "There are two more, and I needn't their names."

"I know, my love. Now speak truthfully."

Amalee demanded truth, yet what was before him was a lie. A lie to which he'd bound his soul.

"Does it matter?" he asked.

"I wanted her dead. You have given your heart to her when it belongs to me!"

"Wrong, Deceiver." He stood, his back straight. "My soul belongs to you."

Amalee giggled. It changed into a hideous sound as she rose taller than even Renmier. The perfect flesh transformed into a sickly gray, and her maw expanded into a wide, toothy grin. "You are correct about that, Knight." Her voice filled the twisted forest, yet bounced off the black mists.

Renmier retreated, almost tripping on the fallen log. He had never seen the demoness in her true form, and now wished he hadn't challenged her deception.

Sebysula's horrific stench surrounded him as she glided her clawed hand to his back, pulling him nearer; he withheld the urge to gag. "Two more deaths, Knight. Two more!" she said. "Then you are mine to feast upon for eternity. A bargain is a bargain, and no god will answer your pleas."

There was no denying the verity of those words. Renmier had fallen into the Sulaens' promises and sought their help to obtain vengeance. He had believed they'd introduce him to Chaos, the creator of this Realm of Darkness, but they assured him that he'd meet his goal through Sebysula, the Soul Eater. It took minor consideration then—Renmier wanted the murderers to suffer for taking Amalee. Before he knew it, the shaman and his ilk surrounded him. The Darklanders chanted words and names while the shaman sliced Renmier's arm, offering his soul to the bitch demoness now standing in front of him. Yes, revenge was nearly met, but at the cost of losing a part of himself with each of those deaths.

And after killing, he returned to the Darklands and repeated the ritual to learn the name of the next remembered face. Except now, Renmier needn't more chants nor Sulaens. He knew the next targets' names, faces, and location.

"Kill them." Sebysula was Amalee once again. "And we shall spend eternity together."

He bowed his head. "We shall."

Javesse remained on well-traveled roads, stayed at taverns for the nights, and arose with the sun's first light. There were the lesser-known paths, but being alone might draw attacks. With many journeyers on the main roads during the day-lit hours, bandits were less inclined to strike. Javesse reached the Delvarian border within six-and-a-half days.

Half a mile outside Dawiryn Woodland, she sheathed the sword on the saddle. Fifty yards from the tree line, someone called.

"Hold there, Human!"

Javesse slowed and presented her empty hands. "It is Javesse Tavarelle," she replied in the Elven Tongue. "I seek King Rainlisyr's aid."

"Lady Javesse?"

"Yes."

Within two minutes, half a dozen horsemen broke from the woods and rode toward her. Three of them scanned the area while the remainder approached.

"My lady," one said, jumping from his horse. "We believed the Darklanders had killed you with the others, but the lack of your body led us to assume your capture."

Javesse pushed away the horrible memory. "The loss of my friends, particularly Lord Beresly, shatters my heart."

"What happened?"

"Is this the place?" She frowned. "I would think His Majesty should like to hear my account."

"You are correct. Forgive me." The border guard bowed, his gaze lingering on her face. "I am... just surprised, yet delighted, by your return."

They permitted her to keep her sword and led her into the woods.

"Might we make haste?" Javesse asked. "Time is not my ally."

"What is it, my lady?" the same guard asked. "Is someone after you?"

"My comrade is in need. King Rainlisyr is the only one I believe can help."

"I see. Of course." He turned to the others. "I shall ride with Lady Javesse to His Majesty."

"Yes, sir," a few of them replied. Others eyed her suspiciously.

The guard, apparently the head of the squad, bobbed his head in the direction they were riding. "Come, my lady. We shall take a path less hindered."

"I am grateful."

For three hours they traveled through the forest. Her escort spoke words of magic before they rode through one lush or branchy arch after traversing five miles prior to reaching another arch. After each pass, different trees and familiar scents and visions forgotten to Javesse surrounded them. Firs, maples, oaks, and many nut or fruit baring trees, filled the air with their aroma. She almost wept at how much she missed Delvarian. After the sixth arch, they arrived at Emerasia, the capital city of the Serine Elven Nation. By normal travel, it took over four days to reach the city, but the magic expedited the trek.

Most abodes of Emerasia were within the enormous trunks or built of fallen wood from the trees, and ivies covered many of the homes with beautiful green. Various bushes and flowers bloomed, their fragrances overflowing onto every path busy with the pale-gray fleshed elves. The leaves rustled above, where birds and smaller animals flew or hopped from branch to branch. Music was constant in the fresh air as the elves talked, sang, or played an instrument. A performance was always on the verge of beginning.

These things Javesse also missed about Delvarian. And although she'd only been gone for six months she felt like an outsider, as many of the elves gawked at her and whispered to one another. She touched her face, which the Delvarians had never seen. There was naught to do now.

The royal residence was an ancient tree larger than any other in the forest. Rainlisyr's entire family lived with him, including his children's families.

At the entrance, the guard spoke with the sentries, then a messenger went inside.

"This is where we part, Lady Javesse," the guard said. "I do hope His Majesty can give insight into your situation."

The words encouraging, she bowed her head. "I appreciate your escort."

He left, likely to return to duty.

Javesse never inquired of his name. The thought hadn't occurred during the ride from the border; her mind had been busy with worry for Renmier.

"Lady Javesse?"

She met the familiar smile of Lord Euralys, an elf lord she had been intimate with before Beresly captured her heart.

"Javesse!" He exited the house and embraced her. "Thank Bryric!" Holding her at arm's length, Euralys viewed her. "We feared you were killed or taken."

"I... I—"

"We shall speak of it later. My uncle wishes to see you, but I had to make certain the guard was not mistaken." Euralys placed her hand within the crook of his arm and walked her inside.

The king's nephew was a fine man, but often used his status to coerce others into conceding to his desires. Beresly was amongst the very few who had refused. The two lords were dear friends, but pride frequently interfered.

After Javesse gained their affections, it was difficult deciding which one to marry. Beresly had been a man of compassion, generosity, and understanding. If she had chosen Euralys as her groom, Beresly would've accepted her decision with grace and maintained a friendship with them both. The king's nephew did not take well to losing.

Javesse tugged on Euralys' arm. "My lord, His Majesty shall like to hear of what I experienced, however, my return is due to—"

"We shall talk of that soon enough, darling." He halted in the carpeted corridor and faced her.

It was strange how cold the wooden walls felt, when in years past, Javesse had often found comfort in the king's home.

"I cannot tell you how relieved I am you have returned. Truly." Euralys kissed both her cheeks. "And I am sorry to hear about Beresly. He was a... good man." He resumed to the audience chamber.

A sour taste developed on Javesse's tongue. She cringed at the lack of respect from Euralys toward his once good friend.

"Beresly was, my lord," she said. "I had agreed to marry him just afore the attack."

Euralys' step faltered. "Is that so?"

"None of that matters since those bloody men murdered him. And—"

"I shall address all concerns in a timely manner." He patted her fingers. "With your return, a new life shall begin."

This couldn't happen. It was obvious he planned to take her as his bride, and she'd yet to speak to the king. Euralys believed being Rainlisyr's nephew gave him favor, but Javesse had never considered his bloodline. And to be truthful, she now hated to have been intimate with him.

"Why are you unveiled, my lady?" Euralys asked.

"Oh. I have been without a veil for the past several months. My captor forbade me to wear one."

"Sulaen bastards." Euralys scowled. "No man should have the privilege to see your face. Except for me, of course."

He'd changed. Euralys must believe no other elf had a chance to win her hand. None of them did.

"They were not Sulaens," she said, "but men from the Columure Duchy of Descension, seeking lighanas."

Disgust skewed Euralys' face. "You? A lighana?"

"M-my captor treated me better than the pleasure slaves suffer, I assure you."

Frowning, he nodded. "Good. Now, my uncle awaits."

They entered Rainlisyr's hall. To an outsider, it might seem unlikely they stood within a tree, for the chamber was vast, the vaulted ceilings high. The walls, pillars, and archways were polished smooth from centuries ago, shining like glass.

Tapestries of Ubrasians and Serine elves lined the circular wall, none behind the king, for there was a tall door beyond the throne. Thankfully, few elves were present: Rainlisyr's personal guard, advisors, and half a dozen men Javesse didn't recognize.

King Rainlisyr stood, his old eyes gleaming. "Lady Javesse, I knew not what to think until I saw you. Though our hearts mourn for the loss of our own, I am joyous you have returned."

Of their own? Hadn't the elves taken Javesse into their home and welcomed her as one of them? Even his nephew made his intentions of marriage obvious.

"Your Majesty." She bowed. "As always, I am grateful for your kindness. I am here with a request for your aid."

He sat, a low groan escaping him. "Nearly half a year has passed. And upon your return you come to me requesting aid?"

"It is of great urgency, Your Majesty."

The king nodded slightly. "I see. What is it I can do for you, my dear?"

How could Javesse ask the favor without revealing too much? "As I told Lord Euralys, the very men who attacked our party took me prisoner—although not Sulaens, but men of Descension, from Columure. For over the past fortnight, I have been in the company of one who has been kind to me."

"Was he returning you to us?"

Did the elves believe Javesse was their property?

"I-if that was his intention, Sire, I know not, yet—"

"What is it you ask of me?"

"He—he was terribly wounded." She pressed her hands to the sides of her thighs, nonchalantly drying her palms. "I left him in the cover of Niwlog Woods."

"In Columure." One or Rainlisyr's brows rose. "And you wish me to leave Delvarian to tend to this man?"

"I know of no other who could help him, Your Majesty."

Displeasure and nervousness showed upon his advisors' faces. Even Euralys appeared uneasy.

"This sounds like a trap," the king said.

Breathless from the horrific accusation, Javesse hesitated before speaking. "Sire, I would never—"

"You were captured by men of ill intent," Rainlisyr said. "You return here nearly six moons later, and request that I leave the safety of my home to tend to a comrade." He relaxed against the throne's high back. "I cannot. I will not."

Tears surfaced, and Javesse couldn't prevent a few from trailing down her cheeks. "I am begging, Your Majesty. I know not if he will live."

"Human matters are of no concern of mine."

"What of mine?" She couldn't hold her composure; her lips trembled. "He matters to me."

The king sighed. "How can I trust you anymore?"

"What have I done to lose your trust?" Javesse whispered. "I have suffered at the hands of those men, and forced into slavery of pleasure. This man was freeing me."

"Yet not returning you to us?"

"What must I do, Sire? How do I gain your help?"

"Marry me," Euralys said.

Irritation marred Rainlisyr's face.

Javesse frowned, yet chills spread down her arms. "Do you give no time for grief of a friend afore asking for my hand?"

"There was never a question of my affection for you," Euralys said. "Marry me and I will ride with my uncle to your comrade's aid."

There was no time to debate, not if she wanted Renmier to live. He refused to change his path for her, so what did it matter if she married Euralys?

She nodded once. "If His Majesty will agree, then I will marry you."

Rainlisyr's expression softened. "Very well then."

"We must leave immediately," she said.

The king's head lowered. "The conditions are not yours to make, my lady." He rose again and gestured to a guard. "Take her to a chamber." Rainlisyr smiled at Javesse. "Rest, my dear. Refresh yourself. I shall gather supplies."

"Thank you, Sire."

It was a large entourage. No doubt the guards discouraged ambush attempts. A dozen rode ahead of the contingent surrounding Javesse, King Rainlisyr, Euralys, and a few of his friends, and another dozen followed. Euralys and his companions shared stories about their feats of outwitting other elves from various regions of Delvarian. Already tired of him, Javesse regretted their agreement.

She sighed. What could she do? To save Renmier—

"You know," Rainlisyr said from beside Javesse, "it saddened me upon learning you and Lord Beresly were to have married."

What a cruel statement.

Her brows low, she pressed her lips into a thin line.

His Majesty noticed her upset. "What I mean, my dear, was that it broke my heart further. Beresly was a tremendously fine man. He would have loved you until your life's end and beyond."

A rush of chills spread over Javesse's arms. She slouched, her heart aching. "I... I loved him."

"They were good friends." He indicated Euralys with a slight motion of his head. "But my nephew envied Beresly for winning your heart."

Javesse nodded.

"Sometimes," the king continued, "I wonder if you had never shown yourself to Euralys—had not bedded him—if his fascination would not have become so strong."

She grazed her teeth together. "Everyone makes mistakes, Sire."

"And now you are bound to him."

The urge to cry built in her throat.

"He will be good to you, my dear," Rainlisyr said matter-of-factly. "Euralys adores you."

Yet I will never love him. She offered a forced smile. "I have no doubt we shall be happy, Your Majesty."

Grinning, he looked forward.

Euralys and his comrades laughed again, their stories continuing.

Javesse's mind filled with worry about Renmier, and if he was where she left him.

She moved to the front party, leading them to the small camp. It was near dusk, but upon spotting the silhouette of the large stallion behind the foliage, Javesse released her breath, easing the tightness in her chest. She dismounted and hurried through the brush.

Renmier was still there, shivering, and he hadn't moved at all.

She knelt and touched his cheek. Fynthiar! He was frigid. "Renmier." Javesse grabbed his shoulders and shook him. "Renmier."

His eyes remained closed.

Leaves shuffled as others neared.

"You jest." Euralys' voice quivered. "*He* is your comrade?"

Without looking at the elf lord, she lay Renmier back and replaced the fur coverlet over him. "He needs help."

"Sir Renmier," Rainlisyr said. "Vulture."

Javesse twisted her neck enough to look at the king. "He has protected me and saved my life."

Euralys grimaced. "I find that hard to believe!"

Rainlisyr's gaze locked to hers, as if reading her thoughts and emotions. He swallowed a noticeable lump. "If I do this, we bind him and leave him."

Javesse shook her head. "Anyone could come along and kill him."

"It is a shame someone has not already! Brydasia would be better for it." Euralys' face darkened and his brows dipped low. "Uncle, I am asking you not to do this."

"If he saved Lady Javesse's life," Rainlisyr said, "the least we can do is save his."

Javesse frowned at Euralys, then addressed the king. "Thank you, Sire."

"After the many lives he has taken?" Euralys shouted. "I cannot condone this!"

"However, we have an agreement." Javesse returned his glare, hoping her tone was strong enough to match. "Are you suggesting your word means nothing?"

Jaw set and eyes shining like sapphires, Euralys spun his back to her.

Javesse gave her attention to Rainlisyr. "I am more grateful than you can possibly know, Your Majesty."

He rolled his sleeves to his elbows. "Euralys, get my satchel."

The elf lord remained unmoving; his fists clenched as he shook his head the slightest. Euralys then stomped to the horses, the weight of his anger lingering.

Rainlisyr knelt beside Javesse. As he leaned toward Renmier, he stilled, his eyes widening. "No." He bolted upright. "I can do nothing for him."

"Why not?"

"This is no man." The king rose slowly. "There is naught to be done."

Quick to her feet, she grabbed his vestment and pulled. "You must do something!"

"Woman!" He clutched her wrists. "He is nearly soulless. It belongs to the Darkness!"

Javesse eased her grip and stared at the pendant on Rainlisyr's chest. "I have seen things with him. Felt... coldness and smelled foul odors—all when he is in the presence of people he feels hatred toward."

"Sir Renmier is bound in a dark contract." Rainlisyr sighed heavily, then glanced at Euralys, who now stood beside him. He placed his hands over Javesse's. "He belongs to the Soul Eater, my dear."

Renmier had already revealed this, but Javesse shuddered to hear it come from Rainlisyr as well.

"His condition reveals to me he recently killed a man of whom he bargained to gain knowledge," the king continued. "Every time Sir Renmier succeeds upon the agreement made with the demoness, she takes more of his soul." He patted her hands. "Upon completion of the bargain, he shall die. He is only a shell carrying little life. Renmier is no man."

She curled the king's robe within her fingers as she formed fists. Javesse stepped away, tugging the fine garment in her anger. "You are wrong! Renmier *is* a man. He lives! I have dined with him, danced, and shared his bed. His body has the warmth of a living man!"

Eyes narrowed, Euralys drew his sword. "Not anymore." He charged at Renmier.

"No!" Javesse lunged to block him.

Rainlisyr grabbed her with one hand and caught his nephew with the other, revealing an unseen strength that belied his appearance. "Euralys! You will not do this!"

"He deserves death!" The elf lord pushed from his uncle's grasp.

"He is already dying!" The king pointed at Euralys. "Still your hand!"

Javesse broke free and lay upon Renmier; his body chilled hers.

Rainlisyr glowered at his kin. "To slaughter one who cannot defend himself is wrong. None of my bloodline, nor my nation, shall act in such a cowardice manner. I will not permit it!"

Euralys' searing hatred shifted from Renmier to Javesse as he sheathed his sword. "I want naught to do with you." He returned to the other elves.

Javesse rested her forehead on Renmier's shuddering chest and wept.

Once the small clearing had quieted, King Rainlisyr spoke. "Come with us. Start your life anew once again."

"I cannot abandon him."

"He has abandoned himself, my dear."

She looked at Renmier's face. Could Javesse save what was left of him? Was there enough soul for him to live a joyous life with her? *Fynthiar, please show mercy.*

Javesse sat up, dried her cheeks, and looked up at Rainlisyr. "I am grateful for your offer, Your Majesty, but I shall remain with Sir Renmier."

Sorrow overtaking his expression, he nodded. The old elf king picked up the satchel, bowed to Javesse, then shuffled from the clearing, appearing frail again.

She waited until the pounding of hooves faded, then surveyed outside the small campsite. No one was there. Javesse tended to Titan—fed, brushed, and spoke with him—then slid beneath the coverlet and held Renmier close. "I love you," she whispered in his ear. "Please come back to me."

Renmier leaned against the fallen trunk and embraced Amalee for... He didn't know how long, for time meant nothing in the Blackening. It was always strange that she felt solid compared to the damned souls he encountered in the realm, although he understood why. She wasn't Amalee and hadn't even been a mortal once. Sebysula was a demoness created by Chaos, and she toyed with her victims. In truth, she made death easier for Renmier. Amalee would never be in this wretched realm, but pretending she was now in his arms gave him the strength to complete his objective.

"*I love you.*" Javesse sounded distant. "*Please come back to me.*"

From where he sat, Renmier twisted toward her words coming from outside the misshaped trees.

"Ignore it," Amalee said. "Ignore *her*."

"You cannot have me yet," he said. "I'm not finished."

She sighed, a growl heard at the end. "*She* cannot have you. You are already mine."

"If you think I'm unaware, you're wrong."

Giggling like a delighted maiden, Amalee rolled in his arms to face him. "I cannot wait until you join me here for eternity."

Renmier didn't share in her joy.

"I'm leaving now." Rising, he forced Amalee from between his legs.

She looked up at him. "Remember what I said."

"I've never forgotten." Renmier walked to the exit of the twisted, dead forest.

Wheat heating beneath the sun's roasting rays filled Renmier's nostrils. From his right, a glorious warmth chased the chill away. Javesse lay against him, sleeping. He wanted this for the rest of his days, but those days were limited and devoted to one purpose. Renmier wished to give Javesse his heart. He wished he could promise years together as a family, yet he had nothing to give anymore. And his mockingbird must understand.

He squinted from the daylight breaking through the canopy. Renmier slipped his fingers through Javesse's soft hair, then kissed it. *And I love you.*

Shattered Teacup

It'd been two weeks since Renmier last brushed Titan—maybe three. He couldn't remember. But how much time had passed was meaningless. Titan's beauty was lost. The chestnut's mane appeared matted and his flesh wrapped tightly to his bones, yet he felt soft. Renmier dropped the brush into the saddlebag, then removed an apple from a sack. Was the fruit in his hand rotten? The shadowy mists outlining his view showed only impending death and darkness. Trees, grass, flowers—anything that lived—were near death. The iciness persisted at his core, a reminder of his awaiting fate. Every breath passing through his nostrils and lips pressed upon his ears louder than the birds flying from the small clearing, as if escaping his presence.

Clouds floated above, giving the sun dominance over the sky and land; its rays seared through the twisted branches of the canopy.

Eyelids squeezed shut, Renmier tried to ignore his throbbing temples as he rested his forehead on Titan's neck. The horse grunted and pulled away. Renmier presented the apple. "Forgive me. I've doomed you, haven't I?" He chuckled, offered the fruit again. "You were going to die either way, weren't you?"

Titan snorted, then jerked the rein back.

"Are you mad at me?"

"*I'm* mad at you," Javesse said from behind.

Her voice was a painful decadence. Soon, he would never hear it again. There was no contentment found after this recovery as with the others. Torment raked its claws through the remnants of Renmier's soul, tearing into the heart of him. He'd never felt so vulnerable after a hunt.

The apple slipped from his hand and landed at the toe of his boot. Was the ground bare of grass or was it lush and soft? His stomach churned at the thought of seeing only death if he was to look at Javesse. Licking his cracked lips, he nodded. "I know."

"How do you know anything? You were unconscious." She stomped closer, her warmth barely touching him. "Look at me!"

Renmier did a languid turn. Cold swept over his flesh, goosebumps rising. He shuddered. It'd just take a few more days to recover this time, he was certain. Squinting to avoid seeing Javesse's flesh peeling away, he tilted his head back.

She retreated a step. After a long silence, she spoke. "King Rainlisyr was correct." Javesse nodded. "You're no longer a man, are you?"

Like the fine point of an assassin's dagger, the question hurt.

Renmier scoffed. "Did you ever believe I was?"

His attempt at humor failed. If only he didn't notice the tears skimming her rotted cheeks.

"What do you see with those black eyes?" Javesse whispered, as if afraid of disturbing the Darkness within him.

He preferred viewing the dead grass, which was better than watching her decompose. "Let's begin the journey."

They remained still within the small copse. Darkness and Sun. Cold and warmth.

Renmier understood his destiny now more than ever. The choice he'd made ensured his fate, and he and Javesse would now continue at odds. Renmier represented the demoness from the freezing and twisted Blackening. Javesse was the light and warmth of everything good Renmier stood to lose before he died. He could blame no one but himself.

After wiping her cheeks with her sleeve, Javesse gathered her items, putting them in Magyia's saddlebags.

Sighing, Renmier grabbed Titan's reins and walked to the path. He paused. "You said King Rainlisyr."

Javesse led the mare past him. "Yes."

"When did he see me?"

She mounted Magyia and waited, her back to Renmier.

"I asked a ques—"

"I rode to Delvarian and requested his aid."

Javesse returned to the elves? For Renmier? Then she came back for him.

The chill now coursing throughout him wasn't from the Darkness pulsating at his center, but the revelation of the knowledge he now held yet could do nothing about. Javesse could've stayed in Delvarian and left Renmier helpless. But she came back and remained at his side, surrendering a future with the elves for a deteriorating love.

There was naught to be done. Except one thing.

"We've a two-day's hard ride to Fyr Port," he said.

Renmier permitted no rest. He had no appetite, but Javesse ate in silence while on horseback. Too much went through his mind—when Sebysula allowed him peace. During most of the ride, her desires for Javesse's death repeated in his ears. It took immense effort, but Renmier pushed the demoness' encouragement into silence and focused on a new plan to free Javesse.

He chose Fyr Port because of its location in southern Brydasia. Not only did it draw the most sea merchants, therefore, more ships than any port city on the Eastern Continent, but it was a three days' ride from Columure. Renmier would send Javesse from Brydasia, then finish his end of the dark contract. If he failed, she should be a safe distance from Darik's grasp. Renmier knew a dozen sea captains, but only trusted four to handle cargo as precious as Javesse. He prayed to whichever god might grant him a favor, he'd find one of those men docked at Fyr Port.

Javesse's quietness was unsettling. To hear her speak was worth every roan Renmier had—even if it was a ridiculous comment about his lips hardly moving. No matter. He shouldn't fret over such things. This was the part of the journey he'd dreaded: time alone with Javesse, silence, being near her. It wouldn't last. The woman was a fighter, and she'd still attempt swaying him off the path from which he couldn't stray.

Renmier pushed their ride past dusk, reaching Arborville, a forested town split by the Kiasier River. It was a community he enjoyed, finding the air fresher than most places. Now it felt heavy and dank, tasting of mold and rotted wood. Each building crumbled amid the twisted and dying trees, yet he knew they stood strong. This new vision made him want death so he'd no longer see it. Renmier still avoided looking at Javesse.

After stabling the horses, he and Javesse headed to the inn. She claimed to have no appetite, so Renmier led her to his reserved room on the second floor.

He left the weapons on the table beneath the window, then strode for the door. "I must collect a few items."

The ropes under the bed rubbed together as she sat on the mattress. "I'm going nowhere."

Renmier grabbed the doorknob; Amalee's taunting overpowered his thoughts. "Good," he whispered, then left.

He raced from the inn, proceeding for the apothecary. The herbalist's shop leaned against the owner's home so service could be immediate.

Amalee's tone lost its softness, changing to Sebysula's low growl. *"I want her dead!"*

Renmier pressed on. *I said I'll not harm Javesse!*

"You will break your promise, and you will do it for her! *Do I mean nothing to you?"*

He saw Amalee's face in his mind, black eyes wide and glistening with sorrow. Sebysula knew how to torment him. Pausing outside the apothecary's home, he leaned against a tree. *She is a life I can never have. You are my destiny.*

Stillness surrounded him. Even the crickets silenced.

"It is good you understand this truth, Sir Renmier."

Laughter sounded from a block away, crickets chirped their night music, and passersby skipped rocks on the path as they walked.

The demoness' presence receded, yet she lingered close enough. Sebysula wasn't letting Renmier get too far when he was so close to completing the contract. The moment the last man responsible for Amalee's death fell, the demoness would snatch his soul.

He drew in a few breaths of stale air, pleased to find a trace of freshness within. Hopefully, the mists be gone from his vision by the morning.

A few townsfolk glanced his way as he resumed to the apothecary's door. After a few solid knocks, it opened enough for the shop owner to see outside.

"Yes? Oh! Sir Renmier." The elderly man swung the door wide. "Come in, my friend."

A genuine smile greeted Renmier, warming him for the briefest moment.

Ducking, he entered the abode. "Master Koslen, forgive me for the late visit."

"Never too late for a visit from you, sir, especially if you're buying potions." Koslen cackled.

Renmier grinned. "Actually, I need a strong herb." He recollected Javesse enjoyed hot tea in the past. "As a tea would be best."

"I see." The herbalist wrinkled his brow. "Come in and tell me the details."

Javesse nibbled on cheese, nuts, and berries from her rations, yet didn't notice the flavors. Ever since seeing Renmier's eyes that morning, she'd been scouring memories of conversations and events to piece together something useful. There must be a way to break the bargain with the Soul Eater. Why did it matter if Renmier kept his side of the agreement? It wasn't as if the demoness was honorable. Creatures of the Darkness were just as conniving and vile as their creator, Chaos. It was a wonder the demigod hadn't attained full godhood yet with the honor he received from the Sulaens.

A piece of cheese fell from her suddenly numb fingers. *Is Renmier a willing sacrifice to Chaos?*

Javesse didn't know how it worked for one to rise amid the ranks of the gods, but Chaos' great power could only grow stronger. Many feared he intended to bring his dark realm to the surface of Emvarr should he gain godhood. Was Renmier's willingness to surrender his soul to Chaos' realm helping the demigod attain such a goal?

She stood and paced, ignoring her scattered rations on the floor. Javesse had to end Renmier's progress. Amalee wasn't enough, for her murder stayed him on the path. Halting, Javesse replayed the night she met Vulture: the chilly air that had radiated from him, the blackness receding from his irises, and the strange stench. The demoness was with him in Darik's presence. And Samris'. She recalled the day she and Renmier left Bashgrahon—he'd been hostile toward Samris. In fact, Renmier told the captain he was going to kill him.

Javesse lowered to the mattress. *Renmier said he was almost done. There are two more men to die: one who was present at the farm, and the man*—She sat upright. "And the man responsible for Amalee's murder. No. How did he...?" A teardrop escaped at the memory of Renmier standing beside Darik Nornt.

A lackey had just delivered a tray holding a steaming pot and two cups. Javesse contemplated the three items while Renmier busied with them at the table. The second cup was odd, considering he didn't like tea. Renmier removed a few contents from a small black case and set them beside the pot: a vial with blueish-green liquid, a brown leather pouch, and a little wooden box. He pressed the pouch to the table until the bottom flattened, opening it as wide as the strings allowed. He lifted a tea-diffuser from the box, then transferred leaves from the bag to the hole-filled steel ball. The diffuser now in a cup, he poured the steaming water, turned, and leaned against the table's ledge, his arms folded over his chest and his head tipped down.

"Look at me," Javesse said.

He clamped his teeth on the corner of his lip. After a moment of obvious deliberation, Renmier raised his eyes to her. The dark mists still lingered along the edges of his eyelids, offering a haunting vision of a man scarcely clinging to this realm of life.

"This whole investigation was a farce right from the beginning," she said. "There never was an assassin to find... was there? Because it's you. You intend to kill Darik. And you started the rumor to disguise your intentions."

He nodded.

Javesse shook her head. *Clever bastard.*

"How do you work for him?" she whispered. "Knowing he sent them to your farm." Javesse sucked in a shaky breath as the blackness grew closer to Renmier's darkening irises. "That's why you looked as you did the night we met," she continued. "*Her* stench—*her* chill surrounded you because you were in *his* presence. You wanted to kill Darik right then. And Samris."

"I wanted to kill them every time I was there." Straightening, Renmier lowered his arms. "But the time wasn't right until now."

She stepped toward him. "And then you'll be *hers.*"

"As was agreed." He lifted the diffuser from the cup. "I'll reunite with Amalee."

Javesse scoffed. "You'll give power to Chaos!"

Laughter was the last reaction she expected. Although her impressions of Renmier at the start of their travels were that he was an evil man, he truly wasn't.

He clinked the spoon on the cup's rim. "Chaos gains nothing from me. The Soul Eater hides living souls from him. I don't know why."

"Then you know Amalee doesn't await you in the Darkness."

Renmier sighed, the sound as heavy as the weight in Javesse's heart. "I do. The demoness' disguise only makes it easier to surrender."

Javesse took the last steps to reach him and clutched his arm. "Then don't! Damn you, Renmier, don't dare surrender to her!"

His voice was surprisingly soft as he said, "I have no choice. I made the bargain."

"If you don't kill them, she can't have you!" Javesse hugged his arm, wept upon it. "Please, sail with me. I promise I'll brave the seas. For you, I'll voyage the oceans again." She guided his face to hers and stared into his black-misted eyes. "Let's start a life together."

Renmier had feared seeing Javesse still decomposing, but death barely touched her now. He had recovered from the hunt, although sluggishly. Or maybe there was a god Who gave him pity. Whatever the reason, the love was definite. It showed in Javesse's eyes, was heard in her voice, and felt in her touch. What little of the soul remaining within Renmier ached for the anguish that crushed her and yearned for a future out of their reach.

If only it was so easy to refuse fulfilling the bargain. If Renmier didn't kill Samris and Darik, he'd remain a tormented being stretched between the icy Blackening and warmth of the living realm. He didn't know whom or what he'd become. Yet to appease Javesse, to make his plan work, he delved into deception.

Renmier palmed her face and kissed her forehead. "Yes. We'll sail to Myndrose." Her eyes brightened, taking more death from what he viewed.

"You—? You'll go with me?"

He forced a smile, only managing a crooked grin. "I'll do anything for you."

The heat of her body fought the chill within him as her arms wrapped around his shoulders and her lips pressed to his. The kiss deepened, sending a jolt to his heart and core. For the first time since killing Rastnin, Renmier felt alive. Desire flickered, moving blood faster throughout him. Arousal soon had him engorged, longing to be with Javesse.

The tea abandoned, they undressed.

Each passing moment of touching and kissing her gave more life to Renmier's vision. The mists lingered just at the boundaries, but she was a magnificent glow. Her flesh against his was an indulgence. The cold remaining inside him pushed to overthrow their heated passion. He resisted. Sebysula couldn't steal this moment from him. Every thrust, bite, suck, and kiss were with purpose and need.

The lovemaking drew out for half an hour before thunderous waves of pleasure overtook them.

Renmier held Javesse afterward. The tea could wait for now. It'd be best to give it to her in Fyr Port anyway.

Excitement of the upcoming voyage brought the return of Javesse's usual chattiness. When no others were on the road, she sang, bringing a sense of peace to Renmier, along with a deep ache. He hated deceiving her, but the woman left him no choice. The 'what ifs' repeated enough times to drive him insane with regret, but no god would give mercy to one who bound himself to a demoness of the Darkness.

"Renmier?"

"Yes?"

"The rumors about you—about Vulture... are they true?"

He withheld a chuckle. "What do you think?"

Javesse's cheeks bloomed soft pink. "Well, I haven't witnessed you consume anyone."

"No one ever had."

"Then why—?"

"One night, after I pommeled a man in a tavern for speaking against Duke Nornt, I removed him from the building and dumped him into a ditch. Upon my return, many noticed his blood on my face, near my mouth." Renmier shrugged. "Whispers about me eating him spread."

"You dumped him?"

"Yes."

"Didn't people see him again afterward?"

He shrugged again. "The rumor spread. To instill that fear, I continued to feed it by removing the unconscious men, or women, and sent them off."

Javesse tugged on the mare's rein. "Sent them off?"

Renmier stopped Titan. "I put them on a ship or a horse and sent them to a port, gave them roans, and told them never to return. If they did, I'd hunt them down and devour them. It was best they continued their lives elsewhere."

"You—?" Her mouth dropped open. "You spared them? Every one?"

"Most." Sighing, he commanded the stallion forward. "Some were foolish and had to die."

Javesse caught up. "What if they weren't willing to go?"

"I poisoned them and dropped them onto a ship."

She fell silent the rest of the way to Fyr Port.

The harbor city was immense and thrived from the markets and businesses spread throughout. Goods arrived on ships from the ports of Myndrose and Yeuroth, the merchants selling many of the items in the local shops before taking them to other communities. The finest shipments were taken to Ravieris, to the emperor and other nobles. Buildings up to three-stories tall crammed the streets to house the businesses, locals, and travelers. Many taverns were near the harbor to accommodate the sailors and their needs, while nicer establishments were away from shore for the more congenial patrons. People crowded the walking paths and roads, forcing carts to standstills, yet Renmier and Javesse could move the horses through with Titan pushing his way.

The orange sun was just touching the waves of the Cobalt Ocean, giving the water a deep blue color beyond its reflection. Monstrous ships swayed along the piers, and recently docked sailors hurried to finish the day's work so they could enjoy a few nights at the taverns and brothels. There were too many vessels to find the particular ones he wanted, so Renmier would search for the captains later.

He rode straight for the stables beside the Amber Hearth, his favorite tavern in Fyr Port. Javesse remained close during the three-block ride, watching the city with curiosity. He wondered how long it'd been since she was last at a port. They boarded the horses and headed for the inn, greeted by the barkeep and his family.

Renmier approached his usual table beside the fireplace and stared at the four men occupying it until they departed. He sat.

"I wish you wouldn't do that," Javesse said, sitting beside him.

"I still have a reputation to maintain." He looked to the bar. "Food! Drink!"

"Yes, sir!" The barkeep was already filling a tall tankard, sending the drink with his daughter.

"There you are, sir." She set the mug down. "Anything for m'lady?"

The girl was fifteen years old, if Renmier remembered correctly. He could never recall her name, even after saving her from an assault by two drunken patrons.

Javesse clasped her hands together. "Wine, please."

"Mama made her special pie, sir. I know it's your favorite."

Renmier nodded. "Very good."

"And for your lady friend?"

He fought the urge to grin as he looked at Javesse. "Meat pie, lady friend?"

She narrowed her eyes at him. "Sounds perfect," she said to the barmaid.

The girl twirled around and hurried to the scullery.

Javesse smirked. "She fancies you."

"I doubt it. Not after what she's witnessed."

The girl returned with a glass of wine. "There you are, m'lady."

"Thank you."

The barmaid's fingers brushed over Renmier's arm on the way to another table.

Javesse giggled. The tavern fell quiet. She'd gained the attention of several men.

"Must I crack this tankard over skulls tonight?" Renmier shouted.

The men looked at their drinks or comrades, conversations soon filling the room.

Shortly after, the barmaid returned with meat pies. As always, it smelled superb. The girl bumped her bottom against his arm as she spun and walked to the bar.

Biting her lip, Javesse fought an obvious laugh. "Not fond of you at all, Renmier."

After supper, he took her to his room. It was one of two on the third floor, and he paid well for it. Amber Hearth was owned by a retired Elite Knight who'd promised to keep Renmier's possessions guarded for a heavy price. There wasn't much within. Other than typical furniture, there was extra clothing, roans, gems, the pouch Tredwyn sent ahead, and his field armor. The very armor Renmier had donned during the war. He always came to Amber Hearth before returning to Columure. This time, the armor would go with him.

Javesse watched while he removed his cloak and leather top, then place the black case on the table. His hair had grown since leaving Darik's home just more than four weeks ago, and he'd not shaved since their first kiss, filling a beard out well enough.

He called for a lackey to bring hot water, then removed the same vial, pouch, and small wooden box. The tea. He'd made it in Arborville, but tossed it the next morning. The whole thing was odd since he didn't drink tea. And Renmier's earlier confession about poisoning unwilling victims only piqued Javesse's suspicions more.

Her attention shifted to the vial. None of that went into either cup before. Was it the tea itself?

"Are you afraid of relaxing?" he asked.

"What do you mean?"

"You're still in your traveling wools."

Viewing her garb, Javesse nodded. She removed the cloak and draped it over his on the chair. "You promised me. Remember?"

"Promised you what?" He opened the pouch and the box.

"That you'd go to Myndrose with me."

He released a slow breath. "I did, Javesse."

A knock thudded on the door. Renmier opened it and motioned for the lackey to set the tray on the table. A steel pot and two clay cups rattled while the young man did as he was bade. After receiving a silver roan, the boy skipped into the dark hall.

Renmier dropped leaves into the diffuser, lowered it into the water, then leaned over it. "You seem... anxious. I know you enjoy tea, and thought it might help you relax."

She retreated. "You're going to poison me."

"What?" He spun, his face crimson. "I did this for you!"

Javesse pointed at the steeping tea. "You'll do what you've done with your past victims!"

Disbelief overtook Renmier's countenance. He removed the diffuser and poured the tea on the floor. "There! You don't trust me? Forget it!" He slammed the cup on the table. "Gods, Javesse! I wanted to do something for you. After everything you did for me, I wanted to return something... I don't know. Pleasant!"

He stomped to the bed and sat. Huffing, Renmier raked his fingers through his hair. "I did what I could to save you from the poison in Ravieris, and now you accuse me of being like them?"

Guilt dried Javesse's mouth as she watched him struggle to explain himself. Had she been wrong?

"What a fine start we're off to," he mumbled.

She moved before him, her fingertips slipping into his dark strands. "Forgive me."

He leaned away.

"I'm sorry, Renmier. Losing you frightens me."

"I promised, didn't I?" he snapped.

Javesse's nails combed through his beard. "I suppose I still have much to learn about you." She kissed the line between his brows. "Please give me more time to know the man behind Vulture."

Renmier parted his legs and pulled her close, kissing her.

Intimacy engulfed them, fast and intense. Their clothing scattered on the mattress and floor, and they embraced as passion claimed them once again.

She lay next to him, stroking the scars on his chest. "I'm thirsty," she said against his skin. "I think I'd like some tea now, if you'll have it with me."

He hesitated. "I'm not fond of it, but I'll drink with you."

Watching Renmier prepare tea while naked was a delight. His fine bottom tightened as his muscles flexed with each motion. He was stunning.

Once the drink was ready, he sat on the bed and offered her one. The dark mists along his eyelids seemed to have grown, but she dismissed it to the shadows in the room.

Raising the cup, Javesse said, "We'll soon begin our new life together."

Sorrow laced his grin. Did he regret his promise?

"I love you, Javesse." He lifted the drink to his mouth.

No. Renmier didn't regret it. He wanted a future with her.

Now at ease, she smelled lavender and aythimus, a rare flower found in the northeast. She had seen the peach bloom twice in her lifetime on Brydasia, and it had a strong, sweet fragrance. Relief soothing her mind, Javesse sipped. It was the best tea she'd ever had. "This is delicious."

He lowered his cup.

She drank until the tea was gone.

Tears pooling, Renmier watched her set the cup on her knee. "Forgive me." He poured his drink onto the floor.

Javesse's heart thudded fast, blood pumping quickly through her veins. "No."

There was a bitterness on her tongue, like poorly made chocolate.

"What have you done?" she asked.

He snatched the cup from her and tossed it against the wall. Grabbing her arms, Renmier stared into her eyes. "I want to go with you more than anything, but I can't."

"No." She attempted to pull free, but he held too tightly. "No!"

Squiggly lines interfered with her vision, her breath came short and quick. No matter her attempts, Javesse's muscles refused to respond. It was useless fighting Renmier as he guided her to lie back. She tried to slug him, but her arms fell to her sides.

"Don't leave me." It sounded as if she spoke from the room's corner.

"I love you," he said. "And I hope you'll one day forgive me."

A pulsating blackness invaded her vision. It consumed everything as a low hum filled her ears. Lips heavy, she couldn't speak. All of her had gone numb as a warmth surrounded her, inducing Javesse into a deep sleep.

Staring at her changed nothing, other than hating himself more. At least Renmier could now grant her freedom. He washed himself, dressed, then did the same for her. Renmier grabbed the pouch sent from Tredwyn, adding the last of his coins and gemstones to it. He kissed Javesse, then left. Downstairs in the tavern, he held a quiet discussion with the barkeep, leaving an emerald in the man's possession under the promise no one disturbed Javesse. It took Renmier less than an hour to accomplish all that since she fell asleep, but it felt the night had already passed.

He hurried to The Sunken Anchor, a tavern patronized by the more refined ship captains while their crew crowded the larger and less savory establishments. The Anchor wasn't quiet. There was plenty of gambling, music, laughter, and women to entertain, but the environment was more relaxed than where crewmen got rougher and louder.

Renmier surveyed the large room, spotting a few familiar faces. Captain Rugard of Myndrose was at a table with three other men, drinking and laughing. Rugard was decent, but his temper could get the best of him, and he often needed to replenish his crew.

Captain Fentelle, also from Myndrose, was a drunk. He stood with one foot planted on the chair while he sang to a local harlot. Although often reliable, he wouldn't do tonight.

Captain Julius, the only one present who hailed from Yeuroth, was a few tables from the hearth. He was in the midst of a teesote game with two women. This man was honorable and true to his word. Rathan Julius carried himself with undeniable confidence, much like Renmier—like a knight. He'd do perfectly.

Renmier headed to Captain Julius' table.

Of ship captains from Yeuroth, very few were not Vhormons, Captain Julius amongst them. An attractive man, he stood only a couple inches shorter than Renmier, yet displayed strength hidden beneath the long black coats he always wore. Rathan Julius kept his dark hair short, and spoke as one with noble upbringing: proper and educated. He ran a devoted crew of Vhormons, the best sailors on Emvarr, and commanded Winged Amyrdene, one of the fastest ships of the seas. Renmier first learned about him in Ravieris, for Captain Julius often did personal transports for the emperor.

Rathan spun the wooden game token, the differently lined sides whirling. Renmier never played teesote, for it was a seaman's game of chance. In the old days, he preferred cards and dice. The captain's forest-green eyes flitted from the token to Renmier, then back to the teesote. Dimples showed upon his clean-shaven cheeks as he grinned at the women whose attention were now on Renmier.

One maiden leaned over the teesote, her breasts interfering with its spin. "G'evening, love. Are you joining our wager? Please say you are."

"No. He's not." A scowl marred Rathan's handsome face. "That three should be your turn, my dear," he said. "I'll have another try." Spinning the token again, he continued ignoring Renmier.

There was no time for this. Renmier thumped his fist on the table.

The teesote flew to the floor, then bounced away. One woman squealed in surprise, the other giggled.

Renmier held Rathan's gaze.

The captain smirked. "Our game has finished, ladies."

"But... what about our wager?" one whined.

"Perhaps another time." Rathan kissed their hands. "Go on now." He slapped their bottoms before they walked away.

Renmier viewed the three mugs. "Wager? I see no roans."

Rathan raised his hands slightly. "Our bets were not of coin." He drank from his tankard, then sighed. "What can I do for you?"

Renmier sat and considered just how much to impart. "I'm in need of your service."

"There are other captains."

"I trust you with this..." Renmier's heart hammered, as if trying to beat through his chest bones. Let it break with the rest of him.

"Cargo?" Rathan said.

"Passenger."

Rathan tilted his head. "A new word for you." Chuckling, he lifted his mug. "Vulture now has a *passenger* he entrusts to me?"

Renmier curled his fingers into fists. "This is no game."

"I don't like you."

"Then why do business with me?"

"Because I help people." Rathan drank again. "And you pay well."

Renmier let his muscles relax. "This shall be our last act of business."

The captain's forehead wrinkled for the slightest second. "The passenger?"

"A woman. She's to go to Myndrose." Renmier untied the heavy pouch from his belt.

Rathan shook his head. "Amyrdene isn't sailing to Myndrose." He nodded toward Rugard. "Captain Rug—"

Renmier tossed the pouch to land in front of Rathan. "She is now."

Neither man moved. Music continued playing, as did the games of chance with cards, teesote, and women.

Rathan opened the pouch enough to peek inside. His eyes momentarily widened. "There's an awful lot of black in there," he said, sitting back. "And some colorful stones."

Renmier nodded. "Just about all I own."

The pouch now cinched, Rathan regarded him as he tucked it under his jacket. "The details, sir."

Two hours later, Renmier approached Winged Amyrdene, carrying Javesse beneath a blanket, and her backpack and sword belt over his shoulder. He had added the remainder of his healing elixirs into her pack, their value too great to let go to waste, along with three large rubies to help Javesse start a new life in Bellinstar.

The payment to Rathan was enough to persuade the ship's crew to return early for duty. Some sailors might grumble within their captain's hearing, even one they feared. The Vhormons did no such thing, at least not in Renmier's presence. The men worked diligently to prepare the ship for departure, a rare evening event, yet appeared it wasn't Winged Amyrdene's first.

He'd never seen a Vhormon until meeting Captain Julius, surprised to learn the shorter humans were behind the crafting of such fantastic machines, especially after hearing them speak. Vhormon dialect sounded like simple-minded chatter. Yet the stout sailors worked hard, proved faithful to duty, and seemed happy with their life at sea.

They paid no mind while Renmier boarded with a covered person, likely used to him dragging bodies onto their stunning ship. Onyx cedar planks formed the vessel from stern to bow, and bowsprit to masts. There was no doubt deep love went into the care of Winged Amyrdene, for she was immaculate, even with a missing figurehead.

Rathan shouted orders from the quarterdeck. Spotting Renmier, he spoke to the Vhormon beside him then headed down to the main deck. "Sir," he said, motioning to the door beneath the stairs.

Renmier scowled. "Your chamber? I think not."

Rathan moved closer, keeping the conversation as private as possible amid the noise. "I didn't believe you intended to drop this passenger right here like the past... cargo," he said. "I imagined you wanted a comfortable voyage."

Renmier eyed the captain. Could he trust Rathan? Discarding the question, he nodded. There wasn't time to doubt him now.

They entered a large dining chamber, the décor in black. The long table could seat ten people, the large chair at the head obviously meant for Captain Julius; carved waves were ready to crash upon the occupant. A few other dark pieces of furniture blurred as the men hurried to a black wall of half-glass and half-wood;

their booted steps softened by the blue rug covering the expanse of the floor. Rathan unlocked the door, then pushed it open to permit Renmier entry.

The bedchamber was exquisite; Rathan certainly spoiled himself. A plush looking bed inlaid in black oak was to the left. To the right was a tall matching chest with five drawers beside a full-length mirror surrounded by golden waves. Two thick-cushioned, ornate chairs were before a large black oak desk where several items rested, a corner wall cabinet was above a table in the shadows behind his desk, and a black rug of Emvarr stretched over the floor. Above the back windows were four paintings of sensual acts between an alluring male sea creature and human or elven women.

The images didn't help settle Renmier's nervousness at leaving Javesse in the captain's care.

Rathan viewed the paintings. "Everything serves a purpose, sir." Nodding once, he flipped the first picture to reveal a partial map of Emvarr, particularly the waters south and east of Myndrose.

"I see." Renmier's gaze swept over the other paintings as he faced the bed. Kneeling, he lowered Javesse to the mattress, dropped the pack and weapon belt, then removed the blanket from her veiled face. His throat tightened.

"A Bellinstarian," Rathan said. "In Brydasia?"

Ignoring him, Renmier grazed her cheek with his fingers. *If there are any gods Who'll listen to my prayer, grant Javesse safe passage home.*

He spun to the captain. "Please take her there... to Bellinstar. She shouldn't awaken until tomorrow afternoon."

Pity showed in Rathan's eyes. "You love her."

Ache, regret, and anger choked Renmier as he swallowed and nodded. His mind went blank with any other response. "Farewell, Captain." He left.

"Sir!"

Renmier hastened through the dining chamber, to the gangplank, and to shore.

A thunderous judder shook Javesse awake. Her sharp breath catching cloth between her lips, she sat up and touched the veil. The rough swaying and shouting outside the unfamiliar dark chamber revealed everything. Renmier had broken his promise.

Tossing the covers aside, she stumbled from the bed. Her head spun. Eyes squeezed shut, Javesse planted her feet on the floor and pressed her palms to her temples, her breath slowing. She must retrain herself to the motions of a ship, and fast.

Her equilibrium becoming familiar with the rocking, her stomach eased and her mind cleared of the anger and hurt—for the most part. She started for the exit. Locked. Javesse pounded on it. "Let me out! I demand you let me out right now!"

After a few more attempts to open the door, she sighed and gave up. Heart heavy, she viewed the surroundings. The Captain's Quarters. It was decorated with expensive wood furniture Javesse recognized was water resistant, if regularly treated, and some of the most gorgeous artwork she'd ever seen, from paintings to baubles. The captain of this ship had amazing taste.

The lock clicked and the knob turned.

Not knowing whom Renmier entrusted her to, Javesse formed fists and readied to fight.

A tall man entered the room. He smiled crookedly, revealing dimples on both cheeks, and bowed his head. Black waves of hair swayed wildly as he straightened, settling around his handsome face. "My lady." He closed the door behind him, his green eyes darting to her fists. "I'm Captain Rathan Julius, and I am your servant."

Javesse lowered her arms. "Excellent. Drop the anchor."

Straightening, he chuckled. "My lady, I hadn't expected you to be awake. So, this is..." He shrugged. "Unexpected."

"Consider it Fynthiar's Will that I *am* awake." She neared the captain. "I must return to... to save him."

Rathan stared at her. "Save *him*? Vulture."

"Renmier." She set her chin. "Sir Renmier."

A brief laugh sounded in his throat. "I had wondered." Rubbing his nape, Rathan dragged his heels over the enormous rug on his way to a table in the corner behind the desk. "Drink?"

"I want to go back to port!"

"Forgive me, but I can't." He poured two short glasses of an amber liquid. It appeared to be a fruzae. "Sir Renmier paid me well. And I gave my word to deliver you safely to Bellinstar."

"I'm not bloody goods!"

Approaching, he offered the drink. "However, I'm a man of my word."

Javesse slapped the glass from his hand; it thudded on the carpet.

Rathan frowned at the mess. "That was uncalled for."

"Renmier is going to die!" She pushed him back, forcing his drink to spill on his hand and fancy sleeve cuff.

Scowling, Rathan banged the glass on the desk. "That's not a concern to me. You are!"

Warm tears trailed into her veil. Annoyed by the heat it created beneath, Javesse removed it.

He sucked in a quick breath. "Gods."

"I don't care," she said.

Blinking, he appeared to break from a spell. "You... You love him."

"I'd give my life for him."

Rathan inched closer. "What is he doing?"

She sniffled, then calmed herself enough to speak clearly. "He's going to kill the last two men responsible for his wife's murder."

The captain's brows dipped low. "I see." He faced the desk, then sank what remained in his glass in one gulp. "I see," he whispered. "I hope he succeeds."

Javesse tugged on his arm. "Even if he does, he'll die. I must stop him so he will live."

Confusion scrunched Rathan's face. "What?"

"I'll tell you everything if you drop the anchor right now."

He considered her demand for a silent moment, then exhaled heavily. "Very well."

"Time is short, Captain Julius. I don't know how long ago Renmier left me here."

He smirked. "Only two hours."

The pounding in her chest was of hope. Javesse could reach Renmier before he arrived at Bashgrahon. "We must go now."

"Not unless I agree. And if I do," he viewed her from head to boots, "I'll not send you alone."

A Lovely Day

Amalee had cut the bread unevenly. Some slices were fat on top and thin on the bottom, or vice versa. Others were half a slice, while some were thick or far too thin. It wasn't anything to be upset about, but she criticized herself for such a small failure. She'd worked so hard baking the bread, doing her best to give Renmier the home and life they had dreamt of since he expressed his love for her. Amalee was no farm girl, yet she gave up her noble life to be one. She collected eggs, fed their small amount of livestock, worked the fields, and prepared meals, even though she'd never done a bit of work in her life before.

Renmier plunged a slice of bread into the sunny egg yolk, then took a bite. "It's delicious, love."

Her hazel-blue eyes brightened behind the blonde locks that had fallen from the loose bun atop her lovely head. "Is it?"

Normally, he'd never lie to her, but Amalee needed the encouragement. They'd been struggling the past fortnight, especially with the builders falling behind schedule. At least the men had completed most of the house and finished the chicken coop, horse barn, and the fences. Renmier and Amalee seeded the fields two moons ago, and the plants were now a few inches tall. It elated the couple to see the progress they'd made. Having grown up on a farm, Renmier knew it'd take time and arduous labor. It was a true challenge to keep his wife optimistic and not disheartened.

He soaked the bread longer to soften the crust. "It is. The dough just needs to sit longer before baking."

Shoulders slumping, Amalee turned her head down. "I see."

Renmier let the bread fall to the plate, then hauled her onto his lap. "Stop this. You're doing a superb job."

"I can't even—"

"I said you're doing wonderfully. I couldn't be happier, my love." He kissed her. "This is exactly what I wanted."

She slid one arm around his shoulder and stroked his beard with her other hand. "I love you, Renmier."

"I love you, my dar—"

A beautiful melody bursted from the open window behind them.

Renmier craned his neck to look at the sill while Amalee peeked over his shoulder. A golden mockingbird sang from her usual perch, her black, gold, and white feathers sleek in the sunlight.

Gasping, Amalee pressed her fingers to Renmier's shoulder. "She's back."

He broke tiny pieces from the slice of bread and dropped them a few inches from the bird. "She trusts us."

"The poor dear." Amalee eased from his lap; he immediately missed her. "I'm glad we found the nest. I just wish we could've saved them all." Squatting by the window, she stared at the bird with the wonderment of a tot.

"As do I." He watched the mockingbird, entranced by her beautiful song. "She reminds me of one I had saved when I was a child."

"A golden mockingbird?"

"Yes." He smirked. "I saw her in a bush. I had believed she was trying to build a nest or something, but noticed she'd been there for far too long flapping her wings wildly. I moved closer and saw the thin branches twisted around her foot."

"The poor darling." Amalee's full attention was now on him while he shared the memory.

Cheeks warming from the way she looked at him, as if he was a hero, Renmier continued. "I spoke gently to her." He dropped another crumb on the sill, but left his hand on the edge. "And carefully unwound the branches."

The mockingbird hopped to his fingertips, ignoring the food.

Surprised, Renmier shook his head. "She flew off, and I thought I'd not see her again."

"Thought?" Amalee's hand warmed his thigh.

Her touch excited him as much as the bird jumping onto his thumb at that moment.

He released a breathy laugh, his heart racing as it had so many years ago. "She returned with at least six others... and they sang to me." His eyes watered at the awe he'd felt that afternoon. "It was the most beautiful music I'd ever heard."

Amalee's hand slid farther up his leg as she drew nearer. "I wish this one would bring more to us, so we may hear their chorus together. To see your face, Renmier, your eyes greener than ever in the sun, and to hear your voice at the memory... it excites me."

Shifting his gaze from the golden mockingbird to his wife, he grinned. "You always excite me, my love."

The bird's song ended abruptly, and she flapped away, screeching. Thumping of approaching horses, many of them, sounded.

Frowning, Renmier looked at Amalee. "Stay here."

He headed to the front window. About a hundred yards away, a dozen men rode from the south. By the dark armor, they appeared to be soldiers. It was difficult from the distance to determine whether they were Imperial or plains patrol.

He glanced at Amalee. The flail was packed beneath his armor under a trapdoor in their bedroom, all of it far too heavy for her to handle. "Get my sword."

She nodded and ran to the hearth room while he trod out the front door.

As the group neared, Renmier recognized the leader. Samris Givins. He'd served in Renmier's unit during the war, but the two had never spoken to one another. Samris was simply a soldier—expendable on the field. Honestly, it surprised Renmier the man still lived, for there was nothing significant about him. Samris fought to keep himself alive, but was unreliable for protecting the soldier at his side, and that's why Renmier never gave a positive report for him. It'd gotten to the point he stopped paying attention to Samris and focused on those who made a difference, who deserved his attention. Samris Givins slipped to the back of the ranks and out of view of Renmier's helmet. He'd forgotten about the soldier. Now Samris sat upon a fine-looking horse, smirking down at him.

"Good day," Samris said.

Renmier scanned the fields for a sign of Titan. Every morning, after feeding the livestock, he let the stallion roam. If he recalled correctly, Titan had run to the west.

Crossing his massive arms over his chest, he glared at Samris while the other men directed their horses into a semi-circle.

Samris' lips twitched. "I'm here to collect."

Collect? Bloody fool. According to His Eminence, every Elite Knight who retired was free of burdens in gratitude for their service.

Renmier dug his heels into the ground. "I owe nothing."

"I beg to differ." Samris' gaze flitted beyond Renmier as the house door opened and closed. Soft footsteps drew nearer from behind. "Duke Darik Nornt now oversees the southern region of Columure. You owe him taxes."

Darik Nornt? He'd also served in Renmier's unit, but above him, under the command of General Repascow. Darik, like Samris Givins, was insignificant.

Renmier grinned back. "I. Owe. Nothing. Get off my land before you regret it."

The men laughed from atop their horses. A few of them drew swords, and two showed their loaded crossbows.

Samris raised his hand in a silent command. "*You'll* regret not paying your dues to His Grace and His Eminence."

Squinting, Renmier spoke through clenched teeth. "Do you know who I am?"

Samris leaned over the saddlebow, looking from Renmier to Amalee. "What I see is an idiot farmer and his fine wife—both of whom are in danger. Your resistance only makes this a better day for us. Especially when we have our way with her." He nodded in Amalee's direction.

There was a rage that often overcame Renmier in battle, something that pushed him beyond recognizing pain. He became a beast looking to tear flesh from bone. However, he didn't have his flail at the ready, so he reached back, feeling the sword hilt in his palm. After closing his fingers around it, he charged, bellowing a roar.

His hair, longer than at the war's end eight months ago, blocked his vision now and then as he swung at horse and man, cutting whoever was in his path. Pain struck, then burned and throbbed at the left side of his back, just below his ribs. Renmier continued swinging. He spun, the sword blurring in a wide arc, and spotted a bolt coming. Ducking, he tilted his head inward, his ear catching the sharp edge of the barbed point. Renmier ignored the warm blood streaking to his chest and kept impaling the blade into men. He took many wounds, but fought on, praying to Valorius for strength to protect his wife and home.

Six men surrounded him. Amalee's scream echoed in his ears.

"Amalee!" Renmier thrust the blade into the soldier in front of him, then kicked him away.

He spotted Amalee fighting Samris, punching and kneeing him while he shook her. Stumbling over the arm of a dead soldier, Renmier charged, slipping on blood-soaked grass. He regained his balance and moved forward, but a sharp, breath-stealing pain brought him to a halt. He looked down to see three inches of a blade sticking from his chest.

Air came out in quick gasps. Blood rose like vomit, falling in streams from his lips.

Amalee shrieked, then cried out. "No! No! Renmier!"

He fell to his knees. The blade pulled free, bringing more pain. A heavy foot thudded on his back, sending him to the patchy grass and dirt. Puffs of dust rushed from beneath his mouth. "Am—Amalee," he managed. Renmier pushed up on his hands and knees, but someone forced him down with their foot.

"Stay there, you big bastard." Scratchy laughter followed.

Three men walked toward Amalee and Samris, while the other kept his weight on Renmier, holding him. Samris shoved Amalee into the arms of a soldier, slapped her—hard.

Blood pooled on the ground beneath Renmier's mouth. He tried to yell, but couldn't find the muscle to do so. It was difficult to breathe.

Samris walked to them, having the two soldiers drag Amalee along. "I told you this was a good day." He tore the front of Amalee's dress. "And I get first spoils."

Valorius, no. Don't let them do this! Renmier gritted his teeth and pressed upward, surprising the man holding him down. He rolled over and grasped his sword hilt.

The soldier who'd stabbed him in the back sat on Renmier's stomach and slugged his face twice, then his temple.

Renmier fought light-headedness as he tried to regain strength to save Amalee, but blackness invaded his vision as well. Fear pushed him when her screams resumed amongst the men's laughter and goading, then her shouts softened into trembling whimpers. His view cleared enough to see Givins assaulting her while another held her arms to the browning grass. "No!" Renmier's shout came out a broken wheeze.

The man atop him struck him again. "Silence, peasant!" He laughed.

Renmier scrutinized the soldier. In fact, he had time to study all of them, for after Samris had his way with Amalee, so did the others. Each took turns pinning Renmier down, taunting him with how good she felt.

Once the last man finished, the one who'd stabbed Renmier in the back returned and sat him up, facing Amalee. Samris lifted her to her knees. She looked bruised and exhausted.

Renmier willed his hand to rise to her in a false sense of comfort. "Ama... Amalee."

Samris placed a blade to her throat. "This moment will teach the other farm peasants a lesson. You don't say no to Duke Nornt."

The steel edge split Amalee's flesh, opening a spring that poured red down her front.

Renmier wished to stop breathing as he watched the life leave her eyes, like clouds drowning the light of the bright sky.

"Amalee," was his last utterance before a knife pierced his heart.

"Leave it," Samris said, as the backstabbing soldier started to pull it out. "I like the idea of him dying slowly while he looks at his wife. What a torment." His laughter filled the yard, soon joined by the other men's.

"What're we taking?" someone asked.

Givins glanced over the property. "Livestock. Coin in the house. I doubt you'll find anything else of value from these peasants." He remained beside Renmier while putting his gloves back on. "And someone put the dead on their horses. I don't want the other farmers to know this one killed any of our men."

A different soldier stepped up to Samris as the others departed to ransack the house. "What do you think he meant—asking if we knew whom he was?"

Samris spat on the ground, the glob landing next to Renmier's face. "I don't care and I'm not worried. He's an idiot farmer."

The men weren't in the house long.

It didn't matter to Renmier what they found. He locked his gaze with Amalee, her pupils expanding to swallow her irises. The ends of her blonde hair looked like a paintbrush dipped in blood; her beautiful face grew pallid. Renmier willed for her to move, whether chest, fingers, eyelids—anything to show she lived. But... would he want her to survive after suffering those men? His Amalee would never be the same.

As time passed, his breaths grew shorter and his mouth hurt from dryness. Warm teardrops fell as he stared at her.

Why, Valorius? Upon entering His Great Feast, Renmier would ask the god. He was a faithful servant, so why did Valorius punish him?

Black and gold fluttered above Amalee before something small landed on her. Renmier tried to focus, but his vision blurred. Then he heard a sorrowful song. The golden mockingbird had lost her family to a predator in the woods, and now she lost this family to a predatory duke and his men. For a fleeting moment, Renmier worried about where his songbird would find safety. Everything went dark, her song fading as he fell into unconsciousness.

Cost of
Vengeance

The memory of that day came unwelcomed. Renmier fought it, but it pressed into his mind, forcing him to relive it until rage consumed him. Fury flowed through his veins, stronger and darker than what he'd known on any battlefield. Pain was no concern. He didn't fear death. Renmier greeted it, for he'd soon reunite with Amalee.

But Javesse... And the future we could have—

Amalee's screams filled his head. Then just like every other time he felt a splinter of hope, she struck him with images of what she suffered because of his failure to protect her. Samris' blade slid over her throat again.

Titan groaned. The stallion seemed as much a remnant of a living being as Renmier. It could've been the extra weight of the plate armor Renmier hadn't donned in seven and a half years, and the battle armor Titan now wore. Thankfully for the native beasts of burden, the metal armor crafted on Brydasia was light, yet maintained the strength of the heavier material found on the other continents. Renmier left his cloak behind, but the axe, sword, flail, and knife were on his person or the horse.

"Renmier!" Amalee's screams echoed.

Each passing scene of the memory brought the freezing air from the depth of the Blackening; Renmier tasted it in his throat. With the end of the bargain drawing closer, Sebysula's hold grew stronger, and death overtook everything he saw through the helmet.

Upon seeing the beastly helm, commoners scurried off the road, clearing the way to the opened gates of the Bashgrahon estate—Duke Darik Nornt's home. The people's rotting flesh peeled from their bones as they grabbed children, spouse, or horse and guided them away, hushed words and gasps floating to the sky. No doubt the vengor helmet was the reason for their utterances.

The black steel worn by His Eminence's Elite gave a foreboding impression, and the helmets designed by each knight struck dread and awe. Renmier's wasn't the most frightening seen on the battlefield, but it spiked terror into the hearts of soldiers and knights when he charged at them. His helmet was in the shape of a mythical beast many claimed roamed the only mountains of Brydasia, located at the northeast corner of the continent. The Venmont Mountains was only a two-day ride from the Forais farmstead, yet Renmier had never been there.

Tales spun about these creatures called vengors, boasting them the most vicious monsters to encounter. The lack of a plains patrol amongst the farming community of the Wragorn Duchy encouraged a rash of rumors about the beasts ranging to the farmsteads for victims. This, of course, deterred raiding parties for decades.

When Renmier was a child, his uncle had told him stories of farmers who claimed to have encountered the beasts—himself included—and described the fine details of the creatures. After those visits, Renmier woke up in the night, seeing a massive form outside the bedroom window. Long hair as brown as the mountain rock covered every inch of the intruder. The dark nostrils sniffed for its young victim trembling under the covers, and saliva stretched between pointed teeth as its mouth opened wide, a low growl rolling from its throat. Renmier saw death in its colorless eyes. He had screamed out, crying for Mother to comfort him. The vengor ducked, its curled horns disappearing as she entered the room. The following days, Mother scolded her brother for telling Renmier such horrible fables.

He'd never seen a vengor, but he couldn't forget the description his uncle shared, nor the visions of the beasts at the window in the late nights. And it was a fitting choice for his helmet. Instead of having a slit like most knights, a boney brow formed openings for clear view, and the stout nose protected Renmier's nose and upper cheeks. The creature's maw showed keen metal teeth—closed enough to prevent a blade from cutting him or an arrow having an easy target. Steel continued down to cover his throat and nape, and the coiled horns coming forward to block attacks to his ears added a touch of vileness. When people saw him, they scurried as if they'd crossed a beast from the Blackening. How odd he fit that likeness more now than ever.

Nearing the estate entrance, Renmier noted three guards with their hands on sword hilts. The view from beneath the helmet showed men who looked like walking corpses.

He untied the shield from the saddle, drew his sword, and commanded Titan into a charge to the arch where the three guards stood. Arrows flew from overhead, but they stuck to the saddle or bounced off the shield and his and the horse's armor.

The men had unsheathed their weapons as he arrived, but Renmier killed one by the time the other two swung. Titan buffeted the guard to the left while Renmier blocked the third with his sword. He impaled the blade into the man's throat, then twisted to the other side of the horse and thrust the shield point onto the last guard's shoulder. Using the shield to block further arrows, he continued forward, leaving the guards wounded or dead.

After listening to Javesse, Rathan refused to give aid because Renmier had made a dark contract with the Soul Eater. She resorted to begging him to consider her love and willingness to fight for Renmier. He seemed torn, but his deliberation was short. He called eight of the strongest crewmen to his chamber for a meeting, gathered his gear, then had his personal dinghy lowered to the water. Rathan rowed the boat himself. Between him and Javesse was a leather pack glistening with oil, which she learned contained his armor.

Renmier had four hours on them, if not more. Vengeance may have driven him to ride with little to no rest, so Javesse insisted they travel just as hard. Still, Bashgrahon was a three-day ride.

Once they docked, Rathan changed into black Brydasian leather, which wasn't simply jerkin and pants. The suit was expensive due to the substantial craftsmanship to not only stitch the leather, but insert the light Brydasian steel chains between it and a layer of Myndrosian wool. It gave the wearer comfort, mobility, and excellent protection. It wasn't plate armor, but it was still fight worthy. Sheathed on his weapon belt were an impressive broadsword and a knife.

The captain was silent for the most part. He appeared unhappy, which confused Javesse, considering his decision to help. She inquired him of it.

Rathan's charming smile revealed his dimples. "Because of your love for him, and his for you." Nodding once, he returned his attention to the road. There was nothing more to say.

Only three miles from the estate and it seemed they'd never reach it in time to prevent Renmier from fulfilling his bargain. People ran past them, heading in the opposite direction.

A man halted, his flesh pale, yet cheeks pink from exertion. "Don't go to the castle! A demon from the Darkness is killing everyone!"

Javesse's stomach twisted. *We're too late.* Without waiting a moment longer, she commanded Magyia into a hard run.

If there were wounds, Renmier wasn't aware. Maybe being too cold to notice was a good thing. He continued swinging, the blood of his victims leaving long trails of red on the black breastplate. His steady heartbeat kept him moving closer to Darik, but first there was Samris. Whether he was with the duke, Renmier didn't know. All that mattered was finding them, which the dark mist made an effortless task.

He wielded the hand axe and knife; the flail remained sheathed, and the sword and shield were left in the entrance hall. He killed three more guards while barely remaining ahead of the rest of the stronghold's force. Pikes punctured the armor, yet he slaughtered another guard, then pushed through the six blocking the study door, knocking one into the doorframe. Renmier bulled his way inside—a guard gaining entry as well—and kicked the door shut. Ignoring the sword strikes on his back, he dropped the bar into place and secured two thick bolts. Renmier then grabbed the guard by his pauldrons and head-butted him, smashing the guard's nose. He pounded the man's face, the steel gauntlets crushing bone and splitting flesh. The guard now dead, Renmier let him collapse.

Thudding and shouts sounded continuously behind him. "The duke's trapped! Get the battering ram! Keep working on this bloody door!"

Footfall faded, but the pounding continued. It would take ten minutes for them to reach the ram, possibly twenty to remove it from the siege supplies, then several more minutes to carry it through the mansion and up the stairs. Renmier had plenty of time.

With exception of the fire in the hearth and the desperate guards in the corridor, the great study was quiet. Renmier had been in the room so many times, he memorized everything in it and their positions. Massive paintings of hunting expeditions took up space on the walls, and a pelt spread between the large desk ahead to Renmier's left and the tables and chairs in front of the fireplace to his right. Darik didn't hunt. He was too bloody frightened to leave the mansion. Like every other window in the building, heavy blue drapes prevented the chilled air from entering the chamber. Other small tables lined the room, holding ridiculous glass baubles. Things Renmier never cared about. A fine quill and inkwell were on the rarely used desk, and an oversized plush chair was behind it. Darik never afforded anyone comfort when they came to see him, and he didn't do business in this room. This was simply for entertainment.

Laughter came from in front of the fireplace.

The gate was open and unmanned; even the walls were bare of guards. Dead and wounded lay scattered on the ground, leaving a long trail to the mansion. Several guards had just carried a battering ram over the short bridge and into the building.

Rathan raised his brows. "Not a good sign. Either Vulture locked himself in a room, or their lord is in danger."

She drew in a deep breath. "We'll follow them to find out where."

"And then?"

"We'll decide when we get there."

He drew his sword and motioned for her to lead.

As they hurried over the bridge, Rathan nodded at her sheathed blade. "Know how to use that?"

She hoped her glare was enough for an answer. "Does it surprise you that a woman knows how to fight?" she whispered as they entered the mansion.

"I know Bellinstarian women learn how to fight. Just not all of them." He quieted when Javesse ducked within a doorway to watch the guards carry the ram through the entry room. "My country has women knights."

She stared at him. "Yeltar?"

"You know of my country?"

"I had wondered about your accent, but thought I was mistaking it for Alohrian."

He frowned. "Our accents are different."

"They sound similar to me." She tapped his arm and followed the men.

"Well... they're still different," he mumbled.

Under different circumstances, Javesse would've laughed.

"How does a Bellinstarian learn so much about Yeurothians anyway?" he pressed as they stepped over bodies.

"Not now, Captain."

"Yes. Of course."

"Hurry!" a guard shouted from ahead; Javesse and Rathan stopped moving and held their breaths. "To the study!"

Javesse released her breath, a sense of relief overtaking her.

"What is it?" Rathan asked.

She squeezed his arm. "There's a way into the study without having to fight the guards."

The captain smirked. "A secret passage known only to those close to the duke."

She arched a brow. How did he know? It didn't matter. They must get to Renmier fast. "Come with me."

Javesse grabbed Rathan's free hand and led him to the dining hall, through the scullery, then up spiraling stairs leading to the servants' quarters. As they walked along the corridor, several doors opened and closed, the servants peeking out.

"Tell me," she glanced back at him, "how did you know about the secret passage?"

He flashed a grin. "What if I said I've had to use one on a few occasions?"

No doubt those dimples got him into a noblewoman's house and had him hurrying out before discovery by her husband.

"How do *you* know about it?" he asked.

Javesse chewed her lip, releasing it as she reached the second from the last door on the left. She opened it, finding the room hadn't changed, the linens and supplies where they should've been. She went directly to the corner at the opposite end. "I was Duke Nornt's lighana."

Amusement melted from Rathan's eyes. "I-I'm sorry."

"Do you care?"

"It's a dreadful life for anyone to suffer." He nodded. "I'm glad Vulture brought you to me to free."

Javesse moved closer to him. "You didn't free me. Renmier did. Don't forget that."

"Of course." He smirked again. "Are we going to save him now?"

There was a great desire to strike him. But how could she after he'd sailed her back to port, then rode with her to Bashgrahon?

The mechanism to the door was hidden behind crates of pillar candles. Javesse pressed on it, her heart thudding as the portal opened.

"You never fail to surprise me, Vulture," Darik said, staring into the flames. He sat in his usual chair at the hearth, swirling an amber drink in a crystal goblet. His flesh peeled from his muscles as he looked to the other chair, its back facing Renmier. "Captain."

Samris Givins stood and drew his sword.

What a shame to see him already withering in death. Renmier hadn't wanted to just kill Samris, but watch the captain die by his hands.

"Sir Ren—" Samris viewed the armor. "Sir Renmier, I-I hadn't expected you to wear field plate."

Renmier removed the vengor helmet, tossed it aside.

Samris' rotting face whitened, his thinned lips parted. "No." He pointed his weapon at Renmier. "We killed you." He looked at Darik. "You never told me it was Renmier on that farm!"

The duke shrugged, his dead, white eyes fixed on the flames again. "You had a job to do." He sighed. "You failed."

Grimacing, Renmier strode forward. "I promised I was going to kill you." He pulled the flail and began its spin.

The captain side-stepped from the chairs, his sword ready. "I never saw your face during the war. If I had, I would've made sure you were dead that day."

Renmier roared, the spiked ball whirring high as he moved swiftly. He brought it in a low arc to strike Samris' leg, but the captain dodged. The flail's momentum persisted. Renmier continued after him, bellowing with each heavy swing.

They battled away from the fireplace, the flail striking the tables, desk, windows, and walls. Glass shattered, stone sprayed, and wood splintered; the captain evaded the attacks.

Samris hurried behind the desk.

Renmier used his reach to wrap the flail over the chair next to the captain and yanked, breaking the back from the supports.

Samris dodged the snapping wood chunks, then whirled around the side of the desk and pierced Renmier's hip; the pain went unnoticed.

Renmier backhanded him, sending him tumbling to the floor. Once the flail was free, he gave chase, but the captain was already on his feet, shaking his head as if to clear it.

"Come now, Samris. You had an opportunity there!" Darik called from the hearth. "Such a shame!"

"Bastard." The captain stepped backwards. His heel slipped on splintered wood, and he fought to maintain balance.

Renmier landed a crunching blow on Samris' left arm, the spikes impaling flesh and the ball breaking bone. He used the weapon and his strength to draw the man closer, but Samris tore free, shouting as he retreated. Seeing the captain's blood surface, Renmier spun the flail with vigor.

Samris swung feebly, his rotting skin changing to a hue of green.

"I never should've counted on you, Captain," Darik said, standing to the side of his chair.

Renmier attacked Samris from an upper angle, crushing the man's right shoulder and forcing him to the floor.

The captain whimpered as he rolled to his stomach and attempted to crawl away.

Renmier used his foot to flip Samris onto his back. Heel pressed on the wounded shoulder and the flail in motion, he focused on the target. The whooshing of the ball and chain was music he missed from the battlefield, and it was strange he hadn't noticed it during the previous hunts.

"*No!*" Amalee shrieked as Samris assaulted her.

The weapon thudded on the man's cock, mashing that and all else around it. Renmier didn't stop. As a strained holler escaped Samris, Renmier did it again. Just as he had pounded Rastnin and the other men into bloody messes, he did the same to Samris' groin, pelvic bone, thigh, anywhere the flail landed.

Blood spurted from the captain's mouth, then he gurgled once or twice.

Once Samris ceased moving and rasping, Renmier planted the spiked ball in the gore and left it there. Dragging his foot over Samris' abdomen, he stumbled a few feet, then blinked to clear his vision.

A bolt pierced through the back ribs of his right side. He staggered to the desk and faced Darik. All of Renmier's weapons were out of reach, except his knife, but Darik wasn't close enough.

The duke dropped the crossbow onto his seat, then he released a slow breath. "Forgive me."

Forgive him? For what he'd done? Renmier spat blood on the floor. "You ordered our deaths."

"That's not true."

"Liar."

"It wasn't me." Sitting on the arm of the chair, Darik pressed his fingers to his lips. "His Eminence made the order."

The bolt's tip had caught beneath the armor, so trying to remove it only promised more damage. Renmier snapped the shaft, grunting from the stinging pain. He stepped closer to Darik. "You're lying."

The duke's eyes raised to his. "I came to believe you were unaware of my involvement." After a sigh, he continued. "I tell you truthfully, I wanted naught to do with it, Renmier. But *you* turned from His Eminence."

Squinting, Renmier shook his head. "Never. Like others, I only wanted to start a new life."

"And like those who suffered, so did you."

Renmier stilled, some of the wounds throbbing. "What do you speak of?"

"When was the last time you saw one of your comrades who retired from the Elite?" Darik poured himself another fruzae, the decanter shaking against the crystal. "Or those wounded in battle? Hm?" He lifted the glass, yet hesitated from taking a drink. "Emperor Larselis had the injured slaughtered, for they proved they weren't worthy to serve in his army."

"No," Renmier said. "His Eminence never—"

"When did you last see any of them?" Darik shouted. Hands quaking, he drank, then swiped his arm across his mouth and continued. "And when several of his Elite moved southward to settle, he sent me to establish myself and quietly deal his wrath." The duke shrugged. "That's why I'm here! To distribute his fury upon those who dared to deny him of his desires. You were amongst many knights targeted by Emperor Larselis, and he sent me as his executioner. I-I even have a recent letter instructing me to slaughter widows and orphans of knights who died in his service. He'll not keep the promise made to support families of those lost in battle! His Eminence is a despicable man."

Renmier looked at the fireplace and considered Darik's words. Then the conversation with Larselis at the ball came to mind.

"Men in power do what they must to maintain an allegiance. Everyone is replaceable. Even you..."

While playing investigator and keeping an eye on Javesse, Renmier hadn't listened. Even Javesse had told him about the letter Darik just mentioned, but he didn't want to believe her.

Darik was being truthful.

"Samris didn't come to collect anything from me." Renmier wiped his eyes with the back of his hands, trying to clear the mists.

"No. To be honest, I hadn't expected him to return." Darik swallowed. He couldn't drown his nervousness with any amount of fruzae. "I wanted him to fail. When he and four others rode through the gate, I knew Brydasia suffered a significant loss." He rose. "Then you arrived two years later. I had believed it was to seek revenge, but you stayed your hand... until now."

Darik neared. "I've seen that dark haze, and I've consulted wise men. I know where you've been and what you've done. Was your soul worth this vengeance?"

The future Renmier wanted with Javesse was naught but a black mist amongst twisted trees, meant to torment him for eternity. No. Losing his soul wasn't worth any of it, but he'd not tell the duke that. He dropped his gaze to the flail, still embedded in Samris' body.

"Where's my songbird?" Darik was too close.

Leather landed on the floor; a scabbard.

Renmier turned his attention to the dancing flames and reminisced being near to Javesse during the Blizzard. How perfectly they had moved together. This wasn't for nothing. He grinned. "She's free."

"Damn you."

White flashed as a blade pierced the black armor. The puncture was painful, driving just below Renmier's chest. He spun, hoping to pull the sword from Darik's grip, but the duke withdrew it. He grasped Darik's wrist as the weapon impaled his side.

The duke's drooping, peeling cheeks trembled in his rage. "I told you she's mine!"

"No." Renmier grabbed Darik's other arm, jerking him closer. "She belongs to no one now. Her voice is her own." He smiled through the pain, knowing his mockingbird was safe. "Her beautiful name... is Javesse. And she loved me."

Darik's jaw tightened. "No!" He pushed the blade in deeper.

Blood flowed under the armor, soaking the clothes beneath. It couldn't end like this. To fulfill the contract, Renmier must kill Darik.

He used all his might to guide the duke's hand back, pulling the sword from his side. At that moment, every wound Renmier had incurred since entering the estate pulsated, bleeding his life out. He fell to his knees, yet maintained his hold on Darik.

The duke hissed, fighting to stop Renmier from twisting the blade between them and pushing it to his throat. Spittle flew from between his gritted teeth. "Die, you bastard!"

"You first," a woman said.

Darik twisted his neck to look behind him. The glint of light flashed off slender steel beyond the duke, swiping up, down, then straight. His grip weakened. "No," he whispered. "My... songbird." He collapsed.

Renmier released Darik's hand and tilted his head back. He didn't want to see Death's toll on Javesse, but fury consumed him. "Bitch!"

A rotting corpse lowered to its knees and cupped his face. "Renmier, lie down."

He shoved her. "You took it from me!"

"It was the only way to save you from—"

Grasping her throat, he squeezed. "You don't know what you've done!"

A heavy force struck him from the side, knocking him over.

A decaying Captain Rathan Julius placed his sword's tip at Renmier's neck. "Are you well, my lady?"

Javesse coughed hard for several seconds.

"My love," Amalee whispered from the shadows beyond the hearth's flickering firelight.

Renmier focused until a dark shape formed within. It remained low to the floor, reaching for him. He stretched out his hand. "Amalee."

Javesse laced her fingers between his. "It's not her." Her mouth was close to his ear, her breath pleasant on his cold flesh. "It's the Deceiver. Not your wife."

"You did well, my love. Come home with me."

"I-I didn't kill Darik. She did."

"It is enough." Amalee pouted. *"Unless... you do not wish to be with me."*

In the Blackening's twisted forest with her was Renmier's destiny, and there was no changing it.

Javesse clutched his head. "Look at me, you bloody fool!"

There was warmth in her golden irises. Not death, but light.

"Don't go, Renmier. I'm begging you." She pressed her forehead to his. "Fynthiar, I implore You, bestow Your Graces."

"It's too late," Rathan said from beside her. "He's lost."

"No." She blinked hard. Teardrops landed on Renmier's cheek, leaving a heated trail into his beard.

"Come, darling. I await."

He stared at Javesse as his heartbeat slowed.

"Lessindra," she whispered, "formed by the very Love of Fynthiar, You are the Goddess of Forgiveness. Please show Your Mercy."

"You can't pray to every god," Rathan snapped.

Renmier rested Javesse's palm over his heart. "I loved you." He looked to the corner. "I'm ready."

Her hand still on his chest, Javesse stared at Renmier. Why? Why did he give up so damn easily? She was right there.

Black wisps emitted from his mouth. He wasn't gone yet.

She punched the breastplate as hard as she could, almost in time with the pounding on the chamber door. "Don't you dare leave me!"

Rathan staggered back.

"Damn you, Renmier. You bastard! Don't leave!" She punched him again. "I'm here!" Sobs racking her body, Javesse lowered her head to his chest. "Please, Fynthiar... Lessindra, please don't take him from me. Have we both not lost enough?" She drew in a quivering breath, released it. "I believed You brought us together, Fynthiar, yet You part us?"

"This was not the gods' doing," Rathan said. "I understand loss, my lady, but *this* is by his choice."

"Leave me," she whispered.

"My lady, I—"

"I appreciate your help, Captain, but I no longer require your services."

Rathan spread his arms wide. "So you'll remain here? It's ridiculous! You've no means to save him! And those men will kill you!"

Javesse straightened. The captain was wrong. Before boarding his dinghy, she'd gone through her pack, searching for useful items. It had surprised Javesse to find Renmier's healing elixirs in a leather case. One vial was of the violet concoction that had healed him after the attack from the Imperial guards. Acreus. She wrapped that and the blue elixir in wool cloths and placed them in her pouch. The acreus was her only hope.

Glancing at Rathan, she yanked on the sack only to have it slip from her hand. Panic and desperation brought on clumsiness.

"My lady?" The captain knelt beside her. "What is it?"

"I have something." She tried to withhold the sob attempting to burst out. "If only I could... I could use my fingers."

He glanced at the chamber door, from where the heavy thudding now rattled it against the frame, then placed his sword on the floor beside him. "We must hurry." He eased her hands from the pouch, then removed the two vials, his eyes widening. "Acreus?" He looked at her. "Excellent."

Once he uncorked it, the vial was in her trembling hand. Javesse prayed to Vynia, the Healing Goddess, then opened Renmier's mouth.

The moment Renmier released his last breath, dark tree limbs curled around his soul and dragged him into the Blackening, pinning his arms and legs to its warped trunk. Amalee was right there, waiting. She thrust her clawed hand into his chest while releasing a deep howl that made him shudder. The freezing pain seared his being and an uncontrolled shiver overtook him.

"You did not expect warmth and love upon your arrival, did you?" The sweetness was gone from Amalee's voice, and a putrid stench floated from her mouth. It burned his soul. "Did you think I might welcome you with an embrace?" Her hand twisted within him before she removed it. "Welcome to your eternal torment, Knight."

Before Renmier was the same clearing where they met after he completed each hunt, but it stretched into a field of wheat at the far end. Like all things in the Blackening, the stalks held no color, but they tried to appear alive. He couldn't make sense of them. Then five gray blobs took form from the ground, each one shifting into the men Renmier had hunted and killed, their shapes soon transparent. The last was Samris, who stood tall and proud, his eyes just as white and lifeless as the others. The souls' heads fell back and they wailed melancholic moans.

"Why?" Renmier shouted. "Why are you here?"

"Because they are a part of your torture," Amalee said, laughter dancing in her voice.

"Love, I-I don't understand."

She looked from him to the approaching souls; Renmier's victims, her murderers. "Strange. I believed you were intelligent." Amalee halted them with a raised hand. "You see, Knight, you shall watch them violate me—"

"No." He slumped within the branches' grips.

"—and witness my death again and again." Amalee simpered. "This is the suffering you shall endure for centuries."

Samris grabbed her arm and hauled her back to the group of soldiers. They slapped her and tore her dress.

"Renmier!" she shrieked. "Help!"

"No!" His face burned from the exertion of his shout. Renmier fought the branches, but they tightened, spreading his arms farther.

A comforting warmth touched upon him from the right, and a soft glow drifted through the twisted forest. "Cease this!"

It was the most glorious voice Renmier had ever heard. And when he tried to raise his head, Amalee was suddenly clutching his cheeks, stilling him.

"Do not look upon Her," she said. The demoness moved between Renmier and the newcomer. "What do You want?"

"You know why I came here... Sebysula."

A growl sounded from Amalee's throat. She crossed her arms, yet kept her back to him while addressing the golden light as it halted in front of her. "He made a dark contract with me. You cannot interfere."

"One that was not completed."

"What do You bloody care?" Amalee's shout was a deep, distorted echo within the clearing. "Too many times You have interfered. This is not Your realm. Leave!"

"I come upon faithful prayers."

"That means nothing to me!" A stench emanated from Amalee as she grew taller, her flesh paling to gray.

"*That* matters not to *Me*." The glowing force closed in, soothing Renmier. "Why do you hide souls from Caleb?"

The demoness shuffled back, her dark eyes widening. "Torment is my pleasure. This one is mine."

"*He* did not fulfill the contract."

Renmier laughed at that truth.

Sebysula struck him. "Silence!"

Pain surged through his jaw, feeling as if it had cracked, but his soul had no bones.

"Leave him!" The glow pulsated.

"Or what, Goddess? Will You send for Chaos again?" The Soul Eater spread her hands. "Do You not know why he created me?"

"I have no time for—"

"It was a mockery of You." Sebysula resumed her transformation, her flesh sagging low, her colorless eyes larger, and her mouth wide and full of sharp teeth. A horrific odor billowed from her maw as she cackled. "Do You not see the likeness?"

The glow floated back ten feet from the demoness.

Sebysula continued. "I am everything You are not. You show love and forgiveness, and I spread hatred and revenge." She slid a claw down Renmier's cheek. "I have no mercy, Goddess."

He turned his quaking head in the direction of the calming light. Lessindra was there for him? *What have I done to deserve Her Mercy?*

"Nothing." Sebysula hummed her amusement.

How did she know his thoughts? He'd have to be careful.

"You... You are a vile creature," the goddess said. "And despite what you just... shared, it does not change the truth."

"I tire of You!"

"Horrid deceiver!"

The light faded, revealing the most beautiful being Renmier had ever seen. His soul ached with desire to weep and lose itself in the vision of Lessindra. Straight golden hair reached Her waist, blue eyes that promised peace darkened beneath a furrowed brow, and lips that he'd kill to kiss pressed into a tight line. But Her body—gods strike him dead again—he'd slaughter all of Brydasia to lie with Her. She was pure perfection. Renmier wanted to love Her as he had never loved anyone. If he lived again, he'd devote his life to Lessindra and no other.

"Gods," he whispered.

Both beings looked at him.

"The Divine and Their egos." Sebysula motioned at Renmier. "He is now forever lost. My torment shall be less painful than what he will suffer because of You. Go frolic in Your garden."

Face red, Lessindra charged with Her delicate hands swinging forward. An unseen energy struck the Soul Eater, sending her from Renmier's view. Not that it mattered, he couldn't take his eyes off the goddess.

Sebysula roared; the tree holding Renmier vibrated. Somehow, she leapt her massive body at Lessindra, her claws arcing. The goddess stood tall and raised Her palm, blocking the attack with a shield of golden light. The demoness landed steadily, her eyes expanding as she leaned forward and spat a glob of slime. Lessindra bent aside, dodging with a flawless, fluid motion, and brought Her fist crashing into Sebysula's flabby cheek. The Soul Eater collapsed, shaking the ground.

The air grew colder, piercing Renmier like dozens of daggers.

"Enough!" a man's voice rang. It was mild, pleasant, yet commanding. And at the end of that one word, a growl sounded.

The goddess and the demoness froze, their heads turning toward Renmier. A man taller than he strode past until standing before the women. The demoness was slow to rise.

"As much as I enjoy Your company, Lessindra," he said, sliding his hand through his long dark hair, "this is the fourth time You have called me here regarding one of my half-brother's knights. Why do You believe I care?"

She glanced at Renmier, who still ogled, wishing to conjure words to express his deep love for Her, but nothing acceptable came to mind. Lessindra neared the stranger. "They had a contract—"

"We did!" Sebysula grabbed the man's hand and pressed it to her wounded cheek.

He jerked free. "Do not interrupt Her!" To the goddess, he spoke with tenderness. "Continue."

She blushed for whomever he was. "It is unfulfilled. Sebysula cannot have him."

His momentary regarding of Renmier revealed an unquestionably stunning face and silver eyes. "This knight deserves the Darkness, does he not?"

"But the bargain was not met," Lessindra said.

The demoness gestured at Renmier. "He fulfilled most of it. I gave him what he wanted and the last man is dead." She glared at Lessindra. "Who cares that it was not by his hand?"

"He did not fulfill the contract," the man said.

"But he..." Sebysula shook her head, her jowls wobbling. "She cannot have Her way again!"

He looked down at his hands. "You shall have other souls. Not this one. This one is mine."

Lessindra scowled.

"Leave us, Sebysula," he said. Nodding at the group of gray soldiers, he added, "Take them with you."

The demoness snarled then stomped to the field and Samris' company. By the time she reached them, she was Amalee again. Turning back, she leered at Renmier. "I will never forgive you for letting them rape and murder me," she said, a teardrop sliding down her cheek. "I will hate you for eternity."

Renmier gasped, his soul withering. "Amalee," he whispered.

She walked amid the men and into the black wheatfield, all of it disappearing to reveal the twisted trees at the other end of the clearing.

"Wicked bitch," the stranger said, then chuckled.

Why did he laugh? Amalee truly did blame Renmier for her death, and she'd hate him forever.

"You shall keep him?" Lessindra asked, regaining Renmier's attention.

If he could gain *Her* heart, perhaps eternity might not be so horrible.

The man sat on a boulder and stared at Renmier, as if determining his value.

The goddess waited a few seconds in silence. "Caleb—"

"Please... I will not answer to that name."

Sorrow passed over Her face. "Your birthname fits you, Wolf Lord." Lessindra's eyes brightened as She took one step toward him.

Why did She look at this... *Caleb* with such affection? He didn't deserve it. He'd never love Her like Renmier would. No one could possibly give as much devotion as Renmier was willing to give Her.

"A name given by a mother who abandoned me in a forest much like this." Caleb raised his hands and twisted from the waist.

"Shaelera was blinded by her adoration for your father."

He grimaced.

"Caleb—"

"Do *not* call me by that name."

"Chaos," She whispered, appearing disappointed. "I do not enjoy it coming from My tongue."

A chill consumed Renmier as he focused on the demigod; the creator of the very realm that now imprisoned him. There was no hope. Not even with the Goddess of Mercy present.

"I am often conflicted," Caleb—no, Chaos—said, "of why I feel the way I do for the goddess formed by the very Love of Fynthiar, when He has felt nothing but loathing for me. Father of All?" He laughed. "All but His own son."

The air within the clearing grew colder, that even Lessindra trembled.

She shook Her head. "I cannot answer for His—"

Chaos flicked his hand in Renmier's direction. "Why this mortal's soul?"

It appeared She debated on answering or finishing what She had been saying. After a long breath, She said, "His lover prayed to Me."

"Did he not reject the gods?"

How did Chaos know?

She drew nearer to the demigod. "Sir Renmier reached out many times over the past several weeks, and I have answered."

Chaos shrugged. "You are too late."

"I have answered him on many occasions. He just did not listen."

A different warmth filled Renmier, and his soul lightened as the tree released him.

The demigod rose, moved closer; the goddess stayed beside him.

"They are healing him." Her face glowed within the dark realm. "An acreus elixir."

"Fascinating," Chaos said. "Yet, they cannot save him."

"Cal—Chaos." She rested Her hand on his chest. "Have mercy."

He cringed. "Mercy? The Five took everything from me." Chaos sneered at the goddess. "And I was given to Lykor for a thousand years—knowing a suffering such as none of You can possibly imagine—afore Fynthiar sent me to this prison! No one ever showed *me* mercy!" He clutched Renmier's shoulder, stilling him.

A groan escaped Renmier as a biting cold snaked into the core of his soul.

Shaking Her head again, Lessindra retreated. "It was *your* choice to kill Raizzia and her babe."

Pain showed in the demigod's gaze. He lowered his hand, freeing Renmier of the agonizing hurt. "I... I knew not of the babe, I swear. I did not even know I had thrust the blade into Raizzia."

Lessindra palmed his cheek. "Your hatred controls you too much."

He closed his eyes and pressed his lips into Her hand. "It surrounds me here," he whispered.

"This was the worst prison Father could have placed you within. Let it not be the knight's. Sebysula's torment—"

"Shall not be his. This mortal shall only know Darkness."

Stepping back, Her hand drop to Her side.

"He has fallen," Chaos said. "Renmier renounced his god... and the Others."

"I would not be here if that was true."

"Your Mercy has no boundaries." The demigod smirked. "However, he is mine."

Renmier lowered his head. "This is the torment I agreed to," he rasped. "The Soul Eater owns me."

"Do not speak in the goddess' presence," Chaos snapped without looking from Lessindra. His voice softened as he continued his conversation with Her. "That he has seen You is another reason he cannot leave, Lessindra. He will go insane with want for only You."

"Is it Sir Renmier to whom you refer? Or yourself?"

A smile was shared between the two. The goddess blinked slowly then dropped Her gaze.

"You speak to me as such while being my half-brother's lover?" the demigod asked, amusement dancing within the words. "And while I am bound here until a living soul frees me. That is unfair and unkind."

The conversation between goddess and demigod seemed far too intimate for Renmier to witness. He shouldn't have been privy to it. And Chaos was not the evil demigod he had expected.

Lessindra's breath came slow, She hesitated to speak. "We can tend to the matter of his seeing Me."

"Why should I free him? He is nothing."

"Not to the woman trying to save him at this very moment. She braved her fear of the oceans, returned to a land in spite of the threat of recapture and slavery, and has begged Me and Father to bring Sir Renmier back to her. Javesse's love is great. So much like another love I once knew."

Chaos' jaw worked left to right, his irises darker.

Did Lessindra speak of him?

"He serves no god," Chaos mumbled.

"Not yet."

"He will not serve me."

"Is that wrong?" She asked.

"Then why should I release him?"

Lessindra was close to Chaos again. "Because I ask you to do so."

The demigod's arms were suddenly around Her, making Renmier seethe with jealousy. "If only I could feel Your warmth within this cold, dark place." Chaos rested his forehead to Hers. "You are the only one Who comes to me here. Grestin... He wants naught to do with me. Yet I cannot blame him, not after the harm I have done."

"Forgiveness can be yours... Caleb."

He skimmed his nose down the length of Hers. "Your Forgiveness. Not Grestin's."

After a moment of silence passed, he released Her and nodded once toward Renmier. "What do I gain from letting this one return to the living?"

Lessindra slid Her fingers between Chaos'. "Compassion."

He tilted his head back and laughed.

"Please?" She guided him to look at Her. "Do this because you know love."

Chaos spun and tramped across the clearing. "I might have once." He looked over his shoulder at Lessindra. "Will I again?"

She clasped Her hands together. "That is not for Me to say at this time."

His snickers floated within the cold air, fitting amid the twisted forest. It settled as he faced Her.

"Will you let Sir Renmier's soul return to his body?" She asked. "Vynia grants Her Healing with the acreus elixir."

He bared his teeth, growling low. "Is this *Her* realm?" Arms sweeping the width of the clearing, he added, "These trees were created by me. Not Vynia."

"*I* ask it of you." Lessindra's warmth reached Renmier.

Chaos' silver eyes fixed on him. "At a heavy cost, Goddess, for he made a dark contract with Sebysula and nearly completed it." The demigod halted Her protest with a gentle wave of his hand. "And because he has seen *You*."

"What shall he forfeit? Sir Renmier has lost so much already."

The demigod walked closer, the chill piercing Renmier again. "Not only shall he forget You," he said, pressing his fingertips to Renmier's forehead, "he shall forget more."

Renmier's eyelids fluttered shut. Thumping sounded in his ears. Steady thumping. Heavy. Faster. Harder.

Renmier drew in a deep, painful breath; a rush of freezing air released with it. From within a black haze, a golden-haired woman was knelt beside him, holding an empty vial. Nearby stood a dark-haired man with a sword at the ready. Heartbeat thudding as if caught in his throat, Renmier recalled two such beings in a place of great misery, but he couldn't remember their faces nor the dark place. Only Darkness and Light. Hatred and Love.

"Renmier?" the woman whispered, tears filling her eyes.

How did she know him?

Her cheek pressed to his, teardrops broken between them. "Praises and thanks to You, Fynthiar and Lessindra. Thank You, Vynia."

Lessindra. He'd heard that name before. It brought him comfort.

"We must go before they bust down that door!" the dark-haired man snapped.

Pounding. The pounding wasn't only Renmier's heartbeat, but something heavy on the chamber door.

The woman petted Renmier's hair. "I need your help, Captain."

"Of course. But we move now."

Her lips were soft against Renmier's. Sure, she was gorgeous, but why was she kissing him? The question was there, ready to be asked, yet he couldn't utter a sound.

The couple helped Renmier rise to his feet, then threw his arms over their shoulders and guided him to the corner of a room torn apart by a skirmish. There were two dead men on the floor, one of them a bloody mess. The woman slid her hand beneath a nearby window's blue curtain.

"We'll leave by way of the scullery," she said as the wall opened inward, revealing a passage. "While they're breaking down the door and searching for Renmier, we'll escape through the gates."

"He'll ride with me," the man said as they moved along a shadowed corridor.

"No." She glanced at him. "Titan knows me. Renmier and I will ride him. You take my horse."

"Very well, my lady."

"Please," she said, opening another door that led to a storage room, "call me Javesse."

Renmier stared at her, a black mist surrounding everything in his view. *Javesse... Who are you?*

Epilogue

Bellinstarian summers were often the hottest in Myndrose. Thankfully, they built their houses from the trees of Taurana where winters lasted throughout most of the year. It was amazing how the lumber kept the trees' cool characteristics, but Javesse wouldn't question the grand works of the Earthen Goddess. She praised Vynia for the bountiful harvest, Fynthiar for her life, and Lessindra for her lover. The gods had been good to her... mostly. She had faith things would continue to improve. Four years was little, considering what Renmier had endured. And she acknowledged he required more time to complete his healing. She hoped it'd not be much longer.

Sitting at the vanity in their bedchamber, she contemplated the changes he'd undergone since the long voyage from Brydasia. It had broken her heart when Renmier finally spoke his first words on the third day at sea; a question inquiring whom she was. Captain Rathan Julius didn't know what caused the memory loss, but suspected it was from the Soul Eater's brief yet wicked torment. After two weeks of sailing, Javesse convinced Renmier they shared a past, he loved her, and they wanted a future together. However, two months dragged before he trusted her, and another three months until he fell in love with her... again.

He wasn't exactly the man she loved before his death, yet she was grateful. Renmier's history was something Javesse guarded for his sake. He learned he had been a knight, he once had a wife whom he adored, and she'd been murdered by the very man who slew him. There was no reason for him to know the exact truth. Vulture didn't need to live on. And if Renmier ever remembered what had truly happened... Javesse would face that moment if it arrived. Every day she prayed that it never would.

This different life wasn't what she had hoped for, but she cherished it nonetheless. Using the three rubies he'd left in her backpack, they purchased a modest farmhouse with eight acres in her beautiful homeland. They gardened a variety of vegetables and tended three dozen sheep, selling the crops and wool to sustain a comfortable living. Renmier took to the tasks with natural skills, showing incredible knowledge, discipline, and focus. He worked hard, and he loved it.

This was the true Renmier; the person unmarred by Emperor Larselis. Yet sometimes he stood in the barn at the pile of corn and stared at the grain flail in his hand while the hired laborers waited. Javesse had watched him break the grain from the husks, the wood end striking again and again with force greater than the other men. Rastnin dying flashed in her mind. Prayers then followed that Renmier wouldn't remember his transgressions as an Elite Knight nor as Vulture.

At least now he had faith in Fynthiar and Lessindra, which seemed to bring him peace. Renmier openly showed his affection for Javesse. And gods! The man protected what was his. This, unfortunately, at times reminded her of Vulture when he grew aggressive toward outsiders who ogled her. Bellinstarians had welcomed Renmier, accepted *and* respected the marriage bond between him and Javesse, but foreigners knew nothing of her people's customs. That or they often overlooked it and thought it was brave to say things about her within Renmier's earshot. Idiots. But he did forgive quickly after implementing punishment.

She looked at her handsome husband sleeping under the coverlet.

More scars marred his flesh than when they'd first met, but she was used to them. He kept his hair short, and shaved his face every week, just as she liked and often had to remind him. Javesse had to remind Renmier of many things. It would be easier if he could remember them on his own better.

A foot pressed from within her belly, catching her rib. She massaged the spot until the foot relaxed. "Thank you, my little darling."

Javesse rubbed cream on her cheeks and hands. Turning in the chair, she found Renmier staring at her. "Blessed morning, love," she said.

He drew in a deep breath and blinked rapidly.

If only the Darkness would release him, but it appeared the demoness still tried to reel him in like a catch. At least the Soul Eater's hold had further weakened over the years, and though the black haze lingered, it was less noticeable. When Renmier grew angry, a thin mist spread to his green irises and a slight chill emanated from him. Thankfully, the stench no longer surfaced. Javesse did her best to avoid situations that might produce such reactions from her husband.

"You..." Brows low, he looked at his hand and caressed the simple gold band on his finger with his thumb; Javesse had discarded the black stone ring while he was asleep on Winged Amyrdene. Renmier raised his eyes to her again. "You're my wife... Javesse."

Forcing a smile, she approached him. "Yes, Renmier. I'm your wife."

Relief eased the tense muscles of his face. He remained still as she sat on the edge of the bed. While Javesse massaged his arm and shoulder, Renmier viewed a portion of the room, taking in the furniture, decorations, and colorful cloaks hanging near the door. "We're in Bellinstar?"

"We are."

Sometimes it ached to witness him as this. Why did the demoness affect his most recent memories? They had naught to do with the past.

A small hand slapped above Renmier's ear, the tiny fingers on his cheek.

"We... We have a child," he said. "A-a son."

Javesse glided her fingertip over their son's knuckles; the tot didn't stir from his slumber. "We do."

Renmier sat up, letting the hand fall to the bed. "Jaris," he whispered, touching their son's thick black hair.

She guided Renmier's palm to her belly. "We shall have another babe in two months."

He stared at her stomach as a foot pushed their hands upward. A slow smile formed over his lips. "Wonderful."

This moment was almost wonderful.

"Am I a complete man, Javesse?"

She hated the question. It broke her heart every damn time he asked. Renmier knew part of him was missing, and she couldn't stand to explain it every day. Patting his hand that rested atop her belly, she said, "That is up to you."

He pulled her close, slid his fingers into her hair. "Then I am complete, for you're in my life." He kissed her tenderly.

Javesse prayed for the gods to grant further mercy on her husband and allow him to remember this new life. She and Renmier could leave the days in Brydasia behind. Maybe in another year or two, such mornings for him will fade away.

Until then, Javesse would be there for Renmier to remind him of whom he was now and what they shared.

Emvarr's Moon Cycle

Emvarr's moon cycle consists of twelve thirty-day months, often referred to as 'moons'. Each month is named after its moon. The order is:

Dalin (Wolf)

Amber

Stallion

Hawk

Blossom

Lover's

Burning

Hunter's

Fox

Harvest

Oaken

Cold

Extended Glossary

Characters:

Admona (*Ad-**mō**-na*) – Barmaid at Long Road Tavern in Volthany.

Beresly Greinlyn (***Bair**-es-lē **Grēn**-len*) – Elf lord and Javesse's lover.

Euralys (***Yer**-a-lis*) – King Rainlisyr's nephew.

Fentelle (*Fen-**tel***) and Rugard (***Rew**-gard*) – Other ships' captains.

Heslion (*Hes-**lē**-in*) – Emperor Larselis' Captain of Palace Guards.

Janis (***Yah**-nis*) and Jovil (***Yō**-vil*) – Javesse's brothers.

Jaris (***Yar**-is*) – Bellinstarian Child.

Koslen (***Kos**-lin*) – Apothecarist in Arborville.

Mistress (***Mis**-tris*) – A Serine elf who runs a lighana market, amongst other services.

Pravnus (***Prav**-nis*) and Shargrid (***Shar**-grid*) – Elite Knights of Descension.

Rainlisyr (***Rain**-le-seer*) – King of the Serine Elves and Delvarian.

Raizzia (*Rā-**zē**-uh*) – A victim of Chaos.

Rastnin (***Ras**-nin*) – Renmier's prey.

Rathan Julius (***Rā**-thin Joo-**lē**-is*) – Ship's captain of Winged Amyrdene.

Repascow (*Rē-**pa**-scō*) – Former general of the Elite Knights of Descension during the war.

Sebysula (*Se-**bis**-yoo-la*) – Created by Chaos, the Soul Eater lives in the Darkness.

Serine (*Sir-**ēn***) Elves – Descendants of Ubrasians. Their homeland is Delvarian.

Sulaen (*Soo-**lā**-in*) – Native of Rela Sulae. Also called a Darklander.

Wickitch (***Wik**-ich*) – Kidnapping thug.

Wynna (***Win**-na*) – Barmaid at a small tavern at a minor crossroad community.

Vhormons (***Vor**-mins*) – Short humans from Vhormos of Yeuroth. Renowned sailors.

Magyia (***Mag**-ya*) – Javesse's acquired mare.

Titan (***Tī**-tin*) – Renmier's Elite stallion.

Midsga (*Mids-**ga***) Flies – Small flying insects whose bites leave tiny, itchy bumps.

Vengor (***Ven***-*gor*) – Fabled creature from the Venmont Mountains. Or perhaps they are real.

Places:

Bellinstar (*Bel-**en**-star*) – Northern country of Myndrose. Home of Bellinstarians.

Bilsnir (***Bil***-*snir*) – Growing town on the edge of Faytirn Woodland.

Camnit (***Cam***-*nit*) – Hamlet in the Faytirn Forest.

Charville (***Shar***-*vil*) – Northwestern Duchy of Descension.Emerasia (*Em-er-**ā**-sha*) – Capital of Delvarian.

Dawiryn (*Da-**wer**-in*) Woodland –Delvarian Forest.

Dibukue (*Dī-**buk**-ē*) River – Flows into the Onyx Ocean from Lake Diriahz.

Faytirn (*Fā-**tern***) Woodland – Brydasia's largest forest, stretching along most of the western coast.

Kiasier (*Kī-ā-**zē**-air*) River – Splits from Tebazryl River in Faytirn Woodland, cuts through Arborville.

Lake Diriahz (*Da-**rī**-ez*) – Largest lake in Brydasia.

Lunalla (*Lew-**nah**-la*) – Capital of Bellinstar.

Lymus (***Lī***-*mis*) – Village west of Niwlog Woods.

Newburrows (***New***-*ber-rōz*) – Southeastern Duchy of Descension.

Niwlog (***New***-*il-og*) Woods – Small forest bordering the Columure and Charville Duchies.

Plinuir (*Pli-**new**-er*) – Village west of Tebazryl River.

Salisby (*Sal-**es**-bē*) – Western country of Myndrose.

Talgrian (*Tal-**grē**-en*) Forest – Woodland east of Volthany and on the Dibukue River.

Taurana (*Tuh-**rah**-na*) – Northeastern country of Myndrose.

Tebazryl (*Ta-**bāz**-ril*) River – Longest western river flowing from north to south Brydasia.

Venmont (***Ven***-*mont*) Mountains – The only mountains in Brydasia, found in the Northeast.

Vhormos (***Vor**-mus*) – Northwestern country of Yeuroth.

Volthany (***Vol**-theh-nē*) – Large village outside Talgrian Forest.

Wheathfaire (***Wēth**-fair*) – Town south of Ravieris.

Wragorn (***Wrā**-gorn*) – Northeastern Duchy of Descension.

Yeltar (***Yel**-tar*) – Northeastern country of Yeuroth.

Miscellaneous:

Aythimus (*Ā-**tha**-mis*) – A peach colored flower with a fruity scent known to grow in northeast Brydasia.

Crueberry (*Krew-**bair**-ē*) – A deep red berry tart upon first tasting, then sweet at the finish. Wonderful for desserts and drinks.

Fruzae (*Frew-**zā***) – Expensive liquor of fermented fruits. Flavors are often blended for variety.

Galnikath (*Gel-**ni**-keth*) – A fatal virus for which there is no cure.

Grospies (***Grah**-spēz*) – Goat testicles that are boiled, stewed, simmered, or skewered. One only needs to use their imagination.

Roan (***Rōn***) – Currency system of Emvarr. Black, gold, silver, and copper. Black being the rarest and most valuable, and copper the least.

Swyve (***Swīv***) and Throng– Sexual intercourse.

Teesote (***Tē**-sōt*) – A game of chance that uses a slender wooden token with one to four notches on each side; the fourth the thinnest. Often played by Vhormons and sailors.

Winged Amyrdene (***Am**-er-dēn*) – Captain Rathan Julius' ship.

Acknowledgements

There's been no greater support for me than my husband, Scott. You've been incredible in every possible way. You are my mountain and you mean the world to me. A special thank you to Ron, Erica, and Dana for taking time to read and provide honest feedback. I always tell you I'm grateful. Well I'm putting it in my novel, so I obviously mean it! I appreciate it more than you know. Jeremy, it was a great idea to use the flail! Thanks, Son!

Thank you to those who have supported me in different ways, from offering a wish of luck to enduring minutes or hours of listening to me discuss this story... or maybe I should be apologizing.

About the Author

Introduced to the tabletop roleplaying game Dungeons & Dragons at a young age, and still an active player, Mary developed a love for fantasy books and arts. After years of writing short stories in several genres, she found her niche in fantasy romance. Writers such as Margaret Weis, Tracy Hickman, Terry Brooks, and Richard Knaak, as well as Guy Gavriel Kay's "The Fionavar Tapestry", have been wonderfully inspiring works. Even horror author Dean Koontz was an influence. Mary lives in southeast Michigan with her family, and adores spending time with them, especially playing various types of games and watching movies. Making memories is the best activity together. She loves listening to music while she reads and writes, usually with one or both of her mini dachshunds curled up nearby.

Sign up for Mary's newsletter at her website, where you can also keep up with · events and blogs: maryjnichols.com

Where to find her on Social Media:
Facebook: FatesOfEmvarr
TikTok: Mary J Nichols_author

Emvarr Novels

For Duty & For Love
(2021)

An Unsought Destiny
(2023)

Mockingbird & Vulture
(2023)

The Misfortunate Maiden
(2026)